For The Ones
Who Endure

R. Collins

Samsara Fleet | Book Six

Books By Riley Collins

To learn more about Riley Collins, see an updated list of titles, and join his mailing list go to his webpage at https://www.rileycollins.info.

Samsara Fleet Series

Book One: For the Ones Who Remain
Book Two: For the Ones Who Are Forgotten
Book Three: For the Ones Who Rebel
Book Four: For the Ones Who Liberate
Book Five: For the Ones Who Prevail
Book Six: For the Ones Who Endure

Central Worlds Series

Book One: Escape From the Fringe

Cover Art by: 17 Studio Book Design
Editing by: Lisa Binion

For my readers and everyone who looks to the sky and imagines what may be out there.

Chapter One
Nicole | Hope, New America

Nicole Bergeron looked out at the brilliant white tundra surrounding the small town of Hope. Faint eddies of snow streaked over the ice-frosted ground and she could almost feel daggers of wind on her skin as she stared out the window. Although they were in Hope, Nicole certainly didn't feel it. She glanced around the small apartment and wished she were anywhere but there. It was sparse—a bed, small kitchen area, and some scattered chairs—but enough for what they needed. She'd rented it for double the market rate if no questions were asked. The last thing she wanted were people taking an interest in them.

Nicole and her companion—she wasn't sure what else to call her—Ai had crash-landed in the ocean not far from town. It had taken a few days of surreptitiously asking locals, but they'd finally found a someone willing to take their credits without any identification.

Hope had not been their final destination, merely a place to stop while they tried to find whatever remained of their friends. However, the stop had stretched from days to months. Despite the locals being unwilling or unable to talk about it, Nicole had discovered there had been a rebel base nearby which the Jadid had destroyed when they'd captured the planet.

Blending into a town as small as Hope was no easy feat, and Nicole wondered how successful she'd been; trying to find out information while also remaining inconspicuous was almost impossible. The timing of her arrival didn't help either—she'd come just after the Jadid had taken over the planet.

The Jadid. The purple aliens had once been Samsara Fleet's allies in their fight against the Nasi. The Jadid's Liberation Fleet had worked in concert with Samsara Fleet, fighting the Nasi and driving them from former Human colonies of New America and Patagonia. Just when Nicole had thought they'd won, their allies had decided to stick a knife in their back. They'd declared themselves the new rulers of the Human worlds and started to ruthlessly hunt down any resistance, including their former allies.

In Hope, which was about as remote as you could get on New America, there wasn't much sign of the Jadid government other than a smoking crater in the mountains outside the city. It had been the Fridge, a rebel base and the last known location of Nicole's friends. Everything they'd worked toward was gone and she was still trying to make sense of it all. The worst part of it was that she didn't know who was dead or alive.

But she would stop at nothing to find out. When the Nasi had first appeared, Nicole had been wracked with guilt because she's unwittingly played a part in their rise. That was over. The only things she felt now were concern for her friends and a burning desire for vengeance.

She stood up and walked toward the door. It was almost time.

"Let me know what you find out." Ai didn't look up from

her tablet.

Nicole wished she had the Jadid's sense of detachment about the situation. Like most of her species, the lanky violet woman seemed almost emotionless at times. When the Jadid had suddenly turned against Nicole and the rest of Samsara Fleet, Ai had bravely helped Nicole escape. As far as she was concerned, the woman could be as distant as she wanted, Nicole would always owe her a debt that couldn't be repaid.

"I will." Nicole grabbed her coat and headed out the door.

New America was a planned planet. From space, most of the land looked like a grid with each square dedicated to a different purpose—housing, commerce, industry, and more. Hope was one of the few towns not located in an urban zone. It was there to support the mines scattered in the surrounding mountains. The unplanned nature of the town gave it a rough, almost frontier, vibe. Multistory ramshackle buildings surrounded the streets of packed snow and gravel. The locals—all of them Human—stalked through the streets, wrapping their hoods tightly around their faces to keep out the biting winds.

Nicole trudged through the streets and entered the Escape Shaft. The small restaurant was one of the only two in town. Its interior was a mishmash of discarded mining equipment and the stuffed carcasses of local creatures. She took a seat in a corner of the room, eyeing a nearby disembodied head with two mouths, both lined with arm-length fangs. Its red eyes seemed to leap out amidst the

3

matted fur and were so hypnotic that Nicole had to force herself to look away.

"Whadya want?" asked the server as he strode up to her table. Contrary to his question, the burly man couldn't have seemed to care less what she wanted.

"I'll wait. Someone's 'posed to meet me here."

"You got fifteen minutes. After that, either you order somethin' or you're out." He turned around and walked back to the bar.

Nicole wasn't sure exactly who she was meeting at the Escape Shaft.

She'd spent every day since they'd landed walking the town, trying to simultaneously disappear and stay close enough to hear any intel. The previous day an elderly man had stopped her as she was walking out of a provisions store where she'd been chatting with some of the other patrons.

"Heard you askin' questions." The man leaned in conspiratorially, fixing her with his crystal blue eyes. Nicole could smell a hint of alcohol on his breath despite the scarf wrapped around the lower half of his face and the wind ripping down the street around them. "Why?"

"Just making conversation." She wasn't about to admit a thing.

"Curiosity like that'll get you locked up. Or worse."

Nicole was momentarily at a loss for words. "I'm just talkin' to people. Learnin' about my new home."

"Nah, I think it's more than that. You wanna hear more? You head to the Escape Shaft tomorrow for lunch. There'll be someone there." The man eyed her up and down for a moment. "You seem like you got questions that need answered."

A transport flew past them. The man jumped slightly then turned around and walked away.

Nicole had spent the previous night wrestling with whether she should take the man up on the offer. Was he a collaborator? Would there be a squad of Jadid soldiers waiting for her? Ultimately, she figured the risk was worth it. She was hearing the same things over and over and didn't dare try and get close to where the base had been. She'd already decided to give up and head to Tiradentes, the capital of New America in a couple of days. They'd need to come back for the skip ship, but they were languishing in Hope without any clues as to what to do next.

Nicole watched the front entrance of the Escape Shaft, keeping her head down and a hand close to the kinetic pistol tucked in her waistband. People trickled in, shuffled to their tables, and ordered drinks, chems, or what passed for food from the server. Not a single one paid her a second glance.

Her fifteen-minute limit was nearly up when a young woman with long silvery hair took the seat across from her. The skin on the left side of her face was puckered and raw, a scar from a burn of some sort by Nicole's guess. She was a woman who fit the town perfectly—the vision of a rough and tumble settler.

"How you enjoin' Hope?" the woman asked with a smile.

"Not exactly where I want to be."

5

The woman snickered. "I hear ya. Not the best place for a vacation." She tilted her head. "Is that why you're here? A vacation? Maybe get some fresh air?"

"Something like that," Nicole said.

"You've been asking about the Fridge. Why?"

"Just curious. I got here—"

"No one asks about the Fridge because they're curious." She leaned over the table. "Not safe to be askin' questions like that."

Nicole glanced around the room. No one seemed to be paying them any attention.

"I think I knew people who were there." She'd heard enough to know what had happened. Enough that she pictured it every night in her sleep. Samsara Fleet had sent assault teams to New America to lead an assault on the plasma lances on the surface. Assault teams that included some of the most important people in her life. They'd been successful in taking out the Nasi anti-ship weapons and then had returned to the Fridge. That's when the Jadid Liberation Fleet had betrayed them. Rained missiles and plasma strikes on their location then sent down their troops to mop up. Her friends hadn't stood a chance.

The woman raised an eyebrow. "You from off planet?"

Nicole nodded.

"I know some other people from off planet." The woman abruptly stood, her chair screeching along the floor. "Let's go."

"Cinder, you ain't gonna order?" The server glared at

Nicole as he spoke as if she were the one responsible.

"Nah." Cinder shook her head. "In fact, I wasn't even here."

"Fine. Maybe some credits magically appear in the till though."

"That a threat?" Cinder stopped walking and faced the man.

He shook his head quickly and held up his hands. "Nah. Nah. But ya know, times are tough."

"Don't I know." Cinder turned and walked out the door and Nicole followed.

They strode through the empty street toward the edge of town. Cinder led Nicole up a small series of metal steps and into a small apartment that faced a narrow alleyway.

"So you with Samsara Fleet?" asked Cinder as soon as the door closed behind them.

"Yeah." Nicole produced a small ID chit that was encoded with an encryption key that provided proof of her affiliation with the fleet.

Cinder waved the chit away. "I don't have any way to read that. Almost all your friends are dead or gone." The woman said it so casually that Nicole wanted to smack her. "The Jadid came and cleared house as soon as they destroyed the Nasi. We didn't have a chance." She unconsciously touched the left side of her face. "Bastards."

"You're still alive. There must be some others."

"There's some." Cinder walked to the window of the small room and glanced out. "A few. We've got no idea who remains. The Jadid are still rounding people up."

"You've got to have some idea," Nicole said.

"You know what the bastard Jadid did?" Cinder turned to look back at Nicole. "They destroyed the entire base without a hint of warning. Just launched missiles at us from orbit and took us out. There wasn't time to react. I was lucky. I barely escaped. I'm guessing most people died before they knew what happened."

Nicole banished the image of her friends dying in the blast and focused on the woman in front of her. She'd been desperate to find answers, taking small trips out to the towns and cities across the planet. Each time she'd returned disheartened, without any more information. All the people, safe houses, and drop locations she'd known were gone. All wiped out by the Jadid. This was the break she'd been looking for these past few months.

"You survived at least." Nicole tried not to sound accusing. "There must be others."

Cinder shrugged. "Like I said, there's a few. One second, we were celebrating, the next, the entire world was ending. There certainly aren't a lot of survivors."

It was so cold and calculating. The Jadid wiped out the allies who'd been fighting against the Nasi with them—and who would have become the resistance against them—in one blast.

"So why am I talking to you?" Nicole asked. "If everything's so bad, why are we here?"

Cinder flashed a crooked smile. "Girls gotta try, right?

There're still *some* people who are fighting the Jadid. I figure you might want to talk with them. I don't know how much longer you can stay here with your *friend*"—she said the word with a sneer—"before they find you."

A spike of alarm shot through Nicole. Who else in the small town knew about Ai? They'd been careful to make sure she stayed away from windows and never left their small room. How had she been found out?

"Don't get all bent out of shape," Cinder said. "I'm the only one who knows. At least, I think I am. When you started askin' questions, I had to do my due diligence."

"Okay, what's next? How do I talk with your friends?"

"First things first." Cinder grabbed a small device from the shelf. "We've got to disable that implant of yours."

Nicole stepped back. Without her neural implant, she'd be helpless. Most importantly, if this was an ambush, she wouldn't be able to warn Ai. She'd be completely at Cinder's mercy.

But Nicole wasn't willing to spend another two months waiting for someone to contact her. She nodded and stepped forward. Cinder placed the device against her head, and she felt a small pinch as the device embedded a small disc into her scalp. A wave of nausea swept over her as the small disc severed the omnipresent link between her nervous system and the small implant in her skull.

"Now follow me." Cinder dropped the device into a drawer and walked to the door. "There's someone you should meet."

9

The town of Kipya Kinshasa was only a fifteen-minute flight from Hope. Despite the short distance, Nicole wondered if Cinder's beat-up transport would be able to make the journey. The dented vehicle's engine sputtered as they soared over the craggy landscape, much too close for Nicole's comfort.

Kipya Kinshasa was almost identical to Hope: a frontier town built at the foothills of the polar mountains. However, it was slightly smaller—Nicole guessed about half the size—and slightly more run-down.

"Who are we meeting?" Nicole asked as they walked through the nearly vacant streets. She could have counted the number of people she saw on one hand.

"Just wait," Cinder replied. "Someone your friends probably trusted."

Nicole followed Cinder to a block-sized rusted metal building. She guessed it was used for mineral processing based on the belts and oil-coated machines. They made their way through the facility, winded through the ribbons of belts, skirted around a large piece of machinery, and entered the partially hidden door behind it.

"Nicole Bergeron."

Nicole smiled as Cell Chief Rafaela Pham pushed off a wall and slapped her on the back. The woman was about Nicole's age with piercing blue eyes and the sides of her head shaved to the skin. She was the leader of one of the Tiradentes Liberation Front cells—or at least she'd been before the Jadid had taken over the planet. Nicole doubted the TLF still existed in any meaningful sense. From what she'd heard, the Jadid had cleared out the vast majority of their bases and resources.

"Rafaela." Nicole slapped the woman right back. She couldn't remember the last time she'd been so happy to see someone. "I'm *so* glad to see you."

"You have no idea," Pham said, her smile still playing across her lips. "Things have been hell around here."

"They took Patagonia too," Nicole said.

She noticed a small pair of blue eyes staring at her from a darkened corner of the room. They belonged to a small girl with bedraggled blonde hair twisted into a nest around her angelic face.

"Nicole?" asked the girl.

Nicole nodded.

"You know Kal, right?"

Nicole felt a strange mixture of hope and despair at Kal's name. How did this little girl know him?

"Yes," Nicole replied. "He's my friend." *Is* not *was.*

The girl hesitantly stepped into the light, her hands clutching the hem of her plain gray blouse. "Have you seen him? Did he tell you about me? Asha."

Nicole shook her head. "I'm sorry. I haven't seen him in a while. I'm sure he *would* have told me about you though," She smiled.

Asha bit her lip. "You haven't seen him either, huh? Of course not." She sniffed and her mouth quivered at the edges. "He said he'd come back for me."

"If he said it, then it will happen." Nicole put on her most earnest face.

Asha took a deep breath and smiled nervously. "He told me all about you. You're a diplomat, right? You make treaties and stuff?"

"Something like that. Or at least I used to be."

Nicole *had* been a diplomatic attaché on the Kurz homeworld when the war had started. A lot had happened since then. Things like betraying Humanity, becoming a soldier, losing everything. Now she wasn't sure *what* she was anymore and she didn't care too much. She didn't need a label or a title to know what she wanted.

"You'll get a chance to grill Nicole all you want in a bit." Pham looked down at the little girl. "But I need to talk with her in private right now."

"Grown-up time?" Asha pouted.

Pham nodded and the girl spun on her heel and walked out of the room.

"She's a good girl," Pham said. "Been through a helluva lot but somehow still seems pretty normal."

"She knew Kal?" Nicole wondered how he'd met the young girl. She could imagine what effect Asha would've had on him. He'd lost his family over a decade earlier. Befriending a girl around the age of his children when they'd died must have been hard.

Pham nodded. "She was taken in by one of our agents near the beginning of the war. A Nasi soldier actually." Nicole couldn't believe it. "He was the first parent that she'd ever had. Then she loses him and now she's lost Kal." Pham shook her head.

"We'll get her back to him. Where is he? Where are the Skulls and the rest of the assault teams that came to New America?"

"If I knew where he was or where anyone was, we'd probably be having a different conversation. Right after we'd taken down the plasma lances, the Jadid called for Kal and took him up to their fleet. Almost as soon as he left, the bastards took out the Fridge with orbital fire. Most people didn't stand a chance. Some of us, like Cinder and me, happened to be in the right place at the right time."

"But Kal wasn't there," Nicole said. She tried to hide her joy at the news. "He wasn't in the attack."

"We're still trying to figure out who survived the attack," Pham continued, ignoring Nicole's question. "The TLF—and every other rebel group—is gone. Wiped out. But I found a few people from Samsara Fleet. I figured you'd be happy to know that your Sergeant Kimathi and Corporal Sato are in Tiradentes."

"That's incredible." It was more than that. It was the best news she'd had since she crashed onto the damned planet.

"Indeed," Pham replied flatly. "But with everything else, it still doesn't help us too much. We've got two enemies, the Jadid and Nasi, and no way to fight them. Everything we worked on for the past two years has been destroyed, and we're scattered across the planet."

"Details." Nicole waved the woman's concerns away. After the news she'd heard she felt more optimistic than she had any right to be. "What about Kal? Any word on him?"

Pham studied Nicole for a moment. Nicole could see the reproach and pity in the woman's eyes. "I don't know what to tell you. I know when someone's not thinkin' rationally. Hell, it's happened to me once or twice." She paused, head tilted. "Fine. I would say there's no hope for the good general 'cept that we keep seeing public notices on the Domespat nets."

The Domestic Patrol, or Domespat, was the Human security force that had enacted the edicts of the planet's prior government, the New American Empire. After the Jadid had taken control, they'd quickly eliminated the NAE and its leader, Fulki Choi, but had allowed the Domespat to remain in power. They were the same vicious dogs, but now with a new master.

"What kind of notices?" Nicole asked, a glimmer of hope blossoming in her chest.

"They're offering a pretty nice reward to anyone who can find him," Pham said. "Good news is that they keep sending out the notices over the planetary net, which means they haven't found him. Bad news is that neither have we."

"He's most likely gone off planet." Cinder had flopped down on a bench that had been fashioned out of a few pieces of old machinery and a piece of sheet metal. "I mean, they summoned him to their fleet and now they're looking for him here. He's probably left the system."

"My thoughts too." Pham nodded. "Ultimately it don't

matter since we got no idea where he went and no way to get off planet."

The Jadid had restricted all travel on and off planet, even going so far as to go through the ports disabling any ship with a fold drive. They'd also eliminated most of the communication between planets by taking out the automated drones that carried messages. Now they broadcast patriotic messages over the planetary net promoting the strength and integrity of the New Human Empire as they called it. To Nicole it was a clear and simple strategy, isolate New America and then brainwash the populace until they had no idea what was true or not. She was reminded of a lesson she'd learned as a child: say something long enough and it becomes the truth.

"I think I might have an idea to help with that," Nicole said.

"I'm all ears."

"The Jadid betrayed us on Patagonia as well," Nicole said. "I came here with the help of a Jadid scientist. She was working on a new ship called the *McCullough*, one that's like nothing we've ever imagined. It can fold from anywhere and can travel between the universes."

"A skip ship?" Pham asked.

"More than that," Nicole said excitedly. "It can travel to almost anywhere instantly. And it doesn't need to be away from gravitational fields before it folds."

Pham's excitement grew as she realized what Nicole was saying. "It's like something from a holo," Pham said. "But why are you still here if you got this ship that can go anywhere, anytime?"

"The ship's at the bottom of the ocean outside of Hope. But if we can get it, we can go through any Jadid blockade."

"How're we gonna get the ship from the bottom of the ocean?" Cinder asked when Nicole had finished.

Pham clicked her tongue. "Details. This is something I can work with." She bit her lip in thought. "It's not going to be simple, but it *is* possible."

"Ai said that the ship's components should survive being submerged," Nicole said. "It's built like an asteroid. As long as we can get it out of the ocean, she should be able to get it working pretty quickly."

"This is the break we've been waiting for." Pham clapped her hands together. "Time to get off our asses and get to work."

"I couldn't agree more," Nicole said.

Chapter Two
Nicole | New America

Pham explained it would take a few days to get everything they needed to recover the skip ship and for Nicole to "sit tight" in Hope. She wasn't sure what else she could do. She wouldn't leave Ai alone, and getting the Jadid scientist to another town without being spotted was near impossible.

She spent her time waiting in their shared flat. It was torture. Although Cinder had reactivated her implant, they were under a strict "no comms" policy. Instead, she paced back and forth in the common area, waiting for Pham or Cinder to contact them.

As Nicole expected, Ai handled the uncertainty much better than she did. The scientist had already spent the past several months in the cramped space and was more used to it than her. She spent most of her time curled up on a small chair in the corner pouring over technical diagrams, trying to anticipate any issue they might find once they'd recovered their ship.

After almost a week, Nicole jumped in the air as an insistent pounding against the front door shattered the quiet. Nicole ran over and cracked it open, her sidearm held just out of sight. Two hooded figures stood on the small platform outside. They pushed past her and entered the apartment— almost getting shot in the process—pulling their hoods down in the process.

"Your doorbell's broken, ma'am."

Staff Sergeant Ekon Kimathi stood in front of her, his smile broken by a deep gash that ran across his mouth. The fact that there was a scar was a clear sign he'd been unable to get to proper medical treatment. Next to him stood Corporal Elinor Sato who seemed positively tiny in comparison. She appeared tiny next to almost anyone though.

To their surprise, and a little to her own, she wrapped each of them in an embrace. She didn't even have to think about it. Seeing her friends for the first time in months when she didn't know if they were alive or not was a cathartic event.

Nicole stepped back from the two soldiers and gestured to the rest of the room. "Take a seat. I think we've got water to drink and"—she took a quick mental inventory of their food supply—"water to eat as well."

Ai nodded slightly and the two Humans nodded back before taking seats at the round dining table in the corner of the room.

"Never thought I'd see you again," Ekon said. "But damn glad I was wrong."

"It's a small galaxy." Nicole set a small glass carafe on the table.

"Feels pretty big to me." Sato grabbed a chipped ceramic mug from the table in front of her and inspected it. "And we're stuck on this planet while the Jadid and the Domespat hunt everyone down." She set the mug down with a frown.

"Not to mention the Nasi." Ekon grimaced as he took a small sip from the cup in front of him. "They're still out there."

"One thing at a time," Nicole said. "We'll get there."

"We'd better get our asses moving toward there." Kimathi

scowled. "We've been holed up in the back of a chembar in Tiradentes for months."

Another knock sounded at the door, and Pham and Cinder rushed inside when Nicole opened it.

"Bout time you got here," Ekon said.

"We came as fast as we could," Pham replied flatly. "Now let's get to work."

Pham explained that in order to repair the *McCullough* they'd need to get it out of the polar water and to a repair shop where Ai could work on it. To do that, they'd need two very hard to find things: a salvage ship and a repair facility. Under normal circumstances, finding them would be hard. On an occupied planet like New America, it was nearly impossible. The cell chief revealed that she'd been able to find a salvage ship, no questions asked, through a friend of a friend of a friend. They had a repair facility as well, but it was located in Kipya Kinshasa, which meant they'd have to ferry the ship over the polar mountains and hope they avoided any Domespat or Jadid patrols.

"How long do you think it will take you to fix the *McCullough*?" Pham asked. "Do you know what you need?"

"It's hard to say," Ai replied. "It could be a day or a month. I have no idea what the water has done to the components. Once I inspect it, I can reply with more certainty. Repairing a ship—especially an experimental research vessel—is fraught with complexities. I won't know everything until I've done a full diagnostic."

"Annoying but fair," Pham said. "And supplies?"

19

"I can give you a starting list. I've been working on scenarios."

"I can vouch for that," Nicole added. Sometimes she'd felt like it was the only thing the scientist had been working on.

"Good enough," the cell chief replied. "Pack up and let's go."

"Now?" Nicole asked.

"You want a moment?" Pham asked sarcastically. "Perhaps you want to build a scrapbook for the memories?"

"Shut up."

Pham laughed.

Nicole hadn't expected to have to leave their apartment so quickly. Thankfully she didn't have any possessions to pack other than her sister's starfish necklace and her sidearm. She considered it a silver lining to having nothing in life. The others had already left, departing in pairs so they wouldn't be seen together.

Starting from scratch, Nicole thought to herself as she and Ai walked out the apartment door, *again*.

Ai had draped a bulky winter coat over herself which covered her lithe frame but couldn't hide the fact she was a head taller than anyone else around her. A mask covered the bottom of her face, and she'd pulled the hood of the coat over her head. If a passerby stared, they might see a hint of Ai's violet skin, but the disguise should be good enough to get them to the salvage ship. After that, they'd be away from the town and prying eyes. At least that was what Nicole hoped.

"It will be interesting to see how the *McCullough* has fared under the ocean," Ai said as they reached Hope's central parking area. "I hadn't designed the ship with such a scenario in mind, but I think it will have held up decently well."

"I hope you're right." Nicole looked around, trying to see if there was anyone watching them. The few people nearby didn't seem interested, so she opened the door of the aircar that Pham had left for them and climbed inside.

Moments later, they'd lifted off, heading toward the bluish-gray expanse of ocean that was just outside of town. Although transports could reach several thousand meters into the atmosphere, they normally remained low, just a hundred or so meters off the ground; the high winds could play havoc with the small vehicle's stabilization systems. They decided to go higher than normal in case they needed to take evasive action and Nicole could clearly see how the small town was at the bottom of a bowl created by the mountains around it. In many ways it was beautiful, and she knew that most people in Hope wouldn't want to be anywhere else. But she was not one of them.

"Pham said she had a good lead on the materials," Nicole said. "Your list was pretty extensive, and they have to find salvage to get some of them."

Ai nodded absentmindedly as she scanned the horizon. Nicole could have sworn the scientist was nervous if she hadn't known better. *She* was definitely nervous now that they were actually leaving the town. Were the Jadid aware? Was that speck in the horizon a bird or a fighter?

"When I get some more time and resources, I plan on making several changes to the ship." Ai tapped her tablet. "I've had plenty of time to think about how to improve it. If the central databases haven't been corrupted by the ocean water, then the information and sensor readings will be invaluable to validating some of my hypotheses."

"Sorry, Ai, but can you keep it down?" It was an inopportune time for the Jadid to suddenly decide to chat.

"Sure."

Nicole glanced over at the scientist and realized something. The woman was just as nervous as she was. "Sorry, keep going. What about the ocean water?"

"You sure?"

"Absolutely. I'd love to hear more about the *McCullough's* sensor readings." Nicole plastered a smile on her face. Damn Kal. She could hear his voice droning on about the responsibilities of a leader. Nicole needed Ai on point and ready to go. If letting her babble did it, then Nicole had to accept it.

They landed on a rocky beach and walked to the nearby salvage ship. It looked like someone had taken a normal ship, cut it in half, and then placed a long flat plate between the two pieces. Cinder sat in the cabin, her legs dangling over the side as she studied the controls. Pham was back in Kipya Kinshasa clearing space for the *McCullough* in the repair facility while Kimathi was searching for materials.

"I thought this was gonna be like a regular ship," the woman said as way of greeting. "But the controls are insane."

"Will you just listen to me?" Corporal Sato yelled from inside the cabin. "I keep tryin' to tell you how this thing works."

Cinder turned her head. "I'll figure it out. I don't need your help."

"Then stop complaining."

"How much longer?" Nicole glanced around. There was nothing to see except the ocean in front of them and the mountains behind.

"Hell if I know," Cinder said. "We just gotta make sure we know how to fly this thing." She continued to study the ship's console as if it were an ancient artifact she'd uncovered.

Not a good sign, Nicole thought to herself.

She stood by the vehicle, listening to the cacophony of Ai talking to herself and the other two women shouting back and forth at each other. After several more minutes of back and forth, and several curses, Cinder declared them ready to begin. She hopped out of the cab, strode to the back of the vehicle, and opened a compartment containing several white suits hanging on a rack.

Nicole grabbed one of the suits—which Sato called a viro-suit—and put it on. The material was heavier than Nicole expected, feeling more like a wet blanket than the thin membrane it appeared to be.

"Get aboard, ma'am" Sato said as she climbed up a small

ladder and into a transparent bubble on the back of the ship. Nicole scrambled to follow her, and as soon as she was in, the door shut, and the ship lifted off. They weaved back and forth over the water, while the ship's sensors scanned the ocean floor.

Nicole idly listened to the back and forth between Cinder and Ai over the ship's intercom as they tried to locate the ship. Thankfully Ai had had the foresight to record the approximate location of the *McCullough* when they'd crashed months earlier. Unfortunately, the ocean bed was deeper than expected, and they weren't picking up anything.

Small creatures rose to the surface and followed them as they slowly made their way over the water. They were large—about half the size of the transport—and almost completely round, making it impossible for Nicole to tell which end was the front. Their light gray hides were dappled with dark splotches of blue, and their skin undulated rhythmically as they swam underneath. As Nicole watched she had to reevaluate her initial assessment—there was no front. The animals were slowly rotating as they swam, their "fronts" becoming their "rears" and vice versa as they trailed behind the salvage ship.

"Interesting little things," observed Sato. "Don't see anything like that on Earth."

Don't see anything on Earth anymore, thought Nicole mournfully to herself.

"I think we've found it," Cinder cried out triumphantly over the intercom.

24

The ship dove forward, and Nicole found herself staring at the overcast sky for a moment before they hit the water. Once fully submerged, the ship leveled off and began to descend. The light from the surface grew dimmer, and water slowly poured into the transparent bubble Nicole and Sato were in. Nicole had been in these waters before and had almost died of hypothermia. She was pleased to find the suit completely insulated her from the ice-cold ocean water.

The rotund creatures began bouncing off the side of the salvage vessel with small thuds. A few even bounced against the glass bubble, causing Nicole's heart to pound in her chest.

"They must be defending their territory," Sato observed.

"Yeah." Nicole wondered what the creatures thought of them. Perhaps they saw them as a giant predator, or maybe they were just reacting on instinct. They probably didn't think much of anything.

They continued to descend, and the water grew pitch-black. The small thumps ceased, and it was silent except for the now whispered exchanges between Ai and Cinder. After another minute they gently landed on the silt-covered ocean floor, and the transparent bubble bobbled open.

Ship's to the port side, Cinder said over their net.

Nicole tried to remember which side was port then finally gave up and followed Sato as she bounded along the ocean floor with her headlamp casting a cone of light ahead of her. Soon the *McCullough* appeared before them, looking no worse for wear than when they'd last seen it. The bare metal

25

of the ship's exterior had a fine coating of yellow algae. Other than that, it seemed fully intact from what Nicole could tell.

We need to attach the hauling cables to the ship, Sato said over the net, her voice flat from using her implant.

Nicole followed the corporal and bounded back to the salvage ship. Once there, they grabbed a cable from one of the tall masts that had sprouted up from either side of the central bed. They bounded back to the *McCullough* and attached the flat plate at the end of the cable to the hull. Once Sato had confirmed the cable was locked in place, they ran back to the salvage ship and went through the same process with the other cable.

You're good to go, Sato said.

The cables started to retract and dragged the McCullough toward the salvage ship. As it got close, the salvage ship turned and maneuvered the *McCullough* onto the bed. Several arm-thick bands launched from the underside of the bed, wrapped over the payload, and then secured themselves on the other side.

Cargo's secure, Sato said after a quick inspection.

They jumped back into the transparent bubble, and the salvage ship slowly rose from the ocean floor in a small cloud of silt. The round creatures started to bounce against the hull again, clearly angry that their previous attacks hadn't been enough of a deterrent.

As they neared the surface, the ship tilted back, pitching Nicole and Sato forward in their seats and then launched out of the water. The pebble-strewn shore stretched out below them as their ship gained altitude and approached the mountains.

They crested the first ridge and the ship abruptly dropped, causing Nicole to yelp in surprise.

"Hold on," Cinder said over the intercom, "we've got some sort of patrol passing through."

Nicole felt helpless. She had no idea where the patrol Cinder had spotted was since there wasn't a tacmap or console in the bubble. If they were spotted, there wasn't a thing they could do either; a loaded salvage ship wouldn't be a match for even the slowest fighter.

Don't think they've spotted us yet, Cinder said. Or maybe they just don't care.

The salvage ship continued to coast along the mountain slope until it came to rest on a small trickle of water that ran between two glacier-topped ridges. Nicole looked down and studied the small mountain stream beneath the bubble. She guessed she could have touched the water without getting out of the ship if she'd wanted to. Silvery shapes writhed in the water, the sparkles of their scales melding in with the glint of the light from the sun.

"We're holding here," Cinder said with a hushed voice. There was no need, but she, like most people, Nicole included, involuntarily whispered when she was trying to hide, even when hiding inside a large salvage ship. "Sensors on this thing are crap. I've got no idea who they are. But they seem to be looking for something."

Nicole tried to focus on the water beneath her rather than

thinking about what was happening in the air above. She reminded herself that there was nothing she could do, but that thought only made things worse.

After several minutes, Cinder gave the "all clear" and lifted off. They continued forward, this time even closer to the ground than before. Although she didn't have any idea who the patrol was, Nicole was certain they were looking for them.

The Nasi had kept a hands-off approach in the governance of New America. From what she'd seen, the Jadid were not making the same mistake. The local nets had been rife with jingoistic shows about how the Jadid and Humans would rule the galaxy together. In addition to the endless propaganda, they'd been launching many more patrols than the Nasi ever had.

It all added up to one thing. Nicole knew that the longer they stayed on New America, the more danger they were in.

Chapter Three

Nicole | Kipya Kinshasa, New America

After a summary inspection of the *McCullough,* Ai declared she could have the ship fully operational within a week.

The repair facility turned out to be a factory where Pham had cleared out a small area for the scientist to work in. After they'd touched down, it had been no easy feat to move the skip ship through the still occupied areas of factory to the work space, and Nicole knew the longer it took, the more likely it was that prying eyes would see what they were doing.

By the time they maneuvered the ship to the back, Kimathi was already waiting with most of the parts Ai had asked for. She looked through the piles and gave him another list, eliciting a groan in response, then immediately started to work, ripping wiring and components from the ship.

While Ai worked, Nicole took a quick look around the building. She'd learned to always look for avenues of approach and exit points when in a new location. The factory wasn't fully utilized, and several machines had a layer of rust on them, but there were some that had clearly been used recently.

Pham grabbed a handful of TLF agents and told Kimathi to stay inside the factory while she got the parts. Nicole wanted to join them, but a gentle shake of the cell chief's head let her know it wasn't going to be possible. She knew why: if they knew what Kal looked like, there was a decent chance they knew who she was as well.

Feeling useless, Nicole tried to help Ai in repairing the ship, but it quickly became clear she was more a hinderance than a help. The best she could do was hand over tools, but Ai seemed to have everything she needed on the belt she wore across her body. Ekon was in the same boat as her, and so the two of them ended up spending a significant amount of time idly waiting in the back of the factory along with Asha.

"When do you think she'll be done?" Asha asked as Ekon sat behind her and braided her hair.

"I don't know." Nicole tried to keep the exasperation from her voice. Kimathi played the part of the older brother to a tee, but Nicole had a much harder time. He could play the part of big brother, but his family was still alive. Her family, including her younger sister, had died when Earth had been destroyed. She wasn't fully comfortable stepping back into that role.

"I can't wait to see Kal again," Asha said brightly. Ekon hummed noncommittally as he took the girl's braids and encircled her head to make a sort of crown. Nicole didn't say anything; she wished she could share the girl's certainty that he had survived the Jadid purge.

A large pop came from the direction of the *McCullough* and reverberated throughout the building. Asha jumped up with a shout and bolted underneath a nearby piece of equipment.

"Do not worry," Ai shouted. "If anything was going to explode, it would have by now."

Asha crawled back from under the equipment, eyes wide

in embarrassment, and sat back down. Kimathi continued working on her hair as if nothing had happened.

"I get scared sometimes," Asha whispered to Nicole.

"It's okay. We all do." Nicole looked at Ekon. He shook his head ruefully. Asha had been through more than most adults ever would.

"What is this place anyways?" Nicole asked, trying to change the subject.

"It's a mineral processing plant." Ekon continued to concentrate on trying to get the intricate braids to stay on Asha's head.

"I don't see any rocks or dust." Asha stood up halfway, causing Kimathi to grunt in frustration.

"They don't mine rocks," he said. "They mine creatures."

Nicole looked at him in surprise. "What do you mean, creatures?"

"You know, the things that live around here in the mountains and glaciers." Kimathi tilted his head. "They're mostly mineral. The creatures eat the metals and stone in the ground. Then the miners catch them and…er…process them. It's easier to catch them and extract the minerals than extract it from the ground."

"That's…horrible." Asha turned to look at him with a scowl, eliciting another grunt of annoyance.

"Sit still." Kimathi gently turned her head so she was facing forward again and continued his work. "Why is it horrible? We use animals for food all the time. I remember you saying how much you liked eating pigs."

31

"I'd never had them before," Asha protested, her cheeks reddening even more. "Besides, we need food. We don't need eat innocent animals to get the minerals. We could just take it from the ground like you said."

"We don't *have* to eat other animals either," said Nicole. "We choose to. Not saying it's right or wrong, just that it's not much different."

"*I* think it's wrong," Asha said in a tone that seemed to indicate the point had been decided.

"Gotta moment?" Pham asked as she leaned against the wall and gave a quick wave to Asha.

"Sure," Nicole replied.

She stood and followed the cell chief around the *McCullough*. They walked around a large piece of machinery that reminded Nicole of a shuttle stood on one end.

"Any luck with Ai's list?" Nicole asked when they were out of earshot.

Pham nodded. "I got my stuff. Still got a few people out there looking." She turned and looked at the *McCullough*. "Ship's lookin' good. First Bo and now Ai. Are these Jadid all brilliant?"

Bowen Nguyen, a Jadid scientist who had become a part of their team, was still missing. According to Pham, she'd lost track of him even before the Jadid had attacked the Fridge. He was the only person, Human or Jadid, that could match Ai's intelligence.

"Well, Ai is one of the Jadid's top scientists. But yeah, it'd be nice to meet a dumb Jadid for once."

Pham laughed. "Yeah, one that can't figure out how to use or spoon or needs help bathing."

"It'd make me feel better about myself and our chances."

"Ain't that the truth." Pham paused. "Look, we need to figure out exactly what we're gonna do once we get this ship workin'."

Nicole was confused. "I thought we'd already said we'd find Kal."

"You think we're doin' all this just to find one man?" Pham asked incredulously. "That's not a plan. Not a good one at least. He's one person who may or may not be alive. I like him as much as the next person, but we got bigger fish to fry."

Nicole had made a promise to herself. She'd vowed she would find Kal if it was the last thing she did. Perhaps because of that, she'd blinded herself to the fact that others may not share the same goal. Sure, Kal had started the resistance against the Nasi, but that didn't mean anything anymore.

"I think he went to Patagonia," Nicole said. She would have bet every single credit on the chit that if he had escaped like she did, he would go to find her on Patagonia. "We need to go there anyway. If there's anything that remains of Samsara Fleet, it would be there."

Pham considered it. "Yeah, that's where I was thinkin'." She seemed placated. "But understand this; I'm here to free New America from the Jadid, Nasi, or any other bastard who thinks they can take what's not theirs. That's what this mission is about."

Nicole nodded. "Of course. Of course." She wasn't going

to argue with the cell chief, but for Nicole, the mission was still about finding Kal. It always had been. The rest of Humanity be damned.

❖

It ended up taking a week and a half for Ai to repair the *McCullough*. After going through a final day of testing, she declared the small vessel ready for action.

The wait had given Nicole and Pham plenty of time to plan out their next steps on Patagonia. Nicole had led the Samsara Fleet assault teams on the planet, and much like Kal, had been separated from her soldiers before the Jadid attacked. Her scout team, Bergeron's Bones, or just the Bones, had *almost* been as elite a unit as the Skulls. Now both were gone.

The last she'd seen them, they'd barely escaped from a subterranean plasma lance facility. She'd been called to orbit by the Jadid for what she'd thought was going to be a strategic planning session and had only just escaped thanks to Ai's help. She didn't know exactly what had happened to her team, but she had a good idea based on what she'd seen on New America. Despite that, she thought there was a good chance at least some of them had escaped, and she knew exactly where to find them.

"We're ready to do this," Pham said, patting the side of the ship reassuringly.

Nicole started to step inside when she felt a firm tug at the back of her shirt. She turned around to see Asha looking up at her.

"Why won't you take me?" Nicole couldn't tell if the girl was purposely making her sky-blue eyes as big as possible. She was pretty sure the pouty lower lip was intentional.

When the girl had found out she couldn't join them, she'd spent days alternating between crying and throwing small fits. Finally, Kimathi had pulled her aside. When they'd returned, her hand nestled in his, she had seemed to finally accept it.

"You know why," Nicole said, placing her hand on the girl's shoulder. "But we'll be back. I promise."

"You'd better." Asha started to cry, her face melting with trails of tears coming down her cheeks. She buried her face into Nicole's chest.

Nicole let the girl cry and then softly pulled away, stepping back into the ship. She looked back to see Ekon bend down and give the girl a final bear hug. She could see tears coming from both their eyes as he stepped past her into the ship.

The *McCullough* had originally been a research vessel, intended to study deep space anomalies. Because of this, it had been completely over-engineered with an incredibly thick hull and struts crossing through the interior. The ship was much smaller than the normal scout corvettes Nicole was used to and barely fit the five people they had on board: Nicole, Cinder, Ai, Kimathi, and Pham.

"Get strapped in, everyone," Ai instructed as the door closed behind Nicole. "I'll be able to take off in a few minutes."

35

The interior was at once both familiar and strange to Nicole. It was a mix of the organic-looking Jadid technology mixed with the industrial Human. Smooth bare-metal floors met with multihued walls that smoothly flowed back and forth. She walked forward into the cockpit and sat down on the Jadid-sized chair next to Ai. The woman's hands flickered over the controls as she spun up the engines.

For most ships, folding required them to get to a point far away from planets and anything else that might have a gravitational field. Their drives simply couldn't handle the interference of even the smallest gravitational field. Not only could the ship travel between the Human and Jadid universes, it could fold from anywhere. However, it was still not fully tested. Ai had told them that traveling just a few kilometers above the planet's surface would increase their chances of success—and by success she meant them not imploding—a hundredfold. The *McCullough* glided through the hole in the ceiling which the TLF fighters had been cutting the past several days.

"I see you even made some upgrades," Nicole said, pointing to the tactical map that had been bolted to the console.

Ai nodded. "Since we're moving to an operational use, I needed to add some features. Unfortunately, I don't know how they'll interact with the experimental fold drive, but it's worth the risk."

"Any weapons or shields?"

Ai frowned at her. "I'm an engineer, not a miracle

worker."

"Worth asking."

The *McCullough* shot straight up and the mountains surrounding Kipya Kinshasa dropped away. The white and gray polar cap was directly beneath them with the grid-like continents of New America at the planet's edges.

"We've got incoming," Ai remarked casually, pointing to red icons on the tacmap.

"And we're being hailed." Nicole's finger hesitated over the comms control. Did she really want to talk with the Jadid? What was left for them to say?

"Screw it." Nicole smashed her finger against the controls, and a Jadid face appeared on the view screen.

"Experimental ship *McCullough*, you are not authorized to leave New America." The Jadid's words were precise and emotionless. "Immediately power down all systems and wait for further instructions."

"Screw you," Nicole spat back. "We're not—"

Ancient Bao Wang's face suddenly appeared in the view screen. Of course, Nicole's voice and likeness must have been designed to initiate some protocol to alert Wang. She should be flattered he wanted to deal with her personally.

As an Ancient, Bao had been one of the original Humans that had unwillingly been part of an experiment hundreds of years ago to test early fold drives. Rather than sending the test ship that he and the other Ancients had been on to another location, it had sent them to another universe. For hundreds of years, they'd settled their new home and created the Jadid. Another Ancient, Esma Baykara, had spent the time plotting her return to the planet that had wronged her. And when she had, her and her Nasi had destroyed everything.

"Nicole." Bao broke out into a smile. "Glad to see you."

If Nicole hadn't known the man was a psychopath, she wouldn't have realized how insincere that smile truly was.

"Bao."

"Listen, you must realize that wherever you go I'll find you. Let's talk. Stay for a bit and let's figure out a way to resolve this." He made a pained expression. "We've been allies for years, and my soldiers made some errors. All of this is—"

"Is what?" Nicole spat back. "A tragic misunderstanding?"

A flush crept into Bao's cheeks. "An error. A mistake. I thought my soldiers had changed. But you've heard some of our histories. You know what my children had to do in order to survive." Nicole *had* heard some of the Jadid history and knew they *had* faced terrible odds when they had first been stranded on Altterra. "Look. What can I say? There's still time to fix this and fight the *real* enemy: Esma and her Nasi. Just power down and let's talk before this all gets worse."

"Bao, screw you and screw your talking." Nicole leaned toward the console. "We'll talk when I'm damn ready to."

"We've got *something* coming toward us—fast," Ai said.

Nicole could see the faint dots streaking toward them on the tacmap. Whatever they were, they were cloaked.

"And they've figured out cloaking," Nicole said. Another of their advantages, lost.

By her estimation, they had seconds before they hit the

McCullough. Damn Bao. He was just trying to buy time. With a snarl of frustration, Nicole activated the fold drive and New America disappeared from the viewscreen.

❖

The *McCullough* pivoted and turned to face Patagonia. They were a light-week away and Nicole couldn't make out the planet from the stars around it.

To make sure they weren't flying into a Gylock's nest they conducted a phased approach to ensure that they were able to see the Jadid's activities prior to them arriving. It entailed folding within a light-week of the planet, taking optical sensor readings, folding closer again, and then again. It allowed them to see the planet from several time periods before they arrived and know what their enemies had been doing without risking discovery. On most ships it could take a while, but with the *McCullough,* it only added a quarter hour onto their journey.

"Ready for the final fold?" Ai asked.

"Yeah." Nicole turned her head and shouted toward the back of the ship. "Get ready, everyone, the Liberation Fleet's in orbit."

Getting through the fleet to land on the planet would be the most difficult part of their plan. They couldn't simply fold down to the surface. Instead, they'd need to somehow avoid detection or evade the Jadid fleet. Without a cloak of their own, it would require some luck and some pretty clever flying.

The fold drive engaged, and they were instantly millions

of kilometers closer to the planet. Patagonia now occupied a large portion of their viewscreen.

"The fleet's gone," Nicole muttered to herself. There was only a single red dot on the tacmap. The rest of the ships were nowhere to be found. They must have just left since they'd been there when the McCullough folded from a few light hours out.

"Good for us," replied Ai. "Bad for someone else."

It had been several months since Nicole and Ai had fled Patagonia. Based on what had happened on New America, she worried for the people she'd left behind. The Nasi had been merciless but efficient, but the Jadid in Wang's Liberation Fleet were just cruel.

Ai gradually adjusted their heading to avoid the lone Jadid battleship and continued moving toward the planet. Neither the capital ship nor the smaller transports and merchant ships in the area realized they were there.

"What's going on?" Nicole asked herself.

"I doubt they've noticed us," said Ai. "A small Jadid ship like ours tends to blend in with the normal traffic."

"I guess we should be thankful."

"Take any advantage you can," agreed Ai.

They made their way into the planet's atmosphere and soared over the mountains that cut the single continent, Pangea, in two. They flew over a verdant jungle, steering clear of major cities and towns before touching down deep in the forest outside of a small town named Trokar. The town itself sat in a gentle valley, surrounded by rolling farmland and hills rising in the distance.

"The rest of you stay here," Nicole instructed. "You see anything and you take off. Understand?" They nodded. "Sergeant Kimathi, you're with me."

Nicole and Kimathi grabbed their sidearms and left the ship, making their way out of the forest and into the tall plant stalks of a farm—Nicole had no idea what kind they were.

"So you think this woman you're looking for will still be here?" Kimathi asked doubtfully.

"I don't have a better idea," Nicole replied.

When Nicole had been in the small town before, she'd met a woman named Deepta. Although her background was a mystery to Nicole, she was clearly very capable and committed to their cause. If anyone would have survived the Jadid's betrayal, it would be her.

The citizens of Trokar seemed to be unfazed by the events of the war. They walked through the streets, dressed in dirt-dusted farm attire. Nicole and Kimathi drew a few glances, but otherwise, no one seemed to pay them much notice.

"Here goes nothin'," Nicole muttered.

She pressed the call button on a small umber-colored house and looked up at the security camera. A small tinge of worry sizzled through her chest as she waited for a response. If Deepta wasn't there, Nicole wasn't sure who she'd try and find next.

The door clicked open, and Nicole pushed inside with Kimathi fast on her heels. As it shut behind them, she looked around the room and felt a wave of relief as she saw two people looking at her with slight smiles on their faces.

"Well, looks like the general was right," said Deepta. "Guess you're harder to kill than you look."

"General?" Nicole asked hopefully. *Had they found Kal?*

"Sorry, not the one you're looking for." Ishmael placed a hand on her shoulder. "General Samaha is here. We haven't heard anything from anyone else on Samsara Fleet."

"Somehow she knew you'd return," Deepta said. "Guess she wasn't as crazy as I thought."

"What happened?" Nicole asked.

Deepta explained that almost as soon as Nicole had left, the Jadid had begun saturating the area where she'd been with orbital fire. Deepta had found out later they'd carpeted all six Nasi plasma lance sites across the planet at the same time, ostensibly to make sure they were offline—though no one believed that was the *real* reason. It was clear that they'd taken the opportunity to eliminate the legendary Samsara Fleet scout teams and the local resistance at one time.

On New America, all six assault teams had rendezvoused at a single location, the Fridge, when the Jadid struck. Since the forces on Patagonia had still been spread across six locations many of them had survived to Nicole's relief. However, the Jadid had unleashed the same tactics on Patagonia as they had on New America—cutting off travel to and from the planet, sending out a flurry of patrols, and saturating the local nets with propaganda. They'd rounded up many of the fighters that they'd called allies only days before.

"We've been waiting here at General Samaha's request,"

Deepta concluded.

"Doing nothin' I might add," Ishmael added. "Small-town charm my—"

"It's been tough on us both," Deepta interrupted. "Though perhaps a little more on him."

"I finally find Ava and then the general sends me here."

"You found her?" Nicole asked happily. She'd been there when the man had been separated from Ava. The two argued all the time from what she could tell, but she'd never seen two people more clearly in love.

"Yeah. After a few days I wanted to lose 'er again." He rolled his eyes. "But the general said we had to sit out here in the boonies and wait for ya."

"Samaha knew I'd come?" asked Nicole.

"She seemed almost certain of it." Deepta shrugged. "And she was right."

"So now we can get the hell outta here?" Ishmael pulled a small bag off the floor and slung it across his back. "I've been waiting for this moment for weeks."

"You've had your bags packed this entire time?" Kimathi asked.

"Damn straight." Ishmael adjusted the bag's strap. "We had no idea who was gonna come to that door. Best be ready for anything. Or haven't you learned *anything* in the past two years."

"Fair," Kimathi conceded.

"Enough chattin'." Deepta grabbed her own bag and hefted it across her shoulders. "We need to get going. No telling who might've seen you come into town. Samaha's in a base in the mountains. Hopefully she's found a way off planet."

"I wouldn't worry about that," Nicole said. "We've got something to solve that problem."

Chapter Four
Nicole | Patagonia

They touched down inside General Samaha's base and Nicole was overjoyed to see another familiar face. As she was stepping out of the *McCullough* she saw Chief Heather Ramos smiling at her from the doorway of one of the bunkers.

"You're lookin' good, ma'am."

"You too, chief." Nicole embraced the woman. "It's so good to see you."

"General always said you'd show up," Ramos said.

"And I was right," General Aamina Samaha called out as she came out from a bunker. "Damn good to see you, Nicole."

"You too, ma'am." Nicole gestured towards the *McCullough.* "Got a present for you too."

General Samaha slowly walked around the *McCullough* as Nicole told her about what the ship could do and what'd happened to her since they'd last spoke.

"So this thing can fold from *anywhere?*" the general asked once they'd made two full circuits.

"Yup," Nicole replied. She wasn't sure why she felt so proud. It wasn't like *she'd* built the thing.

"And it can get there almost instantly?"

"Yup, it travels through the Jadid's universe. Flight times are a fraction of what they normally are."

Samaha looked up at her. "We could go to Altterra as well?"

"I guess." Nicole wasn't sure why the general would want

45

to go to the Jadid homeworld. All of their forces had already been committed to the Human's universe. Even if the other Ancients were not in league with Bao, they still couldn't do anything to stop him.

"I've talked enough with Bao and the other Ancients to believe that he's operating completely on his own." Samaha turned away from the ship and looked squarely at Nicole. "He's a snake. The only question I have is if there are even any other Ancients left. If there are, they may be willing to help us."

The general stepped back and turned down a small path that wound away from the landing pad and through the sparse undergrowth. They were in a former antiair base that had been used in the violent civil war only a year prior. When the Nasi had arrived, the planetary government had dissolved, leaving chaos in its wake. After a year of fighting, Foyleton, led by the former Skulls pilot, Karl Garcia, had won. For a short period of time there had been peace, and the base they were in, along with the others that dotted Pangea's central mountain range, had been abandoned. Local flora had started to breach the perimeter and there were small piles of rusted equipment stacked against the defensive walls.

"I have to say," Samaha said as they entered the base's central cluster of buildings. "I hadn't expected you to arrive with something like the *McCullough*, but I'm going to sure as hell use it now that it's here."

"What about Kal?" asked Nicole.

"What about him?" Samaha asked breezily.

"We've got to find him."

"Do we?" Samaha pulled open a piece of sheet metal that had been repurposed as a door and entered a small barracks. The opposite end of the building was gone and someone had covered the gaping hole with a patchwork of tarps. "I've found that General Norman tends to appear when you least expect him. I have good money on him being invincible."

Nicole wished that were true. She knew Kal well enough to know that most of the time he wasn't thinking beyond his next action. He'd be the first to admit that ninety percent of his success was due to luck. Actually, he would have said due to his team, but Nicole guessed he was alone now.

"The question I've got right now, is what do *we* do now." Samaha stood in front of a large portable display. "When Samsara Fleet first started, we had allies. We had options. Now with the Nasi confined to the Human colonies, all our allies have disappeared." She grunted in frustration. "Hell, even the Kurz have gone back to their planets to rebuild since their last ship was destroyed. Now it's just us, just Humans left to finish this fight." She slammed her fist against one of the ultracrete walls.

Samaha winced in pain and took a moment to regroup. "Based on your intelligence, the Jadid fleet guarding the planet is gone. If I was going to hazard a guess, they're on their way to capture one of the Nasi-held planets."

That meant Mariga or Wudexingqiu.

"The goddamn civil war has started in the cities again," Ishmael said. "With the Jadid Liberation Fleet gone, it'll only get worse. At least they *tried* to keep the fighting limited."

"Any word on the former government?" Samaha asked. Garcia's government had done a good job in keeping the peace right up until when the Nasi realized they were collaborating with the resistance and "disappeared" everyone in power. As far as Nicole knew, they'd all been imprisoned. But who really knew with the Nasi?

"We've got a decent idea of where most of the survivors are being held," reported Ishmael. "We can't be sure until we go in though."

Nicole looked at the general. "You thinkin' of freeing them?"

"Of course," Samaha said. "We don't leave soldiers behind. And we need them, especially with the Jadid fleet gone. We'll need people to lead this planet once it's free."

"Any word on my team?" Nicole had thought about them every day while stranded on Hope but was afraid to hear what the answer might be.

Samaha nodded. "Yes, the Bones were captured and held as well. We're going to get them *all* back. But we're getting ahead of ourselves. We need to know where that Jadid fleet went."

"We've got to release them," Nicole said. "We don't know what the Jadid will do."

"We will. We will." Samaha placed a hand on Nicole's shoulder. "But we're not going to be able to organize some sort of jailbreak. We need to take out that ship in orbit first. Once we do that, the other dominos will fall. The Jadid garrison here is relatively weak. We take out that ship and then the planet will be ours."

"Couldn't you have done that already?" Ekon asked. "I mean, you're an entire planet here. It's just one ship."

"You think we didn't try, kid?" Ishmael asked gruffly. "They took out an entire town." He shook his head. "Just rained down fire until there was nothing left. Killed everyone, their own people included."

"How are you gonna take out that ship?" Pham raised a skeptical eyebrow. "You didn't even have a way off the planet until we arrived."

"Oh, I've still got a few tricks up my sleeve," Samaha said. "I didn't catch on to Bao until it was too late, but I always make sure to have a backup. The *Ofira* and *Merrimack* folded away as soon as he ordered his fleet to betray us. He had moles in our fleet? Well, I had my own," she nodded towards Ai, "as Nicole knows."

"After everything, I realized that I couldn't trust the Ancients anymore," Ai added. "They've become...corrupt." She tilted her head. "Or perhaps they always were, and we never realized until now."

"Power corrupts," Samaha said. "Not always but often. And for some people, it doesn't matter who they have to kill to get more of it. However, I have two fully operational capital ships ready to fold into the system. But before they can come, I need to know what happened to that Jadid fleet. If our ships take out the remaining ship and the rest of the fleet comes back," she looked at each of them in the eye, "then what happened to that village will pale in comparison."

Nicole imagined Wang's Liberation Fleet decimating Patagonia in retaliation. The lives that would be lost was incomprehensible.

"With the *McCullough*, we can fold ahead of their fleet and see if they are going to Wudexingqiu or Mariga," Samaha continued. "If we know where they are headed, then we have time and perhaps some options."

"I say we go for it," Pham said. "Where else would the fleet have gone? This is our chance. Let's crush the bastards." She raised her open hand in the air and closed it into a fist.

"Easy there," Samaha said. "We could, but we don't have to. We don't need to operate blind. They might have folded away to try and lure our ships back. The *McCullough* changes everything. We can operate at a speed our enemies—" Samaha paused.

"General?" Kimathi asked.

"Sorry. What was I saying?" She shook her head. "We've got an advantage. One that our enemy doesn't realize we have. Let's use it. Nicole, find out where that fleet went."

"It would be my pleasure, ma'am."

General Samaha ordered the technicians at the base to retrofit the *McCullough* with at least rudimentary shields and weapons. When the ship arrived at Mariga or Wudexingqiu, it would be a key target. While they worked on adding the defenses, Ai was able to build and install a cloak in only a day.

She cautioned Nicole that the device wouldn't be as efficient or reliable as what she was used to but should hide them from most sensor scans.

As Ai and the technicians finished their work, Nicole talked with the few soldiers at the base. She expected them to be dejected or defeated. Instead, they were angry. The Liberation Fleet's betrayal had, if anything, made them even more determined.

Their anger was palpable enough that Nicole asked Kimathi and Pham to keep an eye on Ai. She worried that an overzealous soldier might forget whose side she was fighting on. Nicole had been at the receiving end of that kind of zeal before, and she wanted to stop it before it turned deadly.

She found herself in the base's makeshift operations center. Housed inside one of the unused hangers, the center was a hastily thrown together mess of tables, viewscreens, and consoles.

"General Borgeron?" A man stood up from his desk, wide-eyed, and looked at her.

"Yeah," Nicole replied uncertainly.

"Honor to meet you ma'am. I've heard a lot about you."

The man started telling her about how he'd been following her and her team's missions through traffic on the net. As he recounted, in great yet incorrect detail, missions that she'd been on, Nicole found her eyes wandering around the room. She'd seen people fawn over Kal like this, much to his great discomfort, but had never been on the receiving end herself. It wasn't pleasant.

"Wait!" Nicole almost shouted, causing the man to stop mid-sentence.

She pointed to several images on one of the viewscreens. "Why are they up there?" Sergeant Gruppenhiem—or Grupp as everyone called him—and Mother Ju's images were displayed on the screen. They, along with Nicole, had been responsible for disabling the plasma lances on Patagonia and defeating the Nasi there.

"Those are some of our agents in Kasongo, ma'am," the man replied.

"You able to contact them?" Nicole wanted to let her friends know she was still alive.

The man shook his head ruefully. "Sorry, ma'am, we're outside of the comms window. We initiate anything now, and we'd be risking exposure.

"Can you let them know I'm alive next time you speak to them?" Nicole asked.

The technician nodded enthusiastically. "Of course." He chuckled. "I'm gonna let everyone know." He started talking about yet another of Nicole's missions.

Nicole scrambled to think of a way out of the conversation. Finally, she settled on pretending to have received an emergency message through her implant and scrambling out of the center.

As she continued her tour, she thought about the ship above them. Was General Frederick Zhou commanding it? He'd been an officer in Samsara Fleet before joining Wang and betraying them. The bastard had been in command of the fleet around Patagonia when Nicole had escaped the planet. Was he still there? Did he feel any guilt over his actions? He'd been a completely by-the-book officer in the fleet and a rising star. She would never understand how Wang had been able to twist him so.

Nicole shook her head and climbed into the *McCullough*. Zhou would answer for his actions eventually. For now, she had to remain focused on finding the missing fleet—and Kal. Despite what she'd told Samaha, Nicole's primary focus was still on him. That was why she'd decided to go to Mariga first.

Kimathi, Pham, and Deepta were already seated in the ship's cargo bay. Nicole gave them a thumbs-up as she walked past and then entered the cramped cockpit, taking a seat next to Ai.

"Let's head out." Nicole strapped herself in as the Jadid went through final checks. "We'll hit Mariga first."

They lifted off the ground and left Patagonia's exosphere. Nicole wasn't worried about the Jadid ship; even If they were spotted, they could easily fold away. With a small flourish, Ai activated the fold drive and the blue orb of Patagonia disappeared in the rear viewscreen.

Mariga replaced it after a few seconds of travel. Those few seconds would have taken days in a normal ship. They were far enough out that it would have been almost impossible to see the planet with the naked eye. But the *McCullough's* optical sensors were able to zoom in enough that they could see rough details of its ice-capped surface.

"Starting staged approach," Ai called out.

Over the next few minutes, they folded several times, gradually getting closer to the planet. Although the ships changed positions, the Nasi fleet didn't change in number.

"Looks like the Jadid haven't arrived here at least," Nicole observed when they were only a light hour away from the planet. "Let's go in."

Ai activated the fold drive for the final time and Mariga suddenly dominated the viewscreen. A second later, alarms blared through the ship almost instantly, indicating they were within weapons range of the ships.

The seven Nasi capital ships were in multi-geosynchronous orbits around the planet. Unfortunately, there was no sign of General Zhou's fleet of Liberation Fleet ships from Patagonia. They may still be on their way or going to another location.

"Let's head down to the planet," said Nicole. "There's something else I want to check out."

Ice and snow, with the occasional mountain poking through, covered the surface of Mariga. The planet's surface was completely inhospitable to Human life, so the first settlers had gone underground and used its extensive network of caves to house their cities and agriculture. There were landing ports underneath the surface in each city, but they were heavily monitored by the Nasi and a ship like the *McCullough* would be flagged almost immediately.

Nicole studied the detailed map of the planet on her

console looking for somewhere they could land and access the network of caves. There were caverns and small forgotten entrances that allowed access underground, but finding one that wasn't monitored was the tricky part.

"Land here." Nicole pointed at the tacmap.

Ai nodded and adjusted their course. As they descended, atmospheric friction buffeted their small craft and the planets monochromatic landscape unfurled beneath them. Nicole was reminded of the tundra around Hope. But where Hope had some signs of life—a few plants, small animals, dirt and rocks peeking through the snow—Mariga was an ocean of white.

As soon as they'd touched down, Nicole stood up and walked to the back. The others were donning the cold weather gear that had been packed away in one of the storage containers. They were the warmest they could find on Patagonia; she just hoped they'd be enough to withstand the few minutes' walk to the greenhouse she'd found on the map.

"What're we doin', ma'am?" asked Ekon as he pulled on a heavy white coat. "I thought we were just scouting for the fleet."

"We are," Nicole replied as she pulled her own gear from one of the containers built into the bulkhead. "But we need to wait a bit, and I want to see if I can make contact."

"With who?" Pham asked skeptically.

"I believe it's with *whom*," Ekon corrected.

Pham shot him a look that should have turned him to ash.

"Just finished getting your gear on," Nicole said. "There's a greenhouse not far from here."

Pham turned her deadly glare onto Nicole but complied.

As they finished getting ready, Ai walked around the perimeter of the ship, laying out optical projectors. The small cylindrical devices would camouflage the ship, rendering it invisible and shielding it from anything but the most intense scrutiny.

One of the few facilities on Mariga that was near the surface were the hydroponic greenhouses. The natural sunlight was much better for the plants, and the heated glass prevented the shifting snows from covering them. The greenhouses were mainly automated, but each one had a small service tunnel for cultivators and harvesters, perfect for getting below the surface.

They left Ai with the *McCullough* and began tromping toward the greenhouse, the snow reaching up to their thighs at some points. Nicole's legs started to ache as she high-stepped through the waist-high drifts of snow. She noticed Kimathi and Pham having the same issues. Pham's short stature made it worse for her, the snow sometimes reaching above her waist, requiring Nicole and Kimathi to help pull her along through the deep drifts. Finally, Nicole saw the glint of sun reflecting off the oval dome of a greenhouse.

Despite her cold weather gear, Nicole had lost most of the feeling in her hands and feet. Her outfit was designed for the polar caps of New America, not the deep snow-covered valleys of Patagonia. Wetness from the snow seeped into her lower torso, amplifying the effect of the warmth-sucking wind.

They reached the multipaned oval dome and peered

inside, keeping their heads as low as possible. All Nicole could see were rows and rows of head-high white hydroponic towers. Tendrils of green poured down from them and ran along the deep brown of the mineral enhanced soil.

"Looks nice," said Kimathi, his face hidden behind a white balaclava. "Warm."

"Just get us inside," Nicole instructed.

The sergeant pulled a small plasma cutter from his pants pocket and began to slice through the centimeter-thick glass. As he was halfway through his cut, the entire pane shattered, sending shards onto the ground below.

"Well, shit." Ekon hastily put the cutter back in his pocket and hopped through the opening, landing gracefully on dirt ground beneath. Nicole and Pham followed.

"Spread out," Nicole whispered. "If there's anyone here, they definitely heard us come in."

The wind sailing across the opening created a low moan that reverberated throughout the room. The smell of earth and fertilizer immediately filled Nicole's nose. She pulled her sidearm out, ready for a shout or plasma fire to sail past. The rows of hydroponic towers stretched before her, blocking out everything except the wall in the far distance. The greenhouse had been dug directly from the ground, with small excavation marks the only evidence that Human hands had been there. The bright Marigan sun shone above them, cascading through the thick glass ceiling.

Nicole jumped as a mesh shutter suddenly sprang from the bottom of dome and grew upwards until the entire greenhouse was engulfed in darkness.

"What the—"

Lights on the ceiling came on, cutting off Pham and casting shadows around the room with a ghastly faux sunlight. Nicole felt an unnatural warmth emanating from above.

"Hell?" Pham finished. She had her sidearm raised and was licking her lips nervously.

"It's the broken window," Nicole said, trying to appear calm. "We must have triggered a failsafe designed to protect the plants."

"Makes sense." Kimathi didn't sound convinced. His weapon was out as well, and his eyes darted around the room.

"Let's just get out of here," Nicole said. She hoped there would be some sort of utility vehicle or *something* they could use to get to the nearest town. They'd reached the limit of her plan.

At least we're inside, she thought to herself.

They made their way through the rows of plants, walking in a line with each person taking a separate aisle. Nerves were affecting all of them. Kimathi kept spinning around as he walked, coming close to falling down several times. Pham's nervous energy was channeled to her hands; she continually flipped her sidearm from hand to hand. Nicole found herself biting on her lower lip so hard it started to ache.

"There." Nicole pointed. A rectangular metal door was embedded into the rock wall. According to their maps, it led to a tunnel that descended through the rock and eventually met up with the network of caves where the inhabitants lived.

They were out of luck; aside from several canisters filled with what Nicole guessed was fertilizer, there was nothing by the door. A small screen embedded into the wall flashed the words "containment breach error" in red.

"The door's locked shut," Pham said.

"I'm guessing we must have tripped a security or safety protocol." Kimathi had knelt near the door. "There may be a quick release or something."

Nicole and Pham spread out to look for any sort of control, but there wasn't a single panel or switch visible on the rough rock wall. As Nicole stood up and shouted in frustration, the door opened with a hiss. She heard an approaching vehicle and saw the reflection of its headlights against the wall outside the door.

They ran back into the rows of plants and lay down to take cover. As Nicole's head hit the ground, a tunnel crawler rolled into the room The machine was designed to navigate the sometimes narrow and winding caves of Mariga. Wheels covered every part of its metal frame with the passenger cabin suspended in the center. It could turn and pivot independently, ensuring the passengers were always upright no matter what happened to the vehicle.

Two maintenance workers, a man and woman, lazily stepped out of the vehicle chatting to one another. They clearly didn't seem to be too concerned with the flashing red alert on the console.

"Haven't had one of these in a while," the woman said,

pulling a small device from the crawler.

"It's the wind." The man shook his head. "We always get a few of 'em each season."

As the two began pulling out their tools and equipment, Nicole aimed her kinetic pistol. Although these were just civilian technicians just doing their job, she couldn't risk exposure. Thankfully, she had nonlethal munitions.

Nicole's bolt hit the man center of mass and sliced through the loose coat he was wearing. He went down with a strangled yelp. Kimathi's shot hit the woman a moment later, causing her to drop the device in her hands and fall to the ground with a clatter.

Nicole stood and looked down at the two immobilized workers and had a moment of gratitude for Kal. He had been the one who'd insisted the fleet's scout teams always carry nonlethal ammunition with them. He'd approached the subject with an almost religious ferocity. Nicole knew why; it had been made all too clear by the screams that used to wake her at night in their stateroom aboard the *Ofira*.

"Restrain 'em," Nicole ordered. Kimathi and Pham had already knelt by the two technicians and pulled out restraints. They hastily wrapped them around the two workers' torsos and legs and pressed a button, causing the black bands to snap tight.

"Never thought I get a chance to drive one of these again," Kimathi said with a grin as he eyed the tunnel crawler.

"Last time we almost died," Nicole said.

"*Almost* being the operative word." Kimathi patted the

crawler's frame. "I've gotten better. This time it you'll just say we *could've* died."

"Any chance we can cut straight to *didn't* or just that we had an easy trip?" Pham asked.

Kimathi jumped into the crawler and began to orient himself to the controls. "Don't push it."

Chapter Five
Nicole | Mariga

The ride from the greenhouse in the tunnel crawler reminded Nicole of an amusement park ride. They twisted through the caverns, delving deeper into Mariga's crust as the heavy thrum of the vehicle's engine drowned out almost every noise except the occasional yelp from Pham, who was squeezed between Kimathi and Nicole.

Nicole rapidly typed a set of coordinates into the crawler's nav system. Their destination wasn't far, perhaps a few klicks from the greenhouse.

"We still pretending we're scouting out the planet while waiting for the Jadid fleet?" Kimathi shouted over the engine.

Nicole didn't respond.

"I know where you're taking us, ma'am" Kimathi continued. "It's his hometown. I don't blame you, but what are the chances he's there?"

Nicole knew Kal and thought the chances were pretty good. After ruling out New America and Patagonia, Mariga was the most likely place for him to go to. The other option was too dark for her to contemplate—that Kal had given up and gone back to his previous life, fleeing from Human controlled space. She couldn't accept that.

As they sped deeper, the man-made tunnel widened and merged into a large thoroughfare. Lights on the ceiling illuminated the road, and other vehicles occasionally sped past. There were even a few refueling stations dug into the side of the tunnel.

"So this is Mariga." Pham looked out the window in distaste. "Not exactly a cheery place."

"It's got its perks," Nicole replied.

They arrived at a cave filled wall-to-wall with mid-rise buildings. Pedestrians and transports made their way through the streets, illuminated by lights hanging from the ceiling and the light reflecting from thousands of tiny crystals on the wall.

"What are those?" Pham craned her neck to study the cave walls as they entered the town proper.

"Salt crystals," said Nicole. Kal had told her all about his hometown, Crystal City. It was a mining town, originally created to mine for salt. Later, rare minerals had been found and the town had expanded. Hundreds of small mines were littered throughout the area.

The term "city" was generous. It was more of a midsize town, dwarfed by *real* cities like Kasongo or Mariga's capital, Torgut. Still, the streets were filled with people wearing coveralls emblazoned with the assorted logos of assorted mining companies.

"Okay, I'll bite," Pham said. "You two seem to know what's going on. What are we doing here?"

"It's General Norman's home," Kimathi remarked.

"We're searching for Kal?" Pham screeched, turning toward Nicole. "We've got Humanity's future on the line, and we're looking for your *boyfriend*?"

"He's the key to all of this," Nicole said. "We need to find him."

"For goodness' sake woman," Pham spat. "He's one man.

You're risking everything, including me, for yourself. If he's still alive, which I doubt, he'll come back when he can."

Nicole knew that she was being was stupid and reckless, but she just didn't care. She knew she was right; there was no doubt in her mind. She *wasn't* just doing this for herself. Samsara Fleet needed to find Kal; they needed him back.

"We're already here, so we might as well look around," Kimathi said philosophically as he pulled into one of the available spaces on the side of the road.

"How the hell would we even find him?" asked Pham. "This isn't Tiradentes, but it ain't a small town like Hope either."

Nicole tried to ignore the woman's tone. She had a point. Instead, she opened the crawler's door and stepped out. "Let's split up and walk around. Maybe he'll find us."

Since it was a mining town, Crystal City tended to harbor a certain class of shops. Chembars and pawnshops occupied most shop fronts, broken up by the occasional provisions store or general merchant.

Nicole wasn't sure exactly what she was looking for other than Kal. She hated to admit it, but Pham was right: he could be anywhere—or not there at all. In the stores with Human shopkeepers she asked if they'd seen her "friend," but their answers ranged from "no" to "get the hell outta here if you aren't buyin'."

After an hour she returned to the crawler to find Kimathi

and Pham already leaning against the vehicle idly talking to one another.

"Ready to give this up?" asked Pham. "Wasted enough of our time?"

"I'm sure he'd come back here." As Kal had struggled with the impact of the war, he'd talked about his family and his hometown. When he'd been young, he left Mariga to join the Earth Defense Force and never looked back. Even when they'd run missions on Mariga, he had never returned to his hometown. Nicole wasn't sure why, but she had sensed something when he talked about it, a yearning to go back perhaps. She hoped she hadn't been imagining it.

Kimathi stood up and scratched his nose. "When I first met the general, he was drugged out of his mind. I know you might not wanna hear it, but maybe that's where he is," he motioned to a nearby chembar, "in one of these places."

He was right. Nicole didn't want to hear it. But she couldn't rule it out either. Kal had turned to chems the last time his world had come crashing down.

"Yeah," she reluctantly agreed. "Let's check 'em."

They split up again and began to comb through the depressing underbelly of Crystal City. Although it wasn't the biggest town, it was *filled* with chembars, which meant they had to wade through a lot of misery. Each one of the dingy establishments was the same, filled with half-conscious addicts lying across couches or on the floor, empty vials and paraphernalia spread around them. Servers walked through the area, masks covering their mouths and nose to prevent

65

them from ingesting the deadly chemicals they were distributing to their patrons.

After thirty minutes she'd searched two establishments and was on to the third, a place called Doctor's Orders. When she entered, she was greeted by the same stench of body odor and depression as the first two. As her eyes adjusted to the light, she was able to see men and woman lying around her, vacant expressions on their faces as the chems did their trick. She wanted to vomit.

"Whatdya want?" a man gruffly asked as he stepped in front of her. It was the smallest one Nicole had seen yet and he appeared to be the only person there. Although he seemed alert at the moment, he clearly had been on the chems himself. He looked young—maybe Nicole's age—but moved like an elderly man and his hair was going prematurely white with a small sprinkling of black that grew denser in the bushy beard that surrounded his mouth.

"You got a menu?" Nicole sputtered. She needed a chance to look around.

"We got the same stuff as any other place. Why don't you go somewhere else, maybe one of the fancy places by the main terminal? We're not exactly a tourist joint."

Nicole looked at the unconscious woman draped across the bar in a small puddle of her own drool next to her. "Yeah, I can see that. I'd still like to see one."

The man grunted then turned and walked toward a small alcove. Doctor's Orders was basically a large room filled with tattered couches and overstuffed chairs. Other than a large psychedelic medical cross that adorned the far wall, it was the least decorated chembar Nicole had been in.

The barkeep tossed Nicole a chipped tablet with a list of chems and their prices. She pretended to study the selection for a moment before settling on the only name she'd heard of before.

"Uh, I'll get a...some Scaff."

The barkeep raised an eyebrow and waved his arm toward the open room. "Find a spot and I'll be over."

Nicole made her way across the room, stepping over the bodies and weaving through the furniture as she searched for Kal's familiar face. She was torn between hoping she would find him and dreading it. She didn't know what she would do if she saw the man she loved lying on the ground, his mind gone. Thankfully, or not, he wasn't there.

Just as Nicole was about to tell the barkeep to cancel her order and leave when the door slid open and two Nasi soldiers strode through. Their movements were smooth and effortless, their silky gait giving the appearance that they were floating rather than walking. Their datons, the Nasi and Jadid version of a plasma rifle, were strapped to their backs, but Nicole knew they could bring them to the ready in a heartbeat.

She collapsed onto the floor next to her, splaying her limbs out at odd angles.

"How may I—"

One of the soldiers pulled their daton out in a smooth motion and pointed it at the barkeep's head. "Stay there.

We're looking for someone."

The man shut his mouth and stepped back, pressing himself as far back into the cashier's alcove as possible while raising his hands. The Nasi strolled through the room, occasionally bending down to turn a body over and study their face. Nicole's mind veered between worrying she was breathing too loudly to wondering if the Nasi's eyesight was better than a Human's.

She couldn't say why, but she was *sure* they were looking for her. The Nasi must have realized they'd come to Mariga. Whether they'd detected the *McCullough* landing on the planet or their breaking into the greenhouse, she couldn't tell.

She dropped her head back down to the floor. She couldn't hear a sound except for the occasional thump of a body being roughly turned over and waited for the sounds of a plasma shot or the rough sensation of one of the soldiers turning her over.

Damn. I wish my pistol wasn't in its holster.

Nicole looked up as she heard the front door swish open. Two Nasi soldiers, carrying an unconscious Human, strode through.

"How may I help—"

"What are you doing here?" asked one of the Nasi who'd been searching the room.

Nicole's breath caught in her throat. The Human was Kal. By the way his head lolled to the side, he was under the influence of something.

Damn it!

Nicole felt a surge of worry and anger. How had she come so close to finding him, the man that—for better or worse—she loved, only to find him helpless and captured.

Kal's head rolled toward Nicole, and he gave her a wink. Joy washed through her body.

"You need to depart the premises immediately. We will let—"

The Nasi soldier was cut off as a plasma round seared through his chest. The other Nasi turned, bringing his daton up. But the Nasi holding Kal were faster and already had their weapons ready, firing several rounds into his chest before he had a chance to respond.

"Kax, check outside," Kal barked. "See where their officer is."

The barkeep nodded and ran out through the door, the small pistol in his hand disappearing up his sleeve.

"Toggs and Melt, frisk the bodies, grab what you can, then make 'em disappear."

The two Nasi who'd entered with Kal nodded and rushed to where the dead Nasi soldiers lay. They quickly patted the bodies down and dragged them across the room. As they approached a couch that rested against the back wall it tilted open, revealing a shadowy compartment. The Nasi threw the bodies into the gaping hole.

"You." Kal looked at Nicole, tears in his eyes. He raised his left hand toward her face and then pulled it back.

"Me." Nicole grabbed his hand and held it for a moment, staring into his dark brown eyes. She had been waiting for this for months, half thinking she'd never see him again but not wanting to believe it. Now that she was there with him, she couldn't find the words.

She looked him over and realized with a shock that his right arm was now bare metal with tubes and wires crossing around it. He'd originally lost the arm years back but had had a prosthesis installed that had been indistinguishable from the real thing.

"Boss, we got issues," Kax called out as he ran back inside. "There's more of those Nasi bastards outside, and they've got an officer with them." One of the Nasi cleared his throat loudly and Kax shrugged. "Present company excluded of course. You guys are great." He gave a thumbs-up.

"I can't believe you're here." Kal shook his head. "We'll have time to talk later. For now, you've got to get out of here."

"Boss?"

Kal turned around to look at Kax. "Right. Right. Let's take advantage of the opportunity. Get ready." He pulled Nicole toward the hidden door.

"Head through here," Kal said. "I'll catch up with you."

Nicole planted her feet and pushed his metallic arm away. "If you think I'm leaving here, you're insane." She pulled her pistol out of its holster. "Now tell me, what do you need me to do?"

"Whatdya need?" Kax said as a group of three Nasi strode

through the door.

Nicole could tell the woman in the center was an officer because of the elaborate silvery tattoos—called Shishen—that snaked across her body. Based on the intricacy of the loops and swirls, she was a high-ranking officer to boot. It confused Nicole as to why the woman would be in a dingy chembar in a backwater town, but there she was, and Kal had a plan to take advantage of that fact.

"Where are my soldiers?" the woman demanded.

"I don't kn—"

Kax's words were cut off by a powerful slap. Nicole knew how strong Nasi were and guessed the blow was enough to break the man's jaw. Kax flew back and crashed against the back wall, landing on the floor in a heap. She just hoped he would be able to get up eventually.

"Where are the soldiers who entered here?" the woman shouted with a snarl.

The room remained as silent as a grave.

"Look around," she ordered as she stepped forward to examine the small alcove where Kax lay. "Places like this make me sick."

That makes two of us, Nicole thought to herself.

She was lying on a small nest of cushions with a pile of used vials next to her. Her hand was beneath her, wrapped around the grip of her pistol. She watched as the two soldiers moved through the room in parallel paths, bending to examine the patrons just like the previous soldiers had done.

Toggs screamed in terror from the back of the room. It

was an act designed to draw the other Nasi farther into the room. They didn't care about the soldiers, but they needed the officer away from the front door. Their mission wasn't to kill *her*; they wanted her alive.

"Damn chemmies," snarled one of the soldiers. "And a Nasi one at that."

"Shut him up," the officer ordered, still examining the contents of the alcove.

Nicole tensed. Would the soldiers just shoot Toggs? If so, should she stop them? *Could* she stop them?

Thankfully, instead of shooting the screaming Nasi, the soldier kicked him viciously in the side, knocking him back several meters and causing him to elicit a groan of pain.

"That got through to him," laughed the other soldier, walking to a spot where Nicole could no longer see him.

The officer threw something down with a clatter and strode to the center of the room. With a loud shriek of annoyance, she spun her daton around and fired at the walls in a display of sheer frustration. It shocked Nicole. She'd never seen a Nasi—an officer no less—act in such a nakedly *emotional* way. Her anger and hatred were bared for all to see.

"I will kill every single person in this room unless someone starts talking," the woman shouted. "Where are my soldiers?"

Nicole's breath caught in her throat. The situation was perched at the edge of a precipice and was about to topple over. In the dim light it was impossible for her to distinguish Kal and his Nasi allies from the other patrons. She didn't have a clean shot on the officer but had a decent line of sight on one of the soldiers—if she could bring her weapon to bear.

"This goddamn planet," the officer cursed as she pointed her daton at the floor. Nicole couldn't tell who or what she was pointing at.

Kinetic shots rang out, and the Nasi soldier in front of Nicole dove to the side while bringing his daton up and firing to her left. The padded furniture of the room might have been great for addicts to drape themselves over, but it was terrible cover for a firefight. Nicole would have one chance for a shot. After that, she'd be completely exposed.

Screw it.

She brought her sidearm up and lined up a shot, remembering the long training sessions she'd had with Sergeant Kimathi. Aim. Breathe. Squeeze. Her hours in the range had made the entire process muscle memory at that point.

Her shot was true and hit the Nasi soldier in the midsection, sending him down to the ground. Nicole rolled to the side right before a plasma bolt hit her location, instantly turning the synthetic material of the couch into a mass of charred goo.

Nicole turned to see the Nasi officer only paces away, her eyes focused on Nicole and her daton swinging toward her. Toggs and Melt tackled the woman from behind, grasping for her hands. Plasma shots leapt from the daton and coated the wall above Nicole's head with a sizzle. The three Nasi became a mass of limbs as they struggled.

73

Finally, they stopped struggling, and the Nasi officer lay facedown on the floor, her hands bound behind her back and legs bound together. Toggs and Melt lay on the floor next to her, winded from the fight.

"Okay, get her out of here," Kal ordered.

Melt dragged the bodies of the soldiers through the hidden exit while Toggs pressed a stunner against the Nasi officer's neck, knocking her out, then followed Melt out, dragging her limp body. Kal ran to where Kax lay on the ground and helped him up. Nicole was shocked at how well the man was taking the vicious hit.

"We...get 'er?" Kax asked, placing a hand gingerly against his jaw.

"We did," Kal said. "You did good."

"Worth it." Kax stumbled toward the hidden exit, using the furniture to keep himself upright.

"Come on," Kal said to Nicole. "We've got a lot to talk about."

Kal walked around the room's perimeter, placing small explosives against the wall. "Scorched earth," he said. "We can't leave a trace. The Nasi *will* come back, and if there's anything left, no one will be safe. Even now, this entire city is at danger from retribution." He clenched his jaw. "There's nothin' we can do about that though."

Toggs and Melt had returned and were dragging the chem-addled patrons out the front door by their arms and legs.

"You have a lot to explain," Nicole said. She tried to

sound angry, but her joy at seeing Kal was too great to hide.

Kal smiled back at her. "I know and I will."

Chapter Six

Kal | Mariga

"Kimathi and Pham are here as well," Nicole said in hushed tones to Kal as they strode through a dank alley.

"Never thought I'd be so happy to hear those two are here." Kal meant it too. He'd always had a hard time with Sergeant Kimathi especially, but there was something comforting about knowing the sergeant had come to find him.

"We have a skip ship, a very special one, waiting on the surface with Ai," Nicole said.

Kal was intrigued. What did she mean by special? His questions would have to wait; their current mission was still very much in play.

"See you back at HQ?" asked Toggs.

Kal nodded.

Toggs and Melt veered down a branch of the ally, carrying Kax between them. To a passerby, they would look like two Nasi soldiers dragging an unwilling Human captive. In reality, the poor barkeep could barely stand and needed every bit of help he could get.

"Can we transmit around here?" asked Nicole.

Kal nodded. There was always the risk that a using one's neural implant could give away your location, but in larger towns and cities that risk went way down due to the sheer number of other signals and transmissions. From everything he knew, the Nasi had not been able to break through the encryption the fleet used, so there wasn't too much risk of their communications being intercepted.

They continued through the alley until it ended at the large avenue that encircled Crystal City. Kimathi and Pham leaned against a nearby wall, looking as if they'd just ended a hard day's work in the mines and were passing the time before heading home.

"Let's get back to the *McCullough* and get out of here," Pham said while eyeing the passersby.

"What if they've found it already?" Nicole asked. "Or if they didn't, we could be leading them right to it."

Kal's mind raced as he tried to anticipate what the Nasi's next step would be. Clearly, they were on to Nicole and the others. The good news was they didn't know *exactly* where her ship was. Nicole had already told him they had it cloaked, which bought them some more time.

"They must know your exact location," Kal said. "We can risk getting to your ship and then we can find a place to stash it near Torgut. I need to talk to some people before we do anything else."

Nicole nodded.

"You take lead," Kal said. "I assume you came here in a vehicle of some sort."

Nicole led them back to a crawler—a base-level maintenance model as far as he could tell—and lifted up the cabin door.

"This is a two-seater." Kal bent over to examine the interior. He found the device he was looking for, a small box underneath the driver's seat. It was a tracker, standard on all government-issue crawlers. He ripped it out and tossed it into the engine housing of the vehicle next to them. Hopefully that would buy them some time.

"We already fit three in here," said Pham. "What's one more?"

"All part of the fun of clandestine operations, sir," Kimathi whispered, giving Kal a pat on the back. "Let's get comfy."

It took a few minutes—minutes they didn't have—for all four of them to fit in the vehicle. Kal ended up in the passenger's seat with Nicole and Pham sitting on his lap. He leaned to the side, trying his best to see out the front windshield as they sped out of Crystal City.

"You can't leave the same way you entered," Kal said. "Your little greenhouse break-in was tracked by the Nasi as was the crawler we're in."

"Obviously," said Nicole.

"What's that mean?" Pham turned her head, cracking Kal in the nose in the process.

"We should've expected the Nasi to be looking for us," Nicole said. "If Kal hadn't been there, we'd be in restraints or dead right now."

"You didn't think of that earlier, ma'am?" Kimathi asked.

"There wasn't time," said Nicole. "Besides, we made it out, didn't we?"

"Well, not yet we haven't." Kimathi hit the accelerator, making Kal momentarily ponder the fragility of life.

Having grown up in the area, he knew it well. There'd

been some changes to the tunnels surrounding Crystal City but not many since he'd been a kid running through the mines and caverns. He tapped a series of coordinates into the nav computer.

"Head here," Kal instructed.

"And that is?" Kimathi asked.

"A way out."

Kal had used the path he was sending them on to get to the surface countless times as a kid. He remembered using his father's crawler to sneak away with friends. They would dare each other to see who would go the farthest toward the surface.

They veered off the road and entered a knot of tunnels that crossed over each other, looping and bending, until it was almost impossible to tell where they were. The point he'd entered on the tacmap was just the beginning of the small tunnel he and his friends had used. They'd have to navigate rest of the way from his memory.

"Go left," Kal called out. "No wait, straight."

The crawler sped through an intersection and then began to climb.

"Get ready to go right. Wait, no. It's left. Up ahead, go left."

"You sure you have a clue where we're going, sir?" Kimathi asked in frustration.

"Yes." *No.*

They followed the tunnel to the left and continued climbing. The ceiling lights were long since gone, and the only illumination came from the bank of headlights on the front of the crawler. Small creatures disappeared into the dirt and ice of the cave walls in front of them as their vehicle sped forward, the light glinting off their bodies like small stars.

The tunnel abruptly ended, and the crawler screeched to a stop, almost hitting a wall in front of them.

"You're *sure* you have a clue where we are?" Pham asked.

"I grew up here," Kal said defensively. He would have been more annoyed if he wasn't only half sure of where they were. "Of course I know where we are. Time to get out."

"Get out?" asked Kimathi.

"Yes." Kal managed to hit the door release, and the crawler's front windshield popped open, letting in a blast of cool air. "We walk from here." He took out his light and searched along the cave wall. It had to be there.

"Found it," he called out in triumph.

A small hole, barely large enough for a person to fit through, had been dug into the ice wall of the cave. Kal remembered the first time he'd discovered it. His friends had all been busy and he'd decided to explore the caverns in his dad's crawler to kill time before he had to head home.

Kal knelt and studied the opening. It seemed right, but then again, he remembered being able to feel the icy surface air when going through the tunnel.

"Wait here," Kal instructed.

He crawled through the passageway on his hands and knees, the ray of his handheld light bobbing in front of him. The tunnel came to an end in a cap of ice that glowed with sunlight coming from the other side. Kal used his claw-tipped metallic arm to steadily chip away at the ice.

"Come on through," Kal called to the others, "weather's great."

He squinted as the sun and wind battered his face. He pushed himself forward and stood, pulling his mask over his face. He was covered in several heavy layers, but it still wasn't enough to last long on the inhospitable surface. The others made their way from the hole, gasping as the full fury of the surface wind hit them.

At least it's midday, Kal thought to himself.

"Which way to the ship?" he asked, screaming over the wind.

After consulting her implant, Nicole pointed to their left. "It's a klick this way," she shouted.

She took the lead, and they trudged up the side of a gentle hill, pushing against the slope and the wind that battered them. Kal followed close behind and doggedly focused on her back, trying to ignore the seeping numbness in his hands and feet.

Nicole abruptly vanished from sight only to reappear a moment later, standing outside a strange-looking ship that appeared to be the love child of Jadid and Human technology. Ai stood at the top of the ship's cargo ramp.

"General Norman, glad to see you," Ai shouted over the wind.

Kal nodded. His face felt frozen, which it might have partially been. As soon as they were inside the ship and the ramp closed, Pham wordlessly rushed to a storage compartment and pulled out a stack of medicated bandages. The combination of chems and nanobots in the bandages could heal many wounds or at least dull the pain. Kal grabbed one, pressed it against his head, and looked around.

The ship was like nothing he'd seen before. The strange mix of Human and Jadid technologies that he'd seen on the outside continued through the ship's interior. The base airframe appeared to be Human, but there were so many modifications as to make it almost unrecognizable.

Nicole noticed him looking over the control panels. "Just wait until you see what it can do," she said.

Kal raised an eyebrow. "What do you mean?"

"This ship can fold from anywhere."

"Not anywhere," Ai corrected. "For instance, we are not sure that it would be able to fold from a planet's surface. Additionally, I am quite sure it would not be able to—"

"Seems like more survived than I thought," Kal interjected. Ai was just as bad as Bo sometimes. The thought made him wonder what had happened to his friend who'd disappeared during the assault on New America months ago.

"Not enough," said Kimathi darkly. "The Jadid's attack gutted New America."

Kal would have loved to hear more about the ship, but Kimathi's words brought him back to the present.

"We've got to lift off," Kal said. "The Nasi are clearly tracking you and we've got no idea how far behind they are."

The others started moving with a jolt. Kal followed Nicole

to the cockpit while Ai ran outside to pick up the optical projectors. The strange mix of technology was even more evident in the ship's controls. Human viewscreens sat above Jadid control panels. A small cluster of defensive controls jutted from between the other consoles almost as an afterthought.

"This space worthy?" Kal asked, eying a loose cluster of wires that seemed to go nowhere.

"It works," Nicole said. "In fact, first time we folded was from *inside* a Jadid carrier."

Kal couldn't believe it. From everything he knew, it shouldn't be possible. But then again, he'd seen a lot that he thought wasn't possible. The *McCullough* was essentially priceless, the most advanced ship the galaxy had ever known. It also looked like a wreck, which made him appreciate it even more.

"Glad we came back to get it," Kal said.

With a flick of a switch, the *McCullough* slowly lifted off. Their destination was Torgut, Mariga's capital city, but they couldn't risk a direct route. Instead, they followed along the valley floor with their cloak activated and their eyes glued to the tacmap. From what Kal could gather, the *McCullough* wouldn't last long in a dogfight; evasion was their only strategy.

Occasionally, they saw a dot or icon indicating another ship or transport in the area, but they always disappeared quickly, never knowing the *McCullough* was nearby. Kal wasn't sure if it meant they were in the clear or not, but ultimately, they wouldn't truly know if they'd been detected until it was almost too late. As they made their way, he took solace in the fact that the chances the Nasi knew where they were was low at that point.

'We're far enough away," Kal said. "You can go direct flight."

They lifted out of the snow-filled valley and began to skim over the hills, continuing to fly only meters off the ground. Kal rarely felt any sort of pride for his homeworld, but looking out over the jagged peaks, he felt a sense of appreciation. Mariga's beauty was different than the other Human colonies. At once cold and majestic, it was a planet that kept its most valuable treasures hidden under a cloak of snow. But he knew firsthand that some of the most beautiful creatures and scenery in the galaxy lay below the ice.

"Okay, Kal," Nicole said, interrupting his thoughts. "Now spill. What happened to you?"

Kal struggled as to where to start. It had been months since the Jadid had betrayed them, but in many ways, it felt like years. He'd lost, or thought he'd lost, everything.

"Not sure how much you know," Kal began. "When Ancient Wang ordered me up to his ship, I thought we were going to talk about finishing taking the planet." He shook his head. "I can't believe I fell for it."

"General Zhou did the same thing," Nicole said. "I fell for it just as much as you did."

Kal felt a stab of disappointment. He'd known that Patagonia had suffered the same fate as New America, falling to the Jadid, but it still hurt to hear confirmation that Zhou, a man he'd trusted, had been behind it. He'd heard a few whispers but hadn't wanted them to be true.

"When I saw the Fridge had been destroyed and learned that Patagonia had already fallen, I wasn't sure what to do." Kal was underselling it. He'd been devastated, believing that everyone he knew was dead or as good as dead. "I...I thought you were gone..." It was a thought that had haunted him these past months.

Nicole reassuringly placed her hand over his.

"Like I said, I went to Patagonia," Kal continued, "but there was nothing I could do. The Jadid had already consolidated their hold on the planet and then they started hailing me. I had to escape while I could."

"So you went home," finished Nicole.

Kal nodded. "The Jadid know everything about us. They know our plans, our operatives, our *faces*. Staying on New America or Patagonia wasn't an option, not if we wanted to mount a *real* resistance." He'd remembered the feeling of helplessness and then the final decision to keep going, not to give up. "The Nasi are still a threat, but now they're the lesser of two evils, so I figured it was better to deal with them first."

"You were able to link up with the Odpor?" Ai asked.

The Odpor was the resistance movement on Mariga. Like Patagonia Front and the varied resistance groups on New America, it was a collection of citizens dedicated to overthrowing the Nasi—and now the Jadid as well. As the leader of the Skulls, a Samsara Fleet scout team, Kal had met with them on a few occasions prior to returning to Mariga to receive intel or provide arms from the fleet.

"Yeah, but the Nasi had taken most of them out, same as New America and Patagonia." The leaders had been rounded up and killed, safehouse destroyed, weapons caches plundered. "I found the few people that were left and we got to work.

"Then we had an idea. Why couldn't we find sympathizers inside the Nasi? I knew there were people willing to turn on Esma. They'd seen how twisted she'd become and wanted to stop it. Then there were some of them that just wanted to the war to end and were willing to look the other way. That first contact was hard, I spent way too long staking out various Nasi chembars and trying to find someone who'd say the right thing. But once I'd turned one, it became much easier. Now we've got more than a few Nasi on the inside."

"In just a few months?" Nicole asked in surprise.

Kal nodded. "They're rotting from the inside. So many of them are just done with the war or disillusioned with what Esma has done, even the senior officers."

Kal remembered the initial shock he'd felt when he'd heard the Nasi officers ranting after a few vials of chems. When the Nasi had arrived in their universe, they'd been closer to bots than people. The intervening years had changed them, made them question things that they had taken for granted before.

"So that's how you found us?" Nicole asked.

"The Nasi fleet IDs every ship entering the system.

Anything that they see also makes its way to us thanks to our people on the inside. Your ship didn't immediately raise a red flag but when there was also a breach alert on a nearby greenhouse, the Nasi command got an alert—and so did I. I had to scramble to get there before they did." Actually, he'd risked everything and broken every single protocol the Odpor had in order to get to Crystal City in time.

"Well, glad you did." Nicole flashed a grateful smile. "But we need to leave soon. We're here looking for the Jadid fleet that left orbit around Patagonia. We think they're either coming here or Wudexingqiu."

"Samaha wanted to make sure the Jadid were engaged against the Nasi before moving," Kal said. It made sense. With a ship like the *McCullough*, they were no longer constrained by the multiday journey between planets. They could quickly scout ahead of the fleets. He wasn't surprised that Ancient Wang was going on the offensive. He would want to take Bayaka and the Nasi out while they were still reeling from losing New America and Patagonia. Besides, Esma was nothing else if not crafty; the more time you gave her, the more dangerous she became.

"Yes," Nicole agreed. "If we can determine where the Zhou's portion of the Liberation Fleet has gone, we can know if we're safe to take Patagonia."

"We won't be long, but before we go, I have some people I want you to meet."

❖

It took a couple of hours for them to travel from the *McCullough's* hidden landing spot to the Odpor's base of operations. Situated in an uncharted network of caves a few klicks underneath Torgut, the location allowed them easy access to the city.

The base itself wasn't much even compared to the relatively basic facilities that Kal had seen with the rebel groups on other planets. He'd quickly learned to appreciate the simplicity of their headquarters though. The Odpor never remained in one location for long. They were always moving through the planet's caves, preventing the Nasi from narrowing down their location. It meant they couldn't have the large viewscreens and landing bays that Kal had seen with Patagonia Front and the TLF, but it also meant they were much harder to catch.

On the way, Nicole had filled Kal in on everything that had happened to the fleet on Patagonia and New America. He'd come to realize that although the Jadid attack had been devastating, it hadn't been complete. There were still Humans fighting and lots of them. Humanity was more than Samsara Fleet; it wasn't something that could be snuffed out in a day or even a decade. They also had the *McCullough*, a ship so advanced that Kal would have declared it impossible just a few years earlier.

They were sitting in one of the base's makeshift meeting rooms which had been made by having a couple of Nasi weaves a few meters apart inside one of the tunnels. One of the weave walls had a hole covered in cloth for a door.

Because of the sloping floor of the tunnel, there wasn't room enough for a table. Instead, benches had been affixed to the tunnel walls and a bundle of cable had been run into the room to power the lighting and the single viewscreen.

"I want you to meet some people," Kal said, motioning to the benches and making a call using his implant.

As Nicole, Pham, Kimathi, and Ai sat down, three Nasi glided into the room through the cloth partition. They all had the looping Shishen tattoos across their bodies, indicating they were Nasi of a moderately high rank. After having spent so much time studying and being around the Nasi, Kal was able to read at least a portion of their Shishen—they were not only a sign of rank but contained a story of the wearer's life and career. The three Nasi who entered the room were decorated soldiers who had sworn to defend Esma.

"You've met Toggs and Melt." The two Nasi nodded as Kal said their "friend name"—the Nasi equivalent of nickname. "This is Red."

The woman gave a small wave. The Nasi, who had been fighting Humanity and occupying their planets had become— for lack of a better word—incredibly Human in their behavior. The Jadid, Humanity's supposed allies—until recently at least—had remained generally cold and aloof. To Kal, it was one of the peculiarities of the war. As occupiers, the Nasi had been forced to interact with their new subjects. The interaction had not only affected the Humans but profoundly affected the behavior of the Nasi. He had seen something similar in the Torgham war. Many of the soldiers who'd fought against the Torgham had become infatuated with their culture. Many of them had gone on to become some of Humanity's greatest scholars of the Torgham.

"Nice to meet you," said Red. Silver threads wound through her black Shishen, indicating her high rank. "I've heard that you've traveled here from our brothers and sisters on the other colonies."

"If you mean from New America where your *brothers and sisters* have killed a bunch of my friends, then yeah." Pham's eyes narrowed.

If Red took offense, she didn't show it. "I've also heard that you have a special ship. An experimental skip ship." She studied their faces and nodded to herself.

Kal could feel Nicole's eyes burning into the side of his head. He could almost hear her voice in his head. *Why would you tell them?* But Kal trusted the three Nasi in that room. He'd run countless missions with them, and they'd saved his life more than once. If he couldn't trust them, then they had no hope of winning the war.

"I have a proposal for you," Red continued. "One that I think can change the course of this war." She took a deep breath. "I want to travel to Altterra."

Chapter Seven
Kal | Mariga

"You sure that we can fold from here?" Kal asked
nervously. He trusted Nicole and Ai, but still, they were barely
past the planet's port station.

"Yes, we've done it before," Nicole said confidently.

"'Sure implies absolute certainty, so no we are not sure,"
Ai said at the same time.

Kal looked back and forth at the two women. What they
were doing felt wrong. Folding from within a planet's
gravitational well would be suicide for any other ship than the
one they were on. Add to that, the fact that they were folding
to another universe, and Kal was struggling to keep the small
meal he'd eaten earlier down.

"I'm going to have to trust you on this." He pointed to
several red dots that had appeared on the tacmap.
"Especially since the fleet just launched missiles at us."

"So they did." Ai said it as if someone had told her the
food processor was finished making her muffins.

A few seconds later and Mariga had disappeared; in fact,
the entire universe disappeared. Amber stars flickered on the
viewscreen, and Kal felt himself being gently pulled in
different directions. Physics operated differently in the Jadid's
universe. Gravity, light, electricity—all were affected, and all
operated in a different manner there. Nicole's normally pale
skin appeared almost orange while Kal's was red. Another
strange property of the universe was that they appeared
differently each time they arrived. Jadid could remain violet or

turn green, while Humans would appear orange or red. Kal wasn't normally into science but even he could have spent years studying and trying to understand the differences between the Jadid's universe and his own. Unfortunately, he didn't have years.

"Let's head out."

"Already on it." Nicole pressed a button and the ship's fold drive engaged. A second later, the sea of orange stars was replaced by a planet consisting of a kaleidoscope of colors. Massive blue clouds hovered over Altterra's milky white oceans and vibrant continents. Kal felt a pang of loss as he stared at the planet—the landmasses were identical to those on Earth, their lost home.

"Something is strange," Ai said as they began their descent. "Someone should have hailed us by now. We're entering Tarzirbu's"—the planetary capital—"airspace."

"I'm seeing some strange things on the surface as well," said Nicole. She zoomed in on the viewscreen. It took Kal a moment to understand what he was seeing. It was a city comprised of the classic Jadid buildings—large, multihued, and almost organic in nature—but there were large gray areas where the buildings and foliage had been blasted away."

"Why haven't we heard anything about this?" Ai asked, the color draining from her still violet face.

"I'm guessing Wang didn't want people to know," Nicole said. "Looks like we're not the only ones he's been screwing."

"Can you zoom in on the palace?" Kal asked. The Ancients' Palace was their home and the center of the Jadid government. Ostensibly it'd been built as a place for the Ancients to retire from public life while they let their children, the Jadid, rule. In reality, the Ancients had never been able to fully relinquish their hold on their children and it had become the new seat of power for the Jadid once constructed.

"It's gone," Ai whispered.

The palace had been a large complex of imposing stone buildings. Now only heaps of rubble remained.

"Head to Eden," Kal ordered.

Ai looked scandalized before adjusting their course. Eden was the original birthplace of the Nasi and was an almost a holy place to them. But Kal knew that if the remaining two Ancients were anywhere, it would be there.

"Unknown craft, you are entering Eden airspace, identify yourself."

Ai looked to Nicole uncertainly. She nodded back.

"This is Scientist Ai Martinez with a delegation from…Samsara Fleet. We are here to speak to the Ancients."

The net remained empty for a few seconds before a second voice spoke. "Acknowledged. Transmitting landing instructions." A destination and flight path appeared on the console as the net closed.

As they approached the coordinates, the ground in front of them slowly dilated open, revealing a deep shaft that disappeared into inky blackness.

"Do we do this?" asked Nicole. "Do we know who we're actually going to meet if we go down there? We enter and there's no getting out. Not unless whoever this is lets us."

Kal pressed the comms button. "Eden control, this is Kal Norman. I need to talk to someone I actually know. What's going on there?"

The line remained quiet as the *McCullough* hovered near the still open landing port. Kal braced himself. Was the enemy sighting them in right now? Would they hear the telltale klaxon warning them of missiles heading their way? He could see both Ai and Nicole had their hands hovering a centimeter from the controls, ready to take evasive action if needed.

"Kal Norman, how are you?" The voice was warm and Human. It took Kal a moment to place it. Richard Kingsley, one of the remaining Ancients.

"I've been better," Kal replied.

"Me too." There was a sigh. "You sit in the air like that for too much longer and someone's liable to shoot you down." Was that a threat? "Please land. We've been hoping you'd show up."

When the Ancients had arrived on Altterra, they'd been exposed to a strange and hostile world. Eden had started out simply as a cave they'd used to escape the predators and destructive elements of the planet's surface. As the Ancients established a foothold on the planet and procreated, they'd dug farther into the ground, expanding the simple cave into a town. After a century, the Ancients and their offspring, the Jadid, had mastered the planet and grown too numerous to stay in the tunnels. So they'd returned to the surface and created cities around the planet while keeping Eden as a refuge and center for meditation and reflection.

"The Ancients are eager to see you," said the Jadid escorting Kal, Nicole, and Red. The rest of their team had remained on board the *McCullough* so they would be ready to lift off if needed.

"I can guarantee you that we're eager to see them," Nicole replied.

Kal felt like he'd been sent back in time. The tunnels they walked through had clearly been cut from the stone by hand, the scrapes and gouges of hand tools evident on the walls. Flickering light from sconces affixed to the walls at irregular intervals gave the impression of a torchlight.

The Jadid led them to a spacious circular room with a large table at the center. As they entered, two Humans, the final two remaining Ancients on Altterra, slowly stood up from the table, their movements making them seem frail and old despite their relatively youthful appearance.

"General Norman, we meet again," Ancient Richard Kingsley said. He looked slightly younger than Kal, perhaps in his forties despite being centuries old.

Twelve chairs were bolted to the floor around the perimeter of the table. The setup was an artifact of a better time for the Jadid and Ancients; a time when they'd been unified against the hostile universe they'd found themselves in. Only after they'd conquered Altterra had they faced their greatest threat in the form of one of their own. Kal corrected himself: *two* of their own.

"The fighting you saw when you were last here has spiraled out of control," Ancient Salina Musa said. "Esma and Bao are waging their war across both our universes."

"And our children are caught in the middle," Kingsley added.

Kal had always thought it strange that the Ancients referred to the Jadid as their "children." Although accurate, the Jadid looked nothing like the Ancients. He wondered what the shock must have been like for the first Ancient who'd given birth to find out that their child looked nothing like them, their physiology changed by the strange universe they found themselves in.

"We're *all* caught in the middle," Nicole corrected. "Or have you forgotten about Earth?"

"No, we haven't forgotten," said Kingsley. He opened his mouth and closed it, clearly struggling to find the words. "You must understand. Over the centuries, we'd…grown accustomed to the idea that we were alone. Stranded. Earth and Humanity became a distant memory."

"At least for most of us," Musa said.

Kingsley nodded. "True. Clearly Esma and Bao never forgot."

"I only spent a fraction of my life on Earth," Musa said. "Everything I've known for the past several hundred years is here on Altterra. If we seem distant, it's because we literally are. We know that this is a tragedy, what our fellow Ancients have done, but it's in another universe. We learned long ago that we needed to be ruthless to survive. We didn't have the luxury of pity or the like. We thought we were making ourselves stronger, but it's clear that we were doing more than that."

"It's certainly come back to us now," Kingsley agreed.

"Seems like there's been some heavy fighting here on Altterra," Kal remarked.

Musa nodded. "Yes. The fighting you saw when you were last here has only gotten worse. Esma and Bao's forces have reopened the gateways and are traveling between our universes at will." The gateways were devices that maintained a persistent wormhole between the universes, allowing people and equipment to move freely between them. Kal knew that in his universe, the gateways were located in the Nasi Footholds on the Human colonies. He had no idea where they were located on Altterra.

"There are two sides here on Altterra," continued Musa. "Esma's Nasi and Bao's Isolationists."

"Guess they weren't as isolationist as they said they were," Kal said.

"They're Bao's?" Nicole asked. "He saved us from them." Bao had led the rescue mission that had helped them escape from Eden.

"One of his many lies." Kingsley balled his fists in anger. "They were always his. The man sewed chaos so we wouldn't see what he was truly doing until it was too late. Now he has his fleet in your universe and an army in ours. The rest of us, the true Jadid and Ancients, are in the middle."

"And growing weaker by the day," Musa added. "We're

barely able to hold on to Eden. Our forces are slowly being worn down from both sides."

"Esma and Bao aren't content to just destroy each other, they want to kill us as well." There was a heavy layer of bitterness in Kingsley's words. Kal couldn't blame him.

"But we came to seek *your* help." Red said. Kal looked over to the Jadid sitting next to him. The woman's face was drained of all color, her mouth slightly open. "Surely you can do something."

"I'm sorry my child," Kingsley said gently. "But we are barely able to save ourselves." To the man's credit his remorse seemed genuine. A parent who'd failed his child. "Ancient Musa and I are powerless."

"There—"

The sound of explosions thundered from outside the room. It was impossible for Kal to tell how close they were, but he was sure they were coming from inside Eden's caves.

They sat in stunned disbelief for a few seconds after the explosion. A small group of Jadid, datons raised to the ready, rushed through the door and fanned out to encircle the room.

"Eden has been compromised," the leader said. Kal recognized her as Madeline Huang, the governor—or former governor he guessed—of Altterra.

Her words jolted them, and everyone jumped to their feet. Kal felt helpless. His sidearm would be useless in this universe. They needed to leave.

"Who is it?" asked Musa as they all stood up.

"Unclear as of now." Huang and the soldiers gracefully moved to surround the two Ancients. "But based on where the breach occurred, I believe they are targeting you."

"Seems like this is their endgame," Musa said with venom.

"Don't you have any way to fight back?" asked Nicole.

"Unfortunately, no." Kingsley reluctantly shook his head. "There are only a few hundred children left who aren't under Esma's or Bao's control."

"What about them?" asked Kal.

"Most of them have been assigned to secure the outer perimeter," Huang explained. "If the attackers have breached Eden, then there is nothing they can do to help."

"We've got to get back to the *McCullough*," Nicole said.

Kingsley and Musa started moving toward the door with the Jadid guards around them, their eyes focused outward as if their enemies would just appear out of thin air.

"Understood. Good luck." Huang turned and strode to the door, her retinue in tow.

"Wait." Kingsley stopped as he reached the door. Huang turned to look at him. "Take us to the landing bay. We're going with them."

The governor looked at him quizzically. "I don't understand."

"We're going with them. There's nothing we can do from here. Protecting us will mean your death. If you don't have to babysit us, you've at least got a chance to escape."

"Richard, what're you saying?" Musa looked at him

beseechingly. "We can't abandon our children."

"We're not. We're doing the only thing we can to save them."

"What exactly are you suggesting?" Kal asked. He wasn't sure they even had room in the tiny ship.

"It's pretty simple. I'm asking you to take us with you. Bao and Esma are back in your universe. They are the key to this. And our only chance is to convince them or the Jadid that follow them to let the rest of us exist in peace."

"You're not going to get them to stop fighting," Nicole said.

"I'm not trying to," Kingsley replied. "Just to stop killing *us*. We don't like what they're doing, but we're powerless to stop them. We just want to be left alone."

"So what? You're just going to ask them nicely?" Kal didn't understand. Was Kingsley so naïve? Why would he expect their help now anyway?

"We've already tried to surrender." Musa shook her head. "They won't let us."

"So you don't care if they kill or conquer *us*, you just care about them leaving you alone?" Nicole asked.

"We care about them leaving our children alone." Kingsley clenched his jaw. "They're destroying everything we built over centuries. Everything they helped to build."

Kal remembered the first time he'd been to Altterra, how these same Ancients had been almost indifferent to the destruction of Earth. "Doesn't seem like that's our problem."

"Don't you see?" Kingsley asked. "If we can at least talk to them, maybe it can help you out as well. Maybe we can convince them to stop fighting altogether or at least to sew some more doubt in their followers. If you thought you were going to win, you wouldn't be here talking to us right now. You need everything you can get."

Another explosion sounded from somewhere inside the underground city.

"Didn't you just say all you want is for them to leave you alone?" Nicole asked. "How does that help us?"

"If the Nasi or Wang's Isolationists capture Altterra, they will be able to focus all their energies on your universe," Musa replied. "They will be able to indiscriminately use the gateways to travel between your planets and can drain our homeworld of its resources."

Another explosion, closer than the first two, sent tremors through Eden and caused dust to rain down from the ceiling. Kal instinctively ducked then looked around sheepishly as he realized he was the only person who'd reacted.

Nicole glanced at him. "Kal, it's worth a shot."

Kal nodded in surrender. "Fine, let's go."

Huang and her security team rushed them through the caves of Eden as the sounds of fighting echoed from the caves around them.

Once of the scouts she'd sent ahead rushed back toward them. "Governor, there is a heavy fighting position ahead."

"Any way around?"

"No," the soldier shook his head, "the enemy has closed off all other means of entry to the landing bay."

Huang considered it for a moment, tapping at her wrist-mounted comeca then turned to Kingsley and Musa. "Ancients, I suggest we turn back."

"And go where?" asked Kingsley.

"There are other ways to escape."

"Do our children not have any hope of victory?"

Huang shook her head. "There is no way to hold Eden. The enemy force is overwhelming." She looked at Kal accusingly. "They are here because of you."

Kal felt a surge of annoyance. The Ancients and Jadid somehow always returned to Kal or Humanity in general as the source of all their troubles. Despite having brought war to Kal's universe and killing billions, they still thought of themselves as victims. Sitting in their own universe for centuries, their sense of having been wronged had seeped into their very souls.

"I'm getting to the ship one way or another," Kal said. "This is our only chance to make it." He looked to Nicole who nodded back at him.

Kingsley considered it. "Governor, we need you to clear the way. Tell the soldiers still trying to hold the perimeter to disappear and hide in the Savage Plains."

Kal could see that Red was aghast at the Ancient's orders. Nasi and Jadid had no problem running or hiding; they were too pragmatic to care about things like honor. But to see her Ancients, people who were a cross between a parent and a deity forced away, must have been impossible to understand.

"My soldiers will be your shield," Huang declared. She swiveled her daton and then brought it up to her face in a salute.

"Thank you, Governor." Musa laid her hand on Huang's shoulder and shuddered slightly. "Thank you, Maddie." She hugged the Jadid woman—who was at least a couple of heads taller—and the small shudders became sobs.

Kal wasn't sure what to do. He'd never seen such a display from an Ancient. Although they referred to the Jadid as their children, they never had expressed any sort of personal affection. What was going on? "Maddie" seemed as shook as he was.

Kingsley laid a gentle hand on Musa's shoulder, and she pulled back, rubbing away tears with the sleeve of her robe.

The Jadid guard, with Huang at the front, silently formed a line in front of the two Ancients, Kal, Nicole, and Red. The former Nasi still seemed shaken at what she was seeing and wrung her hands together as if trying to wash them.

"On my mark." Huang held a hand up to her shoulder as she crept forward, her daton pointed straight in front of her.

As they crept around a bend, a line of plasma fire splashed against the wall next to them. Huang let her hand drop and rushed forward, the other guards at her heels. As they ran, the air in front of them began to shimmer as they activated their personal energy shields.

The Humans—along with Red—rushed forward, following the Jadid "shield" as they attacked the enemy's defensive position. Automatic plasma fire splashed against the portable energy shields, which flared with each impact. The lead soldier in the formation dropped as her shield failed and a plasma bolt took her square in the chest, but the rest continued on and reached the enemy position, their datons moving so fast, they were almost impossible to see.

In a few short seconds, the battle was over, and Huang stood by the doorway. She tapped a few buttons on her comeca and it opened, revealing the *McCullough* on the other side.

"This way," shouted Huang. Kal didn't need to be asked twice. He ran past the former governor and toward the ship. He could hear the ship's engines humming, ready to take off and get them off the doomed planet. Huang and what remained of her detail followed behind.

"Down," one of the Jadid shouted.

Kal dropped to the ground as a curtain of plasma seared through where he'd been standing. He turned and looked back. Several attackers had taken positions by the door and were unloading with everything they had. Huang's soldiers had already turned around and were moving toward the enemy. But there was no cover in the bay, and their energy shields began to fail as they were overloaded from enemy fire.

"Get to the ship," Huang shouted. She ran toward the door, all the while continuing to fire back at the attackers. With a guttural cry, she jumped through the opening, her daton swinging around her head.

"Get your ass up," Pham shouted from the back of the

McCullough. "The landing bay doors finally opened."

Kal shook his head and pushed himself off the floor. He would have to remember never to pick a fight with Huang. A normal Jadid was already more than a match for a Human. Huang was more like a force of nature than a person.

He joined the others in running toward the ship. As he ran through the hatch he spun around, ready to see a horde of Jadid running toward them. Instead, he saw Madeline Huang sprinting toward the ship, her daton held aloft like a torch. She stopped outside the ship and peered inside.

"You coming?" Kal asked.

"No, I am making sure that Ancients Kingsley and Musa are safe." She scowled. "I do not want to go to your cursed universe. It has brought nothing but pain. I will die here on my home with my brothers and sisters."

Her head snapped toward the landing bay door, and she fired several shots through it. Kal tried to see if he could detect any movement on the other side but couldn't make out anything.

"Protect the Ancients," Huang ordered before turning and running back.

"I'll try." Kal felt he owed her that much.

Chapter Eight
Nicole | Deep Space

The white glow of her own universe's stars was a reassurance to Nicole. Traveling to Altterra was always a disconcerting experience at best, and this time she had left with nothing but a deep sense of despair.

Everyone aboard the *McCullough* seemed to be shook, but none more than Ancient Musa. As soon as she had entered the ship, she'd collapsed on the floor of the cargo bay and remained still as they sped off the planet. To Nicole's surprise, there hadn't been much resistance to them leaving. There had been some ground fire as they left the sunken landing pad and sped into the atmosphere, but there wasn't a single fighter or ship that took pursuit. Perhaps because almost all of Wang's and Baykara's fleets were already in her own universe.

Even after they'd folded, Musa remained on the deck with feet drawn up into her chest and her head bowed, reminding Nicole of a small child. It wasn't the response she'd expected from the normally stoic Ancient. Then she realized what she was seeing; a mother mourning her child. The Jadid were the Ancient's children. But Governor Huang must have been Musa's biological daughter.

Nicole wasn't sure what to say to the woman. Whatever the Ancient was experiencing, it wasn't something she could even fathom. What *could* she say that wouldn't seem trite or insincere? She barely knew the woman. Still, she could feel a surprisingly sharp pain of sorrow as the she looked at her

106

huddled form.

She might not know what to say, but she knew who would. Nicole stepped into the cockpit and found Ai and Kal going through checks to make sure the ship was still working as expected after the fold. Traveling between the universes was becoming more commonplace, but it was still fraught with potential danger.

Nicole tapped Kal's shoulder gently.

"Yeah?" He turned around and looked at her expectantly.

"I think Huang is Musa's daughter," Nicole said quietly.

Ai turned and looked at her. "Yes, that is true. Governor Huang is among the oldest of us. She is one of the first generation."

"Can you say something to her?" Nicole asked Kal.

"Who? To Musa?" Kal ran his hand over his short-cropped hair. "I know why you're asking me, but there's nothing I can say to her to make this better. At least not right now. She's got a *long* road ahead of her. She probably hasn't even processed it yet. Frankly, her situation may be worse: not fully knowing if her daughter will live or die." He swallowed. "It took me a decade to deal with my family's—" He swallowed. "I know you, and this is part of why I love you. But there's nothing I can do that you can't. That any of us can't. If she wants to talk then listen. If she doesn't, that's okay as well. Let her decide."

Even though she could understand it, Nicole hated his answer. There was nothing anyone could have said or could say, that could ease the burden of having lost her sister and

107

parents. Time had dulled the pain, her desire to remove the Nasi had focused it, but nothing had made it go away.

Red was also clearly shaken by their experiences on Altterra. She slumped on one of the benches in the bay staring at her hands.

"You okay?" Nicole asked, sitting down next to the soldier. Based on her seniority, the former Nasi had seen more than her fair share of battle. Nicole would have thought there was nothing that could have caused the woman to act like this.

"We were fools."

"There was no way to know that it had gotten that bad on Altterra," Nicole said gently.

"No, for believing Esma. For believing her lies about restoring Humanity to its rightful place. I see it all so clearly now. What were we thinking? What are my people thinking?" Red gestured to her Shishen. "I've had these for almost seventy years. I saw them as a mark of pride. Each time a new line was added, I felt like had done something great. Now I realize that I was just marking myself as the fool that I am."

"It's a powerful thing."

"What?"

"Believing that you are the victim, that there are forces that have conspired to cast you down. It's one of the most powerful tools that dictators have. Make people believe that someone else, someone different than them, is responsible for all their troubles." Nicole gestured to the Shishen. "You earned these, and you *should* be proud. You should be even more proud of the fact that the blinders that Esma put around your eyes are gone. You can see clearly now."

Red nodded. "Perhaps. But it will take the rest of my life to make up for the things that I have done. I have been a part of destroying planets and killing billions of your people and of my own."

Nicole couldn't argue with that. The woman had a lot to answer for, no doubt. But at least she realized it and wanted to make it right.

"You'll get your chance."

Nicole stood up and walked the few meters to the cockpit.

"We're heading to Wudexingqiu," Kal said as she leaned her head in. "Systems all check out, so we're ready." He called over the ship's intercom for everyone to prepare in case they needed to take evasive action. Nicole sat down in the small jump seat at the back of the cockpit and wedged her legs behind Ai's chair.

They arrived near Wudexingqiu and took a staged approach to the planet. As they folded closer, the Nasi fleet remained in the same position. The planet and the position of the fleet looked identical to the last time Nicole had been there months ago. Their optical sensors scanned the planet's surface and validated there was no evidence of fighting or the Jadid fleet. Their final fold took them just far enough from the planet that they wouldn't risk showing up on the Nasi fleet's sensors.

"Where's that fleet?" Nicole asked.

"How long ago since you left Patagonia?" Kal asked.

Nicole could see the wheels turning in his head.

"I don't know." She thought back. It felt like weeks ago. "Twenty hours or so."

"If they're headed here, then they should be arriving any time. That fleet has to show up somewhere. My hunch is it will be here. "

Nicole thought about it. She had no idea if his hunch was right or not. But their mission had been to determine where the Jadid fleet around Patagonia had gone, and she hadn't confirmed a thing yet.

"You think we can remain undetected for a couple hours?" Nicole asked Ai.

The scientist nodded. "If we remain in this location, it's unlikely they'll find us. If they do, we can fold away."

"Good. We'll hold position and if we don't see the fleet in the next couple of hours, we head back to Mariga to see if they show there."

As a scientific vessel, the *McCullough* was designed to hold only a handful of people. After their visit to Altterra, the ship was practically busting at the seams—Nicole, Kal, Kimathi, Pham, Ai, Red, and the two Ancients. Ai had already reassured Nicole earlier that she'd upgraded the ship's life support system, and it could easily handle the added stress of multiple people, but Nicole still couldn't stop herself from worrying. Add in the discomfort of people having to conduct their private business in the corner of the cargo bay, and she was more than ready to head back to Patagonia.

"I figured they were the same as us, but it's nice to have confirmation," Kal whispered to Nicole as he eyed Red using the ship's biorecycler.

"I can hear you," Red called over her shoulder.

"Sorry." They both hastily turned around.

"You both have issues." Pham said, looking up from the game of cards she was playing with Kimathi. "I'm not angry, just disappointed. You need to respect other's boundaries." Kimathi nodded his head in mock sorrow.

Nicole felt the heat creep up her face. "I think we've waited here as long as we can."

"Just let us talk to our children," Kingsley pleaded for what felt like the hundredth time. He'd been lobbying for Nicole and Kal to let him hail the Nasi fleet and "try to talk some sense into them," as he put it. After several flat refusals, he'd even gone around them and tried to get Ai to allow it. To her credit, the scientist had refused in an extremely polite, but firm, manner.

"We contact them, and we give up our position," Kal replied. "You had your chance for years. Now you'll wait until we tell you we're ready."

Musa had remained quiet throughout the exchange, and for his part, Kingsley clearly realized she was hurting and hadn't tried to rope her into his increasingly desperate attempts.

"There's—"

The *McCullough's* alarms blared, causing Nicole to jump.

"We found the Jadid fleet," Ai shouted from the cockpit. "Unfortunately, like they've also found us. We're already being targeted."

Nicole ran to the cockpit and jumped into the copilot's seat. The tacmap painted a grim picture: the entire Jadid fleet was surrounding them.

"You sure they've noticed us?" Kal asked as he took the chair behind Ai and Nicole.

A stream of plasma from a Jadid fighter shot past them. "Yes, very sure," Ai replied.

"We need to take evasive action," Kal ordered. "Get us clear from the battle right now. The last thing we want is to be in the middle of this. When we get far enough away, we can fold out of here."

"Why?" Nicole asked.

She could hear the confusion in Kal's reply. "What do you mean, why?"

"Remember, we're in the *McCullough;* we can fold from *anywhere*," Nicole said.

"New ships, new tactics." Kal smacked himself in the forehead. "I didn't even think of it. Can you get us out of weapons range?"

"Yes," Ai said. "There is still a margin of error, but I can get us out of immediate harm. Looks like the fighters have already forgotten about us and are heading towards the Nasi."

"Then do it," Nicole ordered. Kal outranked her, but it was her mission, and she gave the orders when it came down to it. If he wanted to take over command, fine, but unless he said something he'd need to sit back and let her give the orders.

The stars flickered on the viewscreen, and they were suddenly several million kilometers away from Wudexingqiu. The tacmap, which had been filled with icons and dots of the Jadid and Nasi fleets, now only showed the Nasi positions.

"We're now a few light minutes from the planet," Ai said. "You can actually see our ship if you zoom in." She adjusted the screen, and Nicole could make out a slight shimmer in front of the planet where the *McCullough* had been a few minutes earlier.

"It's strange," Nicole said. "It's like looking back in time."

"You're actually required to do a similar exercise in the academy." Kal was referring to the officer's academy for the Earth Defense Force. "It *is* a bit strange."

The Jadid fleet appeared around Wudexingqiu and began disgorging fighters while unleashing a barrage of missiles at the Nasi fleet. A moment later, the *McCullough* disappeared.

The Nasi were clearly prepared for the Jadid's Liberation Fleet and immediately raised their shields and returned fire. The Jadid were clustered on one side of the planet, and the Nasi ships were forced to leave orbit and circle around the planet in order to bring their full forces to bear.

"The Nasi seem to be keeping up," Kal commented. Nicole agreed; despite their inferior numbers, the Nasi were holding their own, blow for blow, against the Jadid. However, she knew it wouldn't last long. Already the Nasi ships' shields were weakening, flickering slightly against the darkness of space. "They must've been improving their gravitational shields; the skip missiles are all detonating early."

Skip missiles incorporated a fold drive into a regular missile, allowing them to make miniscule folds toward their target, thereby bypassing point defense systems and detonating *inside* the ship. They were costly and often missed—folding past or around their targets—but were almost impossible to defend. Or at least that was what Samsara Fleet's engineers had thought when they'd developed them. Almost immediately after they first used the missiles the Nasi created a defense; a gravitational field that emanated from their fleet, causing the missiles' fold drives to malfunction.

"All the work I did, and it is now in the hands of our enemies," Ai said with an uncharacteristic edge of anger.

"We knew it would happen," Nicole said.

"All weapons end up being used on the people who created them," Kal added. "Samaha knew that when she had you create them." Nicole felt it was a surprisingly philosophic observation considering they were watching an enormous clash between two fleets.

The ship's viewscreen magnified the battle, and they watched in excruciating detail as the enormous capital ships traded missiles while swarms of fighters flew between them. Small bursts of light peppered the fighter clouds as they met an untimely end.

The Jadid slowly wore away the Nasi fleet until there were

only a few capital ships remaining.

"Not long now," Nicole said. She felt empty inside. Was she supposed to be happy?

"I just hope they end up taking each other out," Kal said.

In Nicole's estimation that wasn't likely. The Jadid had a clear edge in the battle and were steadily wearing away the Nasi fleet.

A red icon appeared on the tacmap, halfway between Wudexingqiu and the system's central star. The *McCullough's* computer couldn't identify what the ship was, only that it wasn't friendly. Nicole zoomed in on her console; it looked to be a Nasi or Jadid destroyer with some sort of sensor array affixed to the hull.

"What is that?" Kal asked.

Ai hummed and began tapping at her controls. She made a small grunt. Nicole looked over at the Jadid; she was frowning as she studied the readouts on her console.

"What is it?" Nicole asked.

"I can't be sure, but…" Ai trailed off.

"But?"

"I think based on the size, location, and some of the readings that the new ship is a dreadnaught." Ai zoomed in on the sensor array attached to the ship. "Also, that looks to be a disruptor, a weapon that can remotely disrupt a star's fusion reaction."

Nicole groaned inwardly.

"I thought we'd destroyed all of them," Kal said.

"As did I," Ai agreed. "But nonetheless, the ship is also

following the standard operating procedure for a dreadnaught. It's far away from the battle with a clear line of sight to the system's star. Also, that array is emitting energy readings that are similar to—"

Before she finished speaking, a stream of brilliant light shot from the bottom of the ship toward the star. As soon as it touched, the sun's surface darkened and began to roil as the ship's weapon disrupted the fusion process.

"Damn Nasi." Kal swore. "They're willing to destroy the entire system just to ensure the Jadid can't capture it."

"How did they get another dreadnaught?" Nicole asked.

"I think the more important question is how do we stop it?" Kal asked. "The Jadid fleet can't fold from their location, but we can."

However, several Jadid ships tried to do just that, fold from the battle toward the Nasi ship. Bursts of light erupted across the battlefield as their fold drives failed, overcome by the gravitational fields of so many ships in such close proximity. One of the battleships even tried to fold, and it burst apart in a gout of green flame.

Ai's fingers flew across the console as she continued to scan the dreadnaught; because of the distance, different sensors received information at different times. "It's a converted Nasi carrier," she said. "Based on the energy coming from the star, we've got minutes until the sun goes critical."

Nicole willed herself to think. They could reach the Nasi carrier instantaneously, but what help would that be? They had no weapons.

"What's going on?" Kingsley stuck his head through the doorway and into the cockpit. "Why are we waiting here while my children are dying?"

"Your *children*?" Kal spun on the man with his face red. "Your *children* are about to exterminate billions of people on this planet."

The color drained from Kingsley's face as he saw the viewscreen and realized what was happening. He was no longer the ancient leader of a race; he was a caged rat, trapped by his own offspring.

"Get us to that ship," Kingsley said. "It's the only way we can stop them. I'll get Musa. Together we can talk some sense into whoever is commanding it."

Kal looked at Nicole. She could see the doubt in his face. But he didn't speak. It was her mission, her decision to make. She didn't know that they had any better option.

"Fine, get her in here."

Kingsley ducked back to the cargo bay to retrieve the other ancient. A moment later, they returned and crammed into the cockpit.

"Get us as close as is safe," Nicole ordered.

The viewscreen flashed and the Nasi dreadnaught appeared in front of them. The ship was massive, almost as large as the Nasi's original dreadnaughts and bigger than any Human ship that had ever been built. It's undulating dark gray hull sheened with an almost rainbow patina. The disruptor's beam, which had already been bright where they'd been, was now almost overwhelming in its pulsing incandescence.

"Hail them," Kingsley ordered. He stood upright and gathered his robes around him, setting his face in an expression of stern disapproval. Musa stood next to him, her eyes puffy and red, with the same look of reproach.

Ai sent out a general hail, saying she had a message from Ancients Musa and Kingsley. Less than a half minute later, the round, almost cherubic, face of Grand Ancient Esma Baykara, leader of the Nasi, filled the screen.

"Richard and Salina, come to talk some sense into me?" Esma asked with a smirk.

Kingsley's face reddened in anger. "Damn you, Esma," he pleaded. "Think of the people on that planet. Think of our *children* still there."

"I *am* thinking of them." Esma continued to smile. "They can always fold away before they're destroyed. As for the Humans"—she waved her hand—"there're always casualties, always compromises that need to be made."

"A planet filled with people is not a compromise to be made," Nicole shouted.

Kingsley fixed her with a stern glare. The message was clear. This was his battle to be fought. Nothing *Nicole* could say would get through to Esma.

"You're throwing away half your resources for spite," Musa said reprovingly. "This is not a sound strategy." Her mouth drew to a hard line. "You need to stop thinking with emotions, Esma, and start using your head."

"I am using my head," Esma shouted back. "Bao—that

little weasel—has been playing us all. He outmaneuvered you, but he won't do the same to me."

"This isn't about winning and losing." Kingsley somehow managed to sound stately. "Give his forces the planet, and then you can figure out your next move. You gain nothing by this."

Esma's smile faded, and for a moment, Nicole felt like the woman might actually be considering the idea. The connection clicked shut and the beam from the Nasi dreadnaught disappeared, leaving a faint afterglow in Nicole's vision.

"Did she just agree to stop?" Kal asked in disbelief.

Musa and Kingsley looked at each other cautiously. Something was off.

"This isn't like Esma," Musa said. "She's doesn't just change her mind so suddenly. "

"Why'd you want to talk to her then?" asked Nicole.

"Hail Mary," Kingsley said. He noticed the questioning stares from Kal and Nicole. "It just means an act of desperation." He waved around the small cockpit. "I think that describes us right now, don't you?"

"I think it's described us since the Nasi arrived," Kal replied.

"Is the ship adjusting course?" Nicole asked Ai. "Any changes?"

"No." Ai continued to tap at the screen. "Nothing has changed."

"See if you can raise Esma again," Kingsley instructed.

Ai spent several minutes trying to raise the Ancient, but there was no response. The beam suddenly sprung back to life, striking the central star and sending its surface into a dark roiling mass of gas.

"Dammit," Nicole swore to herself. What was going on?

"You bastards." Esma's face, flushed with rage, appeared on the viewscreen. "You turn my own children against me?" She didn't wait for a response. "You're in league with Bao, aren't you?"

"They're launching fighters," Ai called out.

"I've left you two relatively alone," Esma continued. "Let you wallow in your own resignation. No more. You are enemies of the Nasi and of the Jadid. I'll hunt you down just like Bao." The transmission ended and Esma's face disappeared.

Kingsley swore and punched the metal bulkhead of the cockpit. Musa remained frozen, staring at the beam from Esma's ship as it inexorably spelled Wudexingqiu's doom.

"We've failed," the Ancient whispered. "After all these centuries, we've failed." She shuddered slightly. "And it's our fault. Not theirs." She motioned to Kal and Nicole. "Esma entered this world and started this war, and Bao came here to capitalize on it. What did we do?"

Kingsley looked at her cautiously.

"We did *nothing*, Richard. Nothing." Musa took a seat on the floor like a child at creche. "We deserve this. But not them." Nicole wasn't sure who the Ancient was referring to. Her and Kal? The innocents that were about to be killed? The

Jadid? There were so many victims of Esma and the Nasi.

The woman had snapped—she was broken. Kingsley wasn't far behind. When faced with their failure, with all they had lost, they had nothing left.

"We need to do *something*," Kal said. "We can't let them get away with this."

"Do what?" Nicole asked. "We don't have any weapons. We're in a science vessel for goodness' sake."

"What about folding *into* the ship?" Kal asked.

"The chances of the *McCullough* being able to fold inside of the dreadnaught is approximately one thousand to one," Ai said.

"We did it before." Kal's voice had an edge of desperation. "We can't just let a planet filled with *billions* be destroyed."

"Say we successfully fold inside the ship, then what?" Nicole asked. "Our only option would be to go full speed and hope we hit something critical before we're vaporized."

"The chances of that are again extremely low," Ai added. "I would suggest we fold away now. The fighters will be within missile range in the next thirty seconds."

"We can't just *let* this happen," Kal face was torn.

"We're not." Ai's voice was surprisingly soft and empathetic. She understood what they were going through. Nicole realized the woman was probably feeling much of the same thing. Just because the Jadid were slow to show their emotions didn't mean they didn't have them.

"She's right." Nicole placed a hand on Kal's shoulder.

"We need to go. Esma and Bao won't stop here."

Kal dropped his head between his knees. "Do it." His voice was muffled. "Get us out of here."

They folded as close to Wudexingqiu as they could and watched the final movements of the inevitable. Nicole felt like there was an unspoken agreement that they had to be the people to watch the final moments of the planet and its people. Although they couldn't do anything to stop its destruction, they could at least pay their respects.

The fighting between the Jadid and Nasi fleets was almost over. The two remaining Nasi vessels were using the planet to shield themselves while the Jadid pursued them, maneuvering to get a clear shot.

"It's almost like they don't realize this entire system is about to be destroyed," Kal said solemnly. "Or I guess they don't care."

"The Jadid want to eliminate the Nasi before the system is destroyed," Ai replied. "Every ship destroyed now is one less that they must fight later. Always press the advantage when you can." She said the last line in rote tones as if it was something that she'd had to memorize, which Nicole guessed she probably had.

"Call Bao's fleet," Kingsley ordered. "Open channel. Let them all hear."

Ai's fingers flew over the console. "Ready," she said.

"My children," Kingsley began and then stopped. He

stopped and looked down with a frown. "Are you my children? I do not know anymore. What has happened today, what's happened these past couple of years, is not something that I would've expected from *my* children. Ancient Wang and Baykara—Bao and Esma—have twisted you into something I no longer recognize. You've become something cruel and heartless. I don't…" Richard faded.

"We don't understand why you continue to do this," Musa continued, her voice strong. "You kill innocents and each other for nothing. You destroy your *targets* while your brethren die beside you. I beg you, stop this madness. You have—"

A Nasi man appeared on the viewscreen, cutting off Musa. Nicole felt a pang of hatred at seeing the angular face and slicked back hair.

"Sharma," Kingsley said in despair.

"He's overridden our signal," Ai said.

"My fellow Jadid, Ancients Kingsley and Musa are in league with the enemy. They've decided to join Ancient Baykara and use their power to subjugate not only this universe but our people as well. Understand this: they are now enemies of the Jadid." Sharma slowly shook his head in regret. "I know that this may be hard, but we've been ordered by Ancient Wang to stop them at all costs." Sharma took a deep breath and stared directly at the camera, his eyes intense. "Ancients Musa and Kingsley, I am sorry it has come to this, but for the sake of everything we have built, please surrender yourselves peacefully."

123

"That bastard," Musa swore. "That absolute piece of garbage."

Nicole was pretty sure she was referring to Wang and not the Jadid officer.

"He's lost as are we all." Kingsley's voice was quiet as he looked out at Wudexingqiu. "There's nothing to do here except to mourn this planet and its people."

The passengers on the *McCullough* silently watched as Wudexingqiu's central star continued to darken and then burst in a rushing wall of fire. As the explosion swept toward them, it vaporized anything in its path: planets, asteroids, ships. The single remaining Nasi ship and the remains of the Liberation Fleet separated and folded away, their battle paused for another time.

"Take us back to Patagonia." Nicole's voice broke slightly. "We'll figure out what to do from there."

Chapter Nine
Kal | Patagonia

They didn't speak as the *McCullough* entered Patagonia's atmosphere. What was there to say? The remaining Jadid ship was still in the exact same location, maintaining a geosynchronous orbit at the planet's equator. They were easily able to avoid detection as they headed to Samaha's base in the mountains outside of Foyleton.

With Bao's betrayal and the waning influence of the Nasi, Kal had forgotten just how evil Esma Baykara could be. The fate of Wudexingqiu was a stark reminder that she was responsible for more death than anyone in the galaxy. Bao's betrayal, while bad, was nothing compared to the billions that she had killed.

They landed inside the perimeter of the abandoned base and solemnly trudged through the entrance to find General Samaha waiting for them.

"General Kal Norman," Samaha drew out his name as she spoke. To Kal's surprise, she seemed genuinely happy to see him. "There're not many things you can count on in this galaxy, but you're one of them. You are one lucky bastard."

"Ma'am, not sure if I should be offended, but it's good to see you again."

"Looks like we're not done yet," the general said. Despite the smile on her face, Kal could read the stress of the past few months written across it. "I don't recall us talking about finding *you*, but for some reason, I'm not surprised to see Nicole return with you." She shot Nicole an amused glance. "I see you also brought some others. Ancients Kingsley and Musa, good to see you again."

The two Ancients bowed their heads in greeting.

"We found the fleet," Nicole said without preamble. "The Nasi destroyed Wudexingqiu rather than let it fall into Bao's hands."

Samaha's smile disappeared. "How?"

"Ancient Baykara has built another dreadnaught," Kal said. "She had it within a fold of the planet. As soon as it was clear she'd lost the battle, she brought it in. Took out the entire system."

"That—" Samaha turned and wiped her sleeve across her face. "All those people."

"What's to stop her from destroying New America or Patagonia?" Cell Chief Pham asked. Kal hadn't realized the woman was still standing behind him.

"Nothing," Samaha said. "Nothing but us."

"She won't do that," Ancient Kingsley said, stepping next to Kal.

"How can you be so damn sure?" Samaha arched an eyebrow. "You just told me she destroyed a planet. Which makes it the second time that…woman has done it."

"Esma still has control over one of your planets." Musa stepped next to Kingsley. "She's ruthless but she's also pragmatic. She'll do everything to hold on to what she has first. Her goal remains to control this universe. She won't throw everything away."

"And if she can't hold on?"

126

Kingsley and Musa looked at each other hesitantly.

"I thought so." Samaha frowned. "Seems like any way we turn, we're screwed. If the Jadid defeat the Nasi, I'd bet everything I have that we'll see that dreadnaught here sooner than later."

"There's only one solution then," Nicole said. "We've got to beat them both."

It would be a lot easier said than done.

The history of Patagonia—and of the galaxy—was written on the walls of Samaha's base. Graffiti and murals that had been scrawled by previous occupants ran throughout the compound. Names of defeated factions, portraits of leaders, and even landscapes were nestled among portable viewscreens. Drab government-standard safety posters emblazoned with the crest of the Earth Defense Force had been left up and used as canvases with catcalls and caricatures making clear what people thought of their former protectors.

Kal wasn't sure, but he thought one of the portraits was supposed to be of him. The artist looked to be talented, but if it was Kal, they had painted him as he might have looked twenty years ago without wrinkles or gray hairs.

General Samaha had asked for Kal and Nicole to join her in her private office after they'd had a chance to recover from their mission. The "office" turned out to be a converted maintenance closet with a few chairs placed against the walls.

"I can't believe those bastards," Samaha said as they sat down. "I should correct myself—I *can* believe it; I just hate that it doesn't surprise me."

"Ai figures they were able to convert one of their existing ships." Nicole sat opposite the general and Kal sat next to her. "How, we're not completely sure, but we're not the only ones with scientists and engineers. The actual weapon itself is relatively crude compared to what they used before."

"It was good enough to get the job done." Samaha sighed. "You already uploaded the sensor data?"

Kal nodded.

"We'll see what my one remaining intel officer can make of it." The general pulled out a tablet and began to scroll through the video. "I'd thought I would never see this again."

"What do you think Wang will do?" Kal asked. "You know him best."

"As well as anyone can know that man," Samaha said. "I doubt even he knows who he is very well. The man's a compulsive liar. Those other two Ancients spent centuries with him—created a civilization with him—and were still caught off guard." Her eyes narrowed. "Unless they're somehow in league."

Kal thought about it. Could Musa and Kingsley somehow be working with Ancient Wang? He recalled their reactions to everything, Kingsley's desperation and Musa's catatonia on the deck of the *McCullough*. It seemed very unlikely.

"Not a chance," Nicole said.

"They could be here to distract us," Samaha said. "You

know, the right hand punches us in the face while we're looking at the left one."

Kal scoffed. "Ma'am, they don't need to distract us. The Nasi or the Jadid could destroy us straight up. They're already punching with both hands."

"Fair point." Samaha twisted her mouth. "Indeed. Well, to answer your question, my guess is Wang will attack. He played at being cool and collected, but in his heart, he's a man of passion and anger. He's ready to take the galaxy and won't wait or stop now."

"Which means he'll be moving his fleet from New America to capture Mariga," Kal said.

"It also means we have an opportunity." Samaha smiled. "Esma and Bao are at each other's throats. We're an afterthought to them."

"For good reason," Kal said. "It's not like we've got much to fight them with."

"On the contrary." Samaha smiled and started counting on her fingers as she spoke. "We've got the most advanced ship in the galaxy—"

"Without any real weapons," Kal interjected.

Samaha waved him away and continued to speak. "A burgeoning network of spies spread across their worlds. The support of the other Ancients." She held up two fingers, then a third and fourth. "And we still have two fully functional capital ships."

Kal's heart leapt at the last sentence. "The Merrimack and Ofira are still around?"

Samaha nodded. "I had a worry about our good friend Bao and I try to never put all my eggs in one basket. The ships folded to deep space as soon as the Jadid started to consolidate power." Her lips twisted in distaste. "There were a few soldiers—Jadid *and* Human spies—that tried to stop them from folding, but they were dealt with. They've been waiting for the signal to return."

"And now we've got an opportunity with the Jadid fleet gone," Nicole finished.

"Exactly." Samaha pointed to the woman. "With the fleet around this planet gone, and their reinforcements on their way to attack the Nasi, we can actually take back Patagonia."

"What about when the fleet returns?" Kal asked.

"If we're able to capture the ship in orbit we'll have a chance to fend them off," Samaha said. "We'll have the advantage of surprise along with superior numbers."

Kal couldn't believe it. How could their fates have changed so quickly? From seeing Wudexingqiu destroyed only hours ago to talking about recapturing Patagonia from the Jadid.

"I may be a bureaucrat," Samaha continued, "but I'm also a soldier. We've got two ships ready and the soldiers to support them. While Bao was placing spies in our ships, I was doing the same on his—and from what I can tell, I was a helluva lot more successful."

"How successful?" Kal tried to keep his hope down.

"Enough that we have a chance." Samaha paused. "*More* than just a chance. We're not only going to take this planet back, but we're also going to take their ship and use it against them."

❖

Kal had to admire the ingenuity of people. Despite being on a mountain plateau in the middle of the Pangean continent, there were still many of the comforts of home. The few soldiers and rebels that were off duty played games, watched holos, or sat together chatting. Samaha had told them to take a few hours to recover.

The base wasn't big enough for dedicated rooms or even beds—people slept in shifts—but he and Nicole were able to find a small alcove where they had at least *some* privacy.

The destruction of Wudexingqiu hung in the back of Kal's mind, but the thrill of being back with the woman he loved overpowered it. Since he'd found Nicole on Mariga, he hadn't had time to really appreciate the fact that she was still alive. Now as he studied her angular features and ivory skin, he allowed himself to push everything else out of his mind and just enjoy the moment. The war—and everything that came with it—would have to wait.

"I can't believe I'm seeing you again," said Nicole breathlessly as she pulled her head back to look at him.

"Ditto." Kal didn't have the words.

As they remained in an embrace, she told him about her time on Hope. It was strange to think she'd spent so much time in that small town so close to the Fridge, the base that had been destroyed by the Jadid immediately after Kal had been taken. As he listened, Kal was impressed—but not surprised—by her complete determination to find him and continue to fight. As long as Nicole Bergeron was alive, the Jadid and Nasi didn't stand a chance. It was a trait he liked to think had somewhat rubbed off on him. When he'd retreated to Mariga, he'd continually heard her voice in his head, urging him to keep going.

They reluctantly decided to get at least *something* to eat and found the small room which was being used as a mess hall. A battered food fabricator stood against a wall and several dingy rectangular tables filled the area in makeshift clusters. The only other people in the mess were Musa and Kingsley. The two Ancients sat opposite each other, talking in hushed tones as they experimentally poked at the food in front of them.

"This is not Manakeesh," Musa said, scandalized. "They've bastardized this dish. There's barely any meat on it."

"I don't think there's any meat on it at all, technically," Kingsley replied, lifting a corner of the round bread covered with what looked like cheese and a gray substance in front of him. "I think it's some sort of chemical concoction."

"That's mostly right," Kal said as he sat down next to them with his food. "The fabricator creates food through synthesizing common proteins, scents, textures, and the like."

Musa pushed her plate away. "Sounds disgusting."

Nicole shrugged as she sat down next to Musa. "It takes some getting used to, but I like it. Growing up in the communes, you were *lucky* to get food at all."

"The communes?" Kingsley looked up from his dish. "Those still exist?"

Nicole nodded. "Well, on the planets that your children haven't destroyed they do."

Both Ancients looked away for a moment. "I would have thought Humanity would have evolved beyond things like communes," Kingsley said.

"Easier said than done," Kal replied.

The Ancient nodded in admission. "True. I guess we never had that issue because we Ancients were always in control."

"We were the creator and savior of our children," Musa said. "Until we became their downfall."

Emotions flickered across the Ancient's face. How much had she lived through? Looking at her, Kal would never have known that the woman was one of the oldest Humans in existence.

Nicole took a bite of her meal and pointed her fork towards Musa and Kingsley. "Thoughts on being back? How long since you've been here?"

"We've never been *here*," Kingsley replied stiffly.

"But this universe," Nicole said. "This is the universe you came from. At least some of it must feel familiar."

Kingsley cleared his throat. "Honestly," he said. "No. It doesn't feel familiar. It feels strange. We've been gone too long. He looked down at his meal. If it hadn't been for Esma and Bao, I never would have returned."

"It's strange—the trees, the light," Musa wiggled slightly in her chair, "the gravity."

"Well, we're not exactly thrilled either," Kal said. "But your buddies had other ideas."

"What Esma and Bao have done is reprehensible," Kingsley admitted. "But not only to your people. Not anymore. They've also done it to ours."

"Listen. The sooner they're dead, the better," Nicole said. Kal glanced at her, surprised at the venom in her words.

"On that, we can agree." Musa took a small bite of the Manakeesh in front of her and made a face.

After several hours, Kal received a summons from General Samaha, asking them to meet her back in her office.

Sergeant Kimathi and Corporal Sato were waiting with the general in the closet-turned-office, chatting quietly to one another. Kal wondered if the ranks were even necessary; was there a Samsara Fleet anymore? He remembered something that Sergeant Asif Jones had told him a long time ago; rank and protocol were there for a reason. They provided reassurance and structure even when everything else might be in chaos.

"Okay, we've got everyone here," Samaha said. "Let's get down to it. I've had my staff looking at the situation and trying to figure out what our Nasi and Jadid friends might do next. The Liberation Fleet's most likely course of action is to return here, to Patagonia. The Nasi will continue to rebuild, hoping that Wang will decide it's not worth it to attack Mariga."

"How long until the fleet gets back here?" Nicole asked.

"We've got a couple of days," the general replied. "No more than that. Hopefully, it will be enough time to capture the Jadid ship in orbit and liberate the planet."

"What happens when the fleet arrives, ma'am?" Kimathi asked.

"Then we deal with them," Samaha said. "They won't be expecting to run right into a fleet of—hopefully—three enemy ships."

"This mission will let you do some old fashion Tac-I work," continued Samaha. "Get to the *Ofira* and *Merrimack* and let them know they can return. When our ships fold in, we hit the ship in orbit, the *Resolute Stand*, and capture it. I have some people on the inside who have provided schematics and stand ready to assist. Once the operation starts, they know to unleash chaos on the ship.

"I've also talked with the two Ancients, and they've agreed to help. They'll be broadcasting to the Jadid, telling them to stand down. If anything, it should at least cause a few to sit this one out."

"Destroying a ship is tough enough," Kimathi said. "Capturing one, especially one this big, is going to be damn near impossible."

"Perhaps," Samaha said. "But like I said, it won't just be you. You'll have help and hopefully that'll make up the difference. We do this all at once and they won't know what hit them."

Kal wasn't sure about that. But he agreed that this was their window. If they waited until the remains of the Jadid

Liberation Fleet returned, any advantage they might have would disintegrate. Looking around the room, he could tell the others were all feeling the same way. They were in a hole, grasping for any rope they could find, and this one seemed to be the most secure.

"Ma'am, one question," asked Corporal Sato. "What do we do when the Jadid fleet returns?"

Samaha sighed. "We'll kill every single one of 'em."

Chapter Ten
Nicole | Patagonia

Chief Ramos slapped the button that activated the *McCullough's* fold drive, and Patagonia blipped off the main viewscreen. A second later, the tacmap pinged as the ship's sensors registered two friendly ships—the *Merrimack* and *Ofira*.

Nicole marveled at how the *McCullough* had changed her perception of the universe. Ai's ship had brought the galaxy closer together than ever. They were on the edge of a new epoch, one where distance no longer mattered. The question was what would it look like? Would it be one ruled by the Nasi or Jadid? Or one where Humanity remained free and in control of their own destiny?

"Identify yourself or we will open fire." The command from the *Ofira's* comms officer was delivered in a clipped tone.

"*Ofira*, this is the *McCullough*," Ramos said, patching through the video feed so the other ship could see her. "We've got General Norman aboard and are requesting permission to land."

There was a pause. Nicole could only imagine what was happening on the *Ofira's* bridge. Although Kal wouldn't admit it, he was a folk hero to the rest of Samsara Fleet, a man who'd been fighting—and winning—against the Nasi from day one. There was even a picture of him painted on a wall in Samaha's base. She wasn't sure how much Kal noticed the furtive glances and open-mouthed stares he received, but she noticed every time. Their old unit, the Skulls, had been a thing of legend within the fleet. Every single Tac-I soldier wanted to be on Kal's scout team. Even if the Skulls had been defeated, Kal Norman remained just as famous if not more so.

"Nicole." Irina Petrov, commander of the *Ofira*, grinned through the video feed. "I can't believe I'm talking with you. Scratch that. Knowing you and General Norman, I do believe it." Her grin widened. "What took you so long?"

"Traffic was a bitch," Nicole replied with a smile.

A few minutes later, they touched down in one of the *Ofira's* enormous landing bays. Petrov stood next to their pad with a small retinue behind her. Maintenance technicians and flight crews were scattered throughout, casting furtive glances towards the *McCullough*. As the small ramp to the *McCullough* thunked onto the metal floor of the bay, Petrov strode up and gave Nicole a warm hug, shocking her.

"About time you showed back up," Petrov said. "We were beginning to wonder if you'd decided to take a vacation."

"Spent a bit of time relaxing in a polar mining town," Nicole said. "Then I realized I *hate* the cold, so I decided to come back."

Kal slapped Petrov on the back with a smile then pointed to her collar. "Good to see you *Brigadier General* Petrov. Congratulations on the promotion."

Petrov wave him off. "I think it's less to do with any sort of skill and more to do with remaining alive."

"Either way, ma'am, congratulations," Nicole said.

"I'm sorry, but we're cutting your vacation short," Kal said.

"We've got a mission for you."

"About time."

They followed the commander through the bay. The pilots and maintenance techs had given up all pretense of doing their work and watched their procession as they weaved through the orderly rows of ships. It was rare for a soldier to have the chance to see a legend.

They made their way through the ship to the command level. Several of the doors along their path were open, and Nicole spied eager faces peering out watching them pass. Everyone was eager to see Kal, to see a hero back in the fight.

"Well. Well." Petrov took a seat at the conference table in her command room. "I'm eager to hear what you've got to say. We've been waiting long enough."

"We don't have a lot of time," Kal said as he sat next to the colonel.

Petrov nodded. "Of course. When have we *ever* had a lot of time?"

Kal quickly filled the *Ofira's* commander in on what had happened and their plan. Petrov listened, absently-mindedly tapping a finger on the table while he spoke. When he told her about the fate of Wudexingqiu, she slammed her hand down on the table as her eyes widened in shock.

"Those bastards." The news hit Petrov especially hard since she was from Wudexingqiu. Nicole wasn't sure if she'd had family still living on the planet, but she had to imagine the general at least had friends who'd died. "Those evil sunnuva bitches."

Nicole placed a hand on her friend's back in consolation. She knew exactly what this felt like. To hear that the place you'd grown up was gone forever, not to mention all the people you'd known and loved there, hurt; it was hard to accept, much less recover from.

After giving Petrov a few moments to adjust to her shock, Kal continued. "I know this is a lot to take in," he finished. "But we need to leave soon. Whatever remains of that Jadid fleet that attacked Wudexingqiu will be returning to Patagonia, and we need to be ready for them."

Petrov nodded slowly, her joy at their arrival gone. "We're on constant standby," she said quietly. "We'll be ready in a few minutes." The general stared into the distance, clearly using her neural implant to communicate with her staff.

"Thank you." Nicole wasn't sure what else to say.

The general stood from the table. "You want to thank me? Then kill every last one of those bastards."

After they'd met with the *Ofira's* commander, Nicole told Kal she'd meet him in the landing bay. There was one stop she *had* to make.

Before the war, capital ships like the *Ofira* didn't have a creche. Who would bring a child onto a carrier or battleship? But Humanity had continued to march along after years of war, and even the Nasi couldn't stop them from reproducing. There wasn't a good way to sneak a child onto a planet— though a few had tried—so they had adapted, turning a section of the ship into a childcare facility.

Before the war, the creche had been an overflow dining facility, intended to be used by the senior officers and NCOs. After removing the tables and adding fabricated toys, play areas, and equipment, it was almost impossible to tell its original purpose.

Jae-Ho giggled as he wobbled along, running away from one of the caretakers. When Nicole had last seen him months ago, he hadn't been able to walk. She knelt close by and watched silently as the boy stumbled around the play area with an enormous smile. She wondered what they did for children like him, children whose parents were missing. He was an orphan, his father had died before he was born, and his mother, Chief Taisha Kanumba, had been the pilot and chief engineer for Nicole's scout team, the Bones. Where the woman was now was anyone's guess. Somewhere on Patagonia, Nicole fervently hoped.

"Ma'am?" asked the caretaker who had been following Jae-Ho.

"Sorry. Just a friend of his mother. Wanted to make sure he was doing okay."

The caretaker looked at her knowingly with a small frown dancing on her lips. "He's doing great. Any word on her?"

"No, but soon, hopefully."

"Well, Jae-Ho will be waiting for her."

True to General Petrov's word, the *Ofira* and *Merrimack*

were ready to depart in less than a half hour. She had one of her aides escort Kal and Nicole to an assault ship. Ai had already left with the *McCullough* to head back to Patagonia. It was way too valuable to risk in an attack, so they would use one of the ships already on the *Ofira* which was designed for just such an operation.

The interior of the assault ship was familiar and somehow strangely comforting. The cargo bay was lined with rows of battle suits and had a narrow bench in the center. It was a no-frills setup designed for only one purpose: to get the augmented suits and their pilots into an enemy vessel as quickly as possible.

"Feel like home, ma'am?" Sergeant Kimathi asked as he stepped up the cargo ramp behind Nicole.

"More than I'd like," she admitted.

He nodded in understanding. "I can't remember life before this war. Seems like a dream. I can't even remember why I ever had a worry in my mind back then."

"We all end up adjusting to our reality. Even if we were in paradise, we'd find things to complain about."

"I'm looking forward to complaining about things like my food being too hot."

"You and me both."

As Nicole used her neural implant to link to one of the suits, the rest of the Tac-I team came up the ramp and started doing the same. When the EDF had still existed, Tac-I soldiers had been the elite of the elite, trained at the hardest school in the EDF and assigned to only the most important missions.

They were trained for small unit insertions—boarding ships, bases, or planet-side infiltration missions. Under Samsara Fleet, Tac-I's remained elite, but they were the ones who'd proven themselves in battle rather than having attended a course.

Sergeant Kimathi, their squad leader, and Corporal Sato, one of their two team leaders, had both been Tac-Is in the Skulls, Kal's old team. Cell Chief Pham, the other team leader, was a hardened resistance fighter in the Tiradentes Liberation Front, and Nicole knew she could more than hold her own. The other three soldiers, who had been picked by General Samaha were the unknowns. Presumably, they'd all faced off against the Jadid or Nasi, but Nicole wasn't sure how they'd react when they were pinned down by enemy fire or had to infiltrate a Jadid capital ship. The most notable addition was Red. As a Jadid, she was inherently stronger and faster than any Human, not including the advanced military training she'd gone through as an elite Nasi warrior. Encased in a pitch-black Jadid battle suit, she would be an unstoppable force.

"We will be arriving at Patagonia in one minute," announced the *Ofira's* bridge.

"See you on the other side," Nicole said to Kimathi as she made her way toward the cockpit. The sergeant nodded quickly at her and resumed his work of getting the Tac-I squad ready.

Chief Ramos and Kal were already in the cockpit conducting their pre-liftoff checks. As soon as the *Ofira* folded into the area around Patagonia, the carrier would disgorge the assault ships and swarms of fighters. Then it would be a race to pass through the Jadid fighters on their way to breaching the capital ship.

"Final fold complete," the *Ofira*'s bridge called over the net. "All ships commence assault."

The enormous landing bay doors opened, revealing a smattering of stars stained a faint blue by the energy shield holding in the atmosphere. They rose from the deck and sailed through the opening with assault ships on either side of them. The swarm of fighters streamed out behind them, heading toward the *Resolute Stand*.

They sped toward the Jadid ship, their optical cloak and electronic defenses activated. If the Jadid's point defense system was able to identify and target them, they wouldn't have time to react before a hypersonic slug cleaved through the thin armor plating of their ship. There were nine other assault ships on parallel courses. Each one would try and breach the enemy ship at a different location. They knew not all of them would make it. But it was a numbers game. If at least half of them did, that would send over fifty highly trained Tac-I soldiers onto the ship.

"They're not doing much," Kal said with a note of wariness.

He was right. Normally, a capital ship like the *Resolute Stand* would immediately fire every missile it had and direct every fighter in its fleet at its attackers. So far, the *Resolute Stand* hadn't done any of that. It remained in a geosynchronous orbit above Patagonia's capital as if nothing was going on.

"Let's hope it stays that way, sir," Ramos said.

Despite how close they'd folded to the planet, it still took precious minutes for them to close the distance to the planet. During most of that time, the Jadid ship remained inert. Then red dots began to appear on the tacmap.

"Looks like they've finally woke up," Nicole said. "We've got at least a dozen skip missiles and a couple hundred fighters heading toward the *Ofira* and *Merrimack*." Skip missiles could theoretically hit any ship in the galaxy from any distance. In practical terms, their effective range wasn't too much farther than a conventional one. "I don't think they're in range though. There's a pretty low probability of them making contact."

"Any sign they've noticed us?" Kal asked.

Nicole studied the tacmap. The cloud of Jadid fighters was heading directly toward the Human fighters to the front starboard side of their ship. There was no sign that the small flotilla of assault ships had been noticed at all.

"No, nothing."

"Let's hope it stays that way."

They continued forward, watching the battle unfold around them as their small ship closed the distance to the Jadid capital ship. There continued to be no sign that the enemy had noticed them.

Kal let out a curse, causing Nicole to jump. "We've got another ship that just folded in," he shouted. "The Jadid ships from Wudexingqiu are folding back."

As soon as the last word was out of his mouth, another ship folded in. They were now outnumbered. What had been a mission to capture an enemy ship had turned into a bid for survival. Despite that, Nicole knew there was nothing they could do except keep going forward. The *Ofira* and *Merrimack* would have to figure out something.

"How long until we're within their point defense range?" Kal asked.

"Not totally sure. Could be anytime." Despite the situation, there wasn't much for Chief Ramos to do. She had already pivoted them on their axis so the rear cargo door was facing the direction of travel and cut their thrust to help conceal them from the Jadid sensors. They had to stay the course, gliding backwards, until they reached the hull of the *Resolute Stand*.

The two Jadid ships that had entered the space around Patagonia began spewing fighters. It appeared that much of their fighter complement had been decimated from the battle around Wudexingqiu, but they still outnumbered the fighters from the *Ofira* and *Merrimack*.

"Attention, my children." The stern faces of Ancients Musa and Kingsley appeared on their viewscreen. They were broadcasting over the open net from the *Ofira*. "Please, stop this fighting. What has it gotten you? We've lost so many already and destroyed so much more. So much of what you had come to this universe to save. We can still—"

The video faded to a heavy static.

"Something on the planet's jamming the signal," Ramos

said.

"Eh, worth a try." Nicole hadn't expected the Ancients' transmission to do much. It hadn't worked at Wudexingqiu. Why should it work at Patagonia?

"I keep waiting for Zhou to respond," Kal said. "I'm wondering if he's here."

"I would have thought he'd be on the net already," Nicole agreed.

She wondered where her former comrade was. Perhaps he'd died with the fleet at Wudexingqiu though she doubted it.

Several alarms blared through the ship.

"What's that?" Nicole asked.

"Their point defense is firing," Ramos replied in a tight voice. "We're in range now."

"Guess there's no use in sitting here." Nicole stood up. "Either we make it, or we don't."

Ramos nodded, and Nicole and Kal rushed to the cargo bay to get into their battle suits. Boarding a ship was all about speed and bringing as much firepower to bear as possible. If they were trapped in a single section of the ship, they'd be sitting ducks; the Jadid could vent the air, remove the gravity, or just detonate the entire section with them in it.

Nicole stepped into the back of her battle suit and activated it with her neural implant. The seams along the arms, legs, and running up the back knitted closed, enclosing her in a cocoon of alloy and cutting-edge technology. She grabbed the helmet from the stand in front of her and placed it on with a soft click.

We're t-minus thirty seconds to contact, Ramos called over the ship's internal net.

Sergeant Kimathi and his two team leaders already had the Tac-I squad in two lines along the edges of the cargo bay. It was impossible to see the faces of the others, but Nicole liked to think that everyone else was as nervous as she was. She tried not to imagine the *Resolute Stand's* point defense blowing them into a mass of bodies and shattered metal. *Tried.*

Ten seconds, Ramos announced.

Ready? Kal asked through a private link to Nicole.

Nicole nodded then realized he couldn't see her—it'd been awhile since she'd been in a suit. *Yeah, let's do this.*

The rear door of the cargo bay slid back revealing the dark hull of the Jadid ship. It took a moment for Nicole's brain to reconcile what she was seeing; the hull seemed to be coming toward them at an almost impossibly fast speed. The assault ship's rear thrusters burst to life, slowing them down until they hit the hull with a soft thump. If there hadn't been inertial dampeners, the change in velocity would have sent everyone in the cargo bay flying out.

Two metal blades swung from the assault ship and cut through the *Resolute Stand's* hull, slicing through the thin weaves with ease. After what felt like an eternity to Nicole, Kimathi flew forward and slammed into the hull, pushing the weaves aside and exposing one of the dark twisting corridors of the Jadid ship.

They were in.

Chapter Eleven
Kal | Patagonia

Although descended from Humans, the Jadid were alien in many ways. It was especially apparent in the layout and design of their ships. Human ships were comprised of metallic straight lines. Jadid ships were made from weaves, organic-looking prefabricated materials that were almost impossibly strong. Rather than traveling in a straight line, the corridors spiraled, rose, and fell. Without his suit's tacmap, Kal would have been impossibly lost.

In addition to superhuman strength, flight, advanced shielding, and weapons, battle suits had the advantage of masking the occupant's face. Kal was grateful Kimathi and the other Tac-I soldiers couldn't see exactly how nervous he was as they rushed through the Jadid ship.

Updates, Kal called over the net.

While Sergeant Kimathi was the commander for their small assault team, Kal was the overall commander for the mission. The other assault team commanders reported in, revealing that seven out of the ten teams—including themselves—had been able to make it through the Jadid point defense—more than Kal had expected. Each team had a predefined objective to capture. If they could control specific areas of the ship, they'd be able to control the entire thing.

It was clear that General Samaha's Jadid spies—or assets as she called them—had already been aiding them. *The Resolute Stand* should have sprung into action much earlier, launching missiles and disgorging their fire. The fact that they'd been able to get seven teams aboard was almost surely due to their efforts.

How are we supposed to know who to kill? a squad member asked over the net.

Dammit, weren't you paying attention during the briefing? asked Kimathi. The friendlies will be wearing blue armbands.

Armbands? the soldier asked with a note of incredulity.

What do you want them to do? Wear signs or something? Kimathi asked. Maybe next time you pay attention to the damn briefing.

We're scraping the bottom of the barrel, the sergeant confided to Kal over a private net.

They entered the Jadid ship's storage areas, a network of enormous cells used to store fuel, food, and the like. The area was sparsely inhabited, which meant they were able to make quick work of the few Jadid they saw on their way through the tunnels. Every time Kal passed a body, he dreaded finding a blue armband. Thankfully, none of them had one.

He had to split his attention between what was happening in the hallways in front of him, the status reports from the other assault teams, and the tactical overlay of the battle around them from the fleet. The assault teams were all making headway while taking on some fire, but Samaha's assets had been effective in sabotaging weapons stores and disabling the Jadid battle armor. The fleet was in worse shape, the *Merrimack* had already taken several missile strikes, and the *Ofira* was barely holding off the cloud of Jadid fighters.

151

Kal fought the urge to tell Kimathi to hurry up. The sergeant was a hardened soldier, he knew what he was doing, and Kal's comments would have only elicited a suggestion of where he could direct further advice.

The corridor ended in what Kal could only think of as a nucleus, a roughly oval-shaped room which contained at least a dozen openings in the walls, floor, and ceiling. He wasn't sure what its function was, but the pre-mission briefing had identified it as the quickest way for them to get to the bridge while circumventing much of the known antipersonnel defenses. He was sure the Jadid knew that as well and expected they were about to face a lot more resistance than they had so far.

They made their way up one of the twisting shafts with Corporal Sato and Alpha Team in the lead. The tunnel was tight but still wide enough that Kal had full use of his suit's weaponry if it came to that. Only problem was he couldn't see past the person in front of him.

An explosion boomed from above. Kal quickly checked the status icons on his suit's display—everyone in the squad was still green.

What's happening? Kimathi barked.

We've got fighting up ahead, Sato replied. Unclear who it is.

It's not one of ours, Kal said. The other assault teams had entered the ship from far away. Although he didn't know their exact locations, the idea that one of them would be this far off course was unlikely at best.

Must be those spies of the general's, said Sergeant Kimathi. *Can you get eyes on?*

Uh. Yeah. Sato's reply took a moment. *Seems like we got a few Jadid surrounding someone.*

Kal pulled up the map he had of the ship's interior— thanks to Samaha's network, they had a complete schematic of almost every square centimeter. *This is a cell block. It's gotta be a prisoner. Can you take out the Jadid?*

Roger, the corporal replied.

A moment later, a crescendo of explosions followed by the pops of high-velocity kinetic rounds came from above. Kal followed the others as they streamed out of the shaft and into a large chamber with several bodies on the floor and filled with a smoke so thick that Kal's suit automatically turned on the thermal imaging.

He could see a single person crouched behind a toppled desk with something—a daton rifle by Kal's guess—in their hand. The two remaining Jadid attackers had taken cover in a couple of the alcoves that lined either side of the room. As Kal entered, two of the soldiers from Alpha squad flew down its length, their suits oriented to the sides, and cut down the Jadid in a hail of plasma.

"You can get up now," Kimathi called through his suit's external speakers as he strode down the length of the room toward where the prisoner was crouched. He kept his weapon at the ready; he knew that the enemy of an enemy wasn't always a friend.

Kimathi, Bravo, check for any survivors. Alpha, get me a

status— Kimathi's transmission shut off like a switch as the person behind the desk stood up. *Holy crap.*

What? Nicole asked. *Who is it?* Kal could sense the hope in her voice.

You'd better come down here and check it out.

By the time they reached the end of the room, Kimathi had already knelt down and taken his helmet off. He looked back at Nicole and Kal with a grin. "Look like anyone we know?"

As they got close, Kal realized it was a Jadid standing behind the desk, their face hidden by the rapidly dissipating smoke that still wreathed through the air. He narrowed his eyes trying to somehow will his suit's optic sensor to discern the features of whoever was standing in front of him.

"Bo," Nicole said through her suit's speaker. "I can't believe it's you."

The smoke finally thinned enough to reveal the smiling face of Bowen Nguyen. The Jadid scientist moved smoothly forward as he slung his daton behind his back and slapped the back of Nicole's suit. "Nicole, I was hoping that I would see you again."

Kal was so overcome by emotion he couldn't speak for a moment. Of all the things he had planned for, seeing his friend whom he'd thought was dead, was not one of them. He pulled his helmet off. "Bo, you made it," Kal's emotions strangled the words as they came from his mouth.

"You can't keep this purple sunnavabitch down," Kimathi laughed.

Bo reached over and patted the back of Kal's suit affectionately. "Guess fate has different plans for me."

"Fate's gonna shove a missile up our asses if we wait around here for much longer," Kimathi said easily. He pulled his helmet on and continued through his suit's speaker. "Bo, you are *definitely* coming with us. We gotta head to the bridge."

"I figured," Bo said, following behind. "This guard"—he gestured at a blue-armband-clad Jadid on the floor— "released me from the cell and gave me a daton. Unfortunately, the other ones were not far behind."

"Anyone else in the cells?" Kal asked hopefully. They were still missing a lot of people. If even one more of his missing soldiers were in that room, Kal would consider it the luckiest event of his life.

"None that I've seen," Bo said. "They only kept Jadid in shipboard cells. All the Human prisoners were to remain planetside."

"Well, guess that makes things easier for us," Kimathi said philosophically. "We're not losing you again, Bo. You stay with the general. He's practically got a horseshoe stuck up his ass."

"Horseshoe?" Bo asked, glancing at Kal.

Kal shrugged in reply.

"You all *really* need to read up on your history," Kimathi said with a huff.

❖

Kal forced himself to push the joy of seeing his friend again to the side. If the mission was a success, there would be time to catch up and revel in the news. If not—well, then none of it mattered anyway.

They still had to work their way up the shaft toward the command area of the ship. Bo straddled the waist of Kal's suit and rode him as they continued to move upwards. The other six teams continued to make progress toward the key control points on the ship and reported some sporadic fighting. The relative speed at which they were all reaching their targets made it clear the blue-armband-wearing collaborators had been exceptionally effective in delaying and muting the Jadid response.

Outside the ship, the battle was not going well. The *Merrimack* had sustained heavy damage, and from what Kal could tell, was on its last legs, and the *Ofira* had been forced into retreat, followed by the fighter swarm. They were only still in the battle because the two Jadid ships that had entered into the system had been damaged from their previous attack on Wudexingqiu, and the Jadid ship they were in, the *Resolute Stand*, was hampered by the actions of Samaha's collaborators.

We're near the command level, Kimathi said. Prepare to breach the bridge. We get up there, we move fast.

Though his view was blocked by the people in battle suits above him, Kal could see a small glow of light at the edges of the conduit. According to the tacmap, they would exit only a few dozen meters from the bridge.

The tunnel gradually curved down and they dropped into a large corridor. As Kal's metallic boots hit the deck, a smattering of plasma fire streamed around them. One of the bolts hit his shield, which flared as it absorbed the blast. Kal jumped to the side of the corridor, bouncing off the wall. Thankfully, Bo had jumped to the side even before the blast had hit the shields.

"Bo, stay down," Kal ordered. The Jadid held his daton at the ready but remained kneeling and nodded back.

Kal could make out a mass of four to five Jadid in front of the oval bridge door. They'd taken cover behind what he guessed were portable barriers and were periodically lobbing shots at the Humans.

Bravo team, move forward, Sergeant Kimathi ordered over the net. Alpha, cover 'em.

We'll cover the back, Kal said, turning his railgun on the hallway to their rear. He kept his back to the wall, allowing him to see in front of them as well as the dozen meters of hallway which ended in a sharp turn behind them.

Corporal Sato and Alpha Team used their thrusters to speed forward, a smattering of antipersonnel missiles proceeding them, while Pham and Bravo Team fired plasma shots beneath. Kal doubted that Bravo could hit a thing in the close quarters, but it would at least encourage the Jadid defenders to keep their heads down.

Red somehow corkscrewed through the corridor ahead of everyone, reminding Kal of some sort of insect as she coasted along walls, ceiling, and floor before dropping in between the defenders. Once inside their perimeter, she became a blur as she swept among them, sending Jadid flying into the walls with sickening crunches.

Clear, Sato called out. Red, you coulda at least waited for us.

I wait for no one, the Nasi replied. Kal had a hard time telling whether she was joking or not. He found it was always a coin toss with the Nasi.

Kal moved forward with the rest of the group, his weapon still trained away from the bridge entrance and took a position behind the barrier. He expected the Jadid were already sending several security crews toward them already. They *had* to get inside the bridge before the reinforcements arrived.

A meter-long blade sprung from the gauntlet of one of the soldiers, and they plunged it into the wall next to the bridge door. The weaves that made up the Nasi ship were incredibly resilient against explosions and plasma but were vulnerable to being cut—especially by a razor-sharp blade operated by a someone in a suit with superhuman strength.

As the soldier cut through the weaves, Kal eyed the end of the hallway waiting for a mass of Jadid, clad in black battle suits, to come streaming toward them. Instead, the only sound that came through the speakers in his helmet was the sound of the serrated blade slowly slicing through the Jadid weave wall.

Alpha, get ready to breach, Kimathi ordered.

The squad took positions around the door, their weapons held to their shoulders. As soon as the entrance was cut open, they'd launch explosives through the opening and follow them through, a tide of chaos and death for any Jadid unlucky enough to be on the other side.

The blade was almost halfway through its course when the bridge door opened. Reflexively, half the team turned and fired into the opening, their plasma bolts sizzling against the consoles and floors of the room.

Halt!

The order had come from Nicole. Kal followed her pointing finger and saw an arm sticking from the side of the doorway, waving a blue armband.

They entered the *Resolute Stand's* bridge to find a row of Jadid crew members in restraints sitting against the wall. Several of them were injured, bleeding, or had limbs turned at an odd angle. The woman who had held out the blue armband introduced herself as Senior Officer Freda Kekoa.

If she felt any guilt or uncertainty over leading a mutiny on her own ship, Kekoa didn't show it. She looked at Kal with fierce green eyes as she explained that her forces had been able to secure most of the ship's key areas.

The plan hadn't been for them to capture the ship in one fell swoop. It was impossible for even a hundred Human assault teams to do that. Instead, they would shut down the ship's key systems, rendering it a lifeless hull. After that, they could slowly decompress each section, giving the occupants the chance to turn themselves in. As long as they held engineering and a few other sections, the Jadid crewmembers would be helpless to stop them.

The battle outside was now completely in favor of the two Jadid ships. The *Ofira* had been forced to stop fleeing but was still barely holding its own, thanks mainly to the heroics of its rapidly dwindling crew of fighters. But the *Merrimack* was now on its last legs. A small trail of debris radiated out from its hull, most likely the result of a recent, almost fatal, skip missile strike.

The three Jadid ships, including the *Resolute Stand*, had taken positions around the two Human ships and were tightening a noose around them so they could fire at them from multiple angles and force them to keep pumping energy to their shields.

"We still able to operate this thing?" Kal asked.

Kekoa nodded. "Yes, though I don't know for how long." She pointed to the three-dimensional wireframe of the ship. Several areas were filled with red. It took Kal a moment to realize the red was *his* forces; the hostile forces which had taken control of the ship. Green dots were streaming toward them, or in some places like engineering, already surrounding them.

"Our mission is a failure if the rest of the fleet's gone," Kal said. "We need to take out those other two ships."

"We'll have one chance." Nicole studied the three-dimensional tacmap at the center of the bridge. "And we need to get closer."

"They know we've been boarded," Kekoa said. "I told

them everything was under control then cut off all external feeds. Still, they'll be on the lookout for any deviation from our plan." If they realized that Kal had control, they wouldn't hesitate to destroy the *Resolute Stand.*

"So we need to make up an excuse for deviating." Kal looked around the bridge hoping something would give him an idea. He saw the engineering readouts on one of the walls and many of them were already in the red. "Any chance we can have an *accident* with the engines?"

"The other ships can also see our internal sensors," Kekoa explained. "We would need to have an actual malfunction. And if that's the case, we won't be able to maneuver afterwards."

"Okay, fair. This is a risky idea," Kal admitted. "*But* it shouldn't raise their suspicions too much."

"I cannot say for certain but...No, I do not think so."

"Good enough for me." Kal tried to ooze confidence in his response. He called down to the assault squad in engineering and explained the situation. After several disbelieving requests for him to repeat himself, the team agreed it *was* possible though not the best idea.

"Do it," Kal ordered.

Panels on the bridge display flashed red as a plume of plasma erupted from the underside of the ship. The blast knocked them from their course circling the two Human ships and put them on a path that would take them between the other two Jadid ships.

"Five minutes until we are within primary weapons range,"

a crew member called out. "Our window to fire will not be long, only a few seconds at maximum."

"Sir, you sure you know what you're doin'?" Kimathi asked as he studied the tacmap.

"No idea," Kal admitted. "But if you got anything, I'm all ears."

"Kinda late for that."

Kal shrugged.

As they neared the *Ofira* and *Merrimack*, Human fighters started to pull off from their battle with the Jadid and strafed the *Resolute Stand*. Almost all of them were picked off by the point defense. Kal still felt a surge of anger and frustration at their deaths.

"I wish we could tell them we're friendly," Nicole said.

"Nothing we can do about it, ma'am" Kimathi said. "We're trying to fool the Jadid but seems like we fooled some of our own people as well."

An alert came from the team occupying engineering. General Norman, we're not gonna be able to hold this position for much longer.

Kal looked at the ship's schematic. A steady wall of green now encircled the engineering section, the green and red touching in a few spots.

You need to hold on for a few more minutes, Kal replied.

As if on cue, an explosion ripped through the half-completed hole in the bridge. Two more followed in quick succession, and a Jadid in a black battle suit flew out of the small cloud of smoke where the bridge entrance had been.

Before Kal could react, half the people in the room had fired at the fighter, sending them sprawling back into the hallway. Everyone moved without orders, taking positions behind the consoles or diving into a prone position and bringing their weapons to the ready. Bo also took cover and aimed his daton at the opening while the Jadid crew members held their positions, waiting for their officer's orders to fire.

Damn it, just one more minute, Kal thought to himself. The *Resolute Stand* would soon be even with the other two Jadid ships. At that point, they could unleash a devastating broadside attack.

Two more Jadid fighters flew through the opening, spraying plasma fire across the bridge as they went through. One of the bolts hit a crew member in the back, sending her smoking body to the floor. Another hit the main viewscreen, burning a hole in the direct center and rendering it useless. Another two Jadid—thankfully without battle suits—leapt through the opening and into the bridge. Their movements were fast and silky smooth as they brought their datons up and fired, their bolts sizzling against the shields of the Human's battle suits.

The whine of railgun slugs greeted the intruders and one of them went down in a heap. Another round struck the torso of one of the armored Jadid with a ping and bounced off.

Kal tried to line up a shot, but the enemy was moving too fast, and the quarters were too close. He unsheathed the sword in his suit's gauntlet and rushed forward, along with the other members of the assault team to protect Kekoa's crew.

Kal found himself locked into a fight with the remaining unarmored Jadid. As he tried to grab a hold of their body while dodging their haphazard fire, his suit registered another Jadid on his back. Several more had entered the bridge and joined the fray.

Keep them off the crew, Kal shouted over the net. We have one chance to destroy the Jadid ships.

He tried to stab at the two Jadid who bounced around him. As he turned, a readout on his suit went red. A point-blank plasma blast had almost pierced through his suit's back armor. Even without battle suits, the Jadid were lethal.

Kal's eye trailed on a charred Human battle suit on the ground, and he saw that three of the icons on his head up display were red. They were losing and fast.

Another Jadid managed to climb onto Kal's back and started stabbing his suit with a plasma knife. With an oath, Kal activated his front thrusters and flew backward, hitting the bulkhead with a crunch that sent shivers down his spine. He didn't need to look back to know the Jadid that had been climbing on his back were dead. He reversed course and sped toward a grouping of three Jadid. They noticed him coming and turned with their weapons raised.

At the last moment, Kal sent his feet flying in front of him and cut the thrust, causing him to slide feetfirst along the deck. He raised his blade and sliced at the Jadid's legs in a single motion, sending all three of them down with screams of pain.

"Fire," Kekoa commanded with an icy calm.

Kal looked up just in time to see a curtain of plasma and missiles streak out from both sides of the *Resolute Stand*. They were close enough that the attack hit the other two ships in seconds, overwhelming their defenses. Explosions blossomed along the sides of the vessels as their hulls were torn away and atmosphere billowed out. A moment later, one of the ships went critical and shattered in two, spraying a cloud of atmosphere and bodies into the void. Seconds later, the *Resolute Stand* groaned as thousands of pieces of debris struck the sides.

The explosion was enough to distract the remaining Jadid defenders on the bridge. The Humans took advantage of the lapse, driving them down with several railgun slugs.

"I have locked out all periphery networks," a Jadid rebel called out.

"What's that mean?" Kal asked.

"It means that the only way to control this ship is to do so from the bridge," Kekoa explained. "All other systems are offline."

"Not like it matters," Kimathi said with a ragged breath from his suit.

"True." Kekoa nodded and turned to her crew. "Lock down the ship and close the breach to the bridge so we can begin decompression." She motioned to the bodies littered about as if they were trash. "And clear this area up." Kal was amazed at the matter-of-fact way the woman spoke after destroying two of her fleet's ships.

165

Two of the blue armband-clad rebels went through the room and dragged the bodies to the side while another began to apply a patch to the large breach. It didn't take long until the hole was gone, and it was impossible for Kal to tell it had been there—one of the many benefits of the Nasi weaves.

Kal looked down and finally gauged the cost his team had paid in the assault. Three battle suits lay on the ground. Two of them were clearly dead with deep craters in the suits where a plasma round had overwhelmed their shields. Kal only knew the third was dead because of the red status icon on his heads-up display. They had been volunteers from Petrov's crew, and he didn't know who they were other than three more people dead on his watch.

Most of the other assault teams were much worse off. Two of them were completely decimated with casualty rates above eighty percent. On the other hand, they'd been successful. Samsara Fleet controlled the *Resolute Stand*, the other two Jadid ships were destroyed, and the *Merrimack* and *Ofira* were heavily damaged but both still in one piece.

Kal pulled of his helmet and dropped it on one of the consoles. He pushed the deaths to the back of his mind and tried to focus on their victory. Somehow—improbably—they were still alive, and the mission had been a success.

Now came the hard part.

Chapter Twelve

Nicole | Patagonia

Clearing the *Resolute Stand* of enemy fighters was a laborious process despite the surgical and merciless way that Senior Officer Kekoa evacuated the ship of atmosphere. Section by section, she called for the enemy fighters to lay down their arms. If they didn't, then she ordered her crew to decompress the entire space and shut the artificial gravity down. After ensuring there were no signs of life, they repressurized the area and moved onto the next.

After the first time she watched the grizzly process on the bridge viewscreen, Nicole vowed to look anywhere but back up there. However, Kal seemed to be fixated and practically stared at the screen as the process unfolded. She wasn't sure what it was about the man; he seemed determined to absorb every ounce of pain and suffering into his soul.

The rest of the Humans followed Nicole's example and focused on anything but the screen, chatting among themselves about anything except what was happening in front of their eyes. There wasn't much for them to do except wait for the process to be finished. But they remained in their battle suits—with their helmets off—just in case.

Nicole joined Sato, Kimathi, Red, and Bowen, attracted by the sound of laughter and their smiling faces.

"Bo," Nicole wrapped the Jadid in a hug then leaned against a console. The last time she had seen the Jadid scientist had been months ago but felt like another lifetime. She'd assumed the worst when she'd heard he hadn't been found. It was such a relief to see him alive and apparently unhurt.

"I am so happy to be talking with you." Bo smiled. "Though when they suddenly released me from my cell, I had an idea I might be seeing you and General Norman."

"Where are the other prisoners?" asked Kimathi. "There're several levels of cells."

"They didn't take any," Bo replied with a shake of his head. "Humans were kept on the planet and the Nasi…"

"They didn't take Nasi prisoners," Nicole finished.

Bo shook his head again.

Nicole shouldn't have been surprised, but she was. Despite everything, she'd thought the Jadid would be different than the Nasi. It was clear that any difference between the two was minimal. It made sense if she thought about it; they both came from the same culture, one that had been steeped in the desperate need to survive in an inhospitable universe. What would that mean if they won? Was there any difference between a Jadid or Nasi victory?

"Why are you here?" Kimathi asked. "You were with us on New America."

"They didn't tell me why," Bo replied. "My guess is that I've earned some notoriety among the Jadid due to my contributions to Samsara Fleet."

Bo told them about his treatment at the hands of the Jadid, a race he'd once considered himself a member of. His despair was palpable as he described what he saw as a fracturing of their society. The schism among the Jadid was evident even in his imprisonment; some of his captors treated him humanely, even generously, while others tortured him mercilessly.

"I was a Jadid," Bo said. "But now, I don't know what I am."

"You're one of the only decent ones of us left," Red whispered.

Bo listened gravely as the others described the Jadid attack on Wudexingqiu and its destruction by the Nasi dreadnaught. After years, Nicole could sense his visceral horror by the way the skin around his eyes crinkled and the tightening of his lips.

"We've entered the darkest period of the Jadid," Bo said when they were done. "There can be no illusions of honor or any hope for victory. We have destroyed ourselves."

After several hours, only a quarter of the *Resolute Stand's* crew agreed to be taken prisoner and more than one of them tried to attack as they were taken into custody. It was a brutal affair, but at the end of the day, the enormous ship was now theirs.

"We ready?" General Samaha asked with an arched eyebrow as she looked at Officer Kekoa.

Once the ship was secure, the general had taken a shuttle from the surface to take command of what little bit of fleet they had. The *Resolute Stand* had a skeleton crew, and the *Merrimack* was undergoing extensive battlefield repairs. The

Ofira was the only operational ship and would be almost useless against any Jadid battleship or destroyer that came into the system. That said, having three capital ships in orbit around the planet gave them a decisive edge against the Jadid ground forces that controlled it. Given enough time, the planet would be theirs. However, time was not something they had a lot of.

"We are ready," Kekoa replied. "Opening up communications to the surface."

General Samaha stood in front of the auxiliary viewscreen and absent-mindedly pulled at the bottom of her blouse, trying to smooth the wrinkles out of her uniform. Nicole glanced uncertainly to Kal as they stood at either side of the general waiting for their hail to be answered.

A moment later, the round face of General Frederick Zhou appeared in front of her. His eyes narrowed as he saw them.

"Frederick." Samaha practically spat the man's name out as if getting rid of something rotten.

Zhou flinched and clenched his jaw. "General Samaha, it is good to see you."

"Good to see me?" Samaha cleared her throat and chuckled mirthlessly. "I doubt that. Or did you forget you tried to have me killed?"

"I never wanted to *kill* you," Zhou said. "Simply help you to understand. Samsara Fleet has done so much to rid our galaxy of the Nasi scum. We're in the final phase now. Ancient Wang has—"

"Ancient Wang is a murderer and psychotic," Kal

interrupted. "And so are you."

"General Norman." Zhou looked at Kal with disappointment. "You understand what we're doing and why it's important. You saw what the Nasi are capable of. You're the one who first helped me understand."

"We know what *you're* capable of," Nicole said heatedly. "We know you decided to slaughter the Nasi prisoners you took."

"Of course, I'm capable of that," Zhou said. "I have to be if I'm going to win. If we're going to win."

"That's a cop out and you know it."

"Colonel Bergeron, I demand you treat me with the respect befitting my rank. I am your superior officer after all." Nicole had to control herself from shouting at the man. He had committed treason of the highest order yet somehow still saw himself as her superior. "It was a simple question of expediency. There was no way for us to keep the Nasi we'd captured around. We don't have the facilities to hold thousands upon thousands of prisoners, especially Nasi ones. It was regrettable"—his tone indicated it wasn't *that* regrettable—"but it was what had to be done."

"It didn't *have* to be done," Samaha said. "You had a choice."

"Ma'am, we've made similar decisions together on behalf of the fleet," Zhou replied. "This is the reality of war. Especially one of survival. How many times did you directly order—or look away—when we used enhanced interrogation? Were you not the one who was prepared to wipe out the Nasi

Footholds to win the war?"

To her credit, Samaha looked away. Nicole could see that Zhou's words had struck home. Nicole had fought against the use of "enhanced interrogation" at the time, but the general had been desperate for information. It was something she always thought about when she saw the general, a black stain on her otherwise stellar opinion.

"There's proportionality, dammit," Kal shouted at the screen. "You murdered people. It's not just black and white."

Zhou waved his hand idly at the screen. Nicole could sense his anger growing with every word; he wasn't speaking like a man defeated. Despite the fleet having been gone from orbit, General Zhou clearly felt he held the upper hand.

"Enough," Samaha didn't shout, but then again, she didn't need to. She instilled enough iron into the word that everyone stopped to wait for what she would say next. "Frederick, you're no longer a general, not in my book. We've wiped out your ships from the planet. You know as well as I do that it's a matter of time before we capture it and you. We'll take out every single one of your Jadid garrisons if we need to."

"Now who's the murderer?" Zhou asked.

"Stow it and save us all some time and a lot of lives. I want your soldiers to leave their bases and report to the coordinates I send you." Nicole had been shocked to learn that Samaha had been planning for this eventuality since the hour after the Jadid had betrayed them. She had a detailed plan for how they would process the Jadid and then hold

172

them for months.

"I'm afraid that's not something I'm going to order my soldiers to do, ma'am," Zhou replied. "I've already sent notice to Ancient Wang, and I imagine you'll have the rest of Liberation Fleet here shortly."

Nicole tried to hide her unease. If even a handful of Jadid vessels arrived, there would be nothing that the dilapidated Samsara Fleet could do to stop them.

Somehow Samaha kept her calm. If anything, she looked content as she smiled slyly at the viewscreen. "Wang's not going to help you, Frederick. He's got to worry about the Nasi. What you *don't* know is that the Nasi have another dreadnaught. Wang'll be more concerned with saving his own skin than yours."

Nicole could tell the message hit home as the former Samsara Fleet general paled, but his expression never wavered. "Dreadnaught or not, we will win. Our fleet will prevail."

"Almost half your fleet was wiped out," Kal said. "I saw it. Your *Ancient* won't be able to help."

"There's—"

"You've got ten minutes, Frederick," Samaha said, cutting him off. "If I don't hear anything back, then we start taking out your forces en masse." She motioned for the connection to be cut.

As soon as the viewscreen had flickered back to a field of stars, the general sighed and ran her hands through her hair.

"You think he's right?" Nicole asked. "Will they move

some of the fleet from New America here instead of attacking Mariga?"

"Doubt it," Samaha said, turning to face Nicole. "Once he hears what's happened at Wudexingqiu, Wang's gonna be scared."

"They'll probably move their fleet away from the planet," Kal said. "Wang's never struck me as someone who is anything but patient and cautious."

"Right up until he stabs you in the back." Samaha nodded in agreement. "He's patient but not always. Liberation Fleet will try and strike the Nasi and take them out." She sighed. "They'd better at least, because if they don't, we won't have a chance in hell."

Zhou wouldn't respond to any of their hails. True to her word, Samaha ordered the ships to fire on the known Jadid bases. Despite their severe damage, the three capital ships were able to make short work of them. It was simple to lob plasma at the planet when you knew they wouldn't fight back. Nicole expected the Jadid soldiers would have already received some sort of evacuation order. Although they couldn't hide among the locals like the Human rebel groups, there was a lot of covered forests and land in Patagonia. The planet wouldn't be truly *theirs* for months.

"I've got a few crews standing by," Samaha said after the initial wave of orbital fire was complete. "They'll start liberating our prisoners. Zhou'll probably slink off to the forests, but we'll find him eventually."

"We'll head to the surface," Kal said. "There's more than enough work to go around down there."

The general nodded. "It's good to see the Skulls back together again." Nicole couldn't have agreed more.

The Skulls headed to one of the *Resolute Stand's* landing bays. It was decided that Bo and Red would remain on the *Ofira* since they didn't know how the locals would react to them, not to mention Bo had a few minor injuries from his captivity.

There was still a large cluster of prisoners in the bay that were in the process of being escorted onto transport ships that would take them to the surface. The Skulls had to wait another hour before they found a transport with space to fit them.

The transport landed in the center of Kasongo, not far from the governor's palace. Nicole's feet had barely touched the ground before it was lifting off over their heads, heading back into space.

"They got their work cut out for them, huh," Sato said as she watched the ship disappear into a bank of clouds.

"We all do," Kal said. "The hard part's over, but the work has just begun."

"Not to mention our good friend Ancient Wang, or our other friend Esma, could show up at any time and blow us all to hell." Sergeant Kimathi whistled cheerily.

"I hope Samaha's right and they'll be too focused on each other to worry about us for a bit," Kal said. "There's some

175

serious hatred between those two."

Nicole nodded in agreement and watched the crowds around talk with each other. News of the Jadid defeat must have reached the people of Patagonia as there was an air of stunned disbelief. Occasionally she heard a shout of joy or the sound of whooping, but mainly it was clusters of people talking to each other in hushed tones and a flurry of waving hands.

"You'd think they'd be happier," Sato remarked, scanning the street.

"They've been through a lot," Kal replied. "They're just hearing it now. Give it some time."

Nicole thought back to the people she'd met across the Human colonies over the past years. For her and the soldiers of Samsara Fleet, the war was all-consuming, but for most people on Patagonia and the other colonies, it was just another thing they had to overcome. Sure, there were revolutionaries, but the average man or woman was more concerned about putting resources in their fabricator than anything else. As multiple people had told her, what did it matter if they were paying taxes to the United Earth Government, the Nasi, or the Jadid? It was an opinion she vehemently disagreed with, but she understood.

The normally well-kept gardens of the governor's palace had been left to go wild. Despite the overgrown hedges and tall grasses, the buildings themselves remained as imposing and grandiose as ever. The crowds hadn't yet started to make their way through the common areas between the buildings, but Nicole suspected they would once they'd digested the news of the Jadid defeat. When she'd first seen the compound, it had surprised Nicole to find out that the Patagonian government hadn't put up fences or gatehouses around the area.

Last time Nicole had been to the palace itself, there had been a ring of Nasi guards surrounding it. Now the dome-topped building seemed almost empty. She saw an occasional Jadid wearing a blue armband and a few Human soldiers pacing around with their weapon at the ready, but other than that, there wasn't much movement in or out of the buildings.

"Who's in charge now?" asked Sato.

"I don't know," Nicole said, "but I hope it's Karl."

Karl Garcia had been the Skulls' pilot. He was the son of one of the most powerful crime syndicates on the planet and had gained control of the government after the planet's brutal civil war. When the Nasi had found he'd been collaborating with Samsara Fleet, he'd disappeared.

"I hope so too," Kal said. His tone clearly indicated what he thought the chances were.

They entered the palace without a single person stopping or even addressing them. The soaring central lobby was ringed with artifacts from the relatively brief history of the planet. The first exosuits worn by the initial settlers stood next to holographic statues of some of the native wildlife. One creature in particular caught Nicole's eye. It reminded her of the dinosaurs she'd read about as a girl on Earth. Intelligent eyes peered out from the bony head that brushed the ceiling of the room. It stood on two legs with a long tail sweeping out behind it. Four sets of dagger-tipped tentacles streamed out in front of it, moving back and forth as if ready to lash out at prey.

"Imagine wearing that"—Kimathi pointed to the suit—"and finding that thing." He pointed back to the giant predator hologram.

"I think the exosuits have a biowaste recycling unit at least," Corporal Sato quipped.

"Gross." Nicole couldn't stop herself from a slight, distinctly unprofessional, snort.

Sato laughed. "Hey, I'm sure it's happened more than once, ma'am."

"Stop where you are and put your hands up."

Nicole grabbed her sidearm and looked around for the source of the voice. A woman stepped from behind a column, her rifle up and pointed at them. Although she was young, she looked more than comfortable holding the weapon.

"We're here from Samsara Fleet," Kal said. "Who are you?"

"Samsara Fleet? I'm gonna need some sort of proof," the woman said, not moving her rifle an inch.

"Well, considering we don't know who the hell you are, that's gonna be hard." Kal rolled his eyes in annoyance. "Call up to the fleet and let them know you're talking with General Norman."

The woman's eyes widened. "General Norman?" *Now her*

rifle dipped slightly. "Kal Norman? Really?"

"Watch out for his laser eyes," Kimathi warned with a grin.

"And don't tell him to turn around since he shoots missiles out of his—"

"Shut up," the woman said in annoyance, pointing her weapon at Sato. "Fine. Follow me."

She slung her rifle across her back and led them through the vacant hallways of the palace. Nicole noticed the woman's hand was never far from the pistol on her thigh. She also made sure to keep to the right of the group so that her firing arm would be clear if needed. Nicole couldn't blame the woman for being cautious. Years of war had taught them all not to let someone get the drop on them.

They arrived at one of the sumptuous meeting rooms which had been retrofitted into a combination of reception area and control center. As they entered, a young man stood and hobbled toward them. The left side of his face had clearly had a makeshift graft placed on it, and the synthetic skin was pale and taut compared to the rest of his face. His left arm and leg were both low-level prostheses, even worse than the metallic arm that Kal had. When he saw them, he smiled—at least half his face did. It looked ghastly to Nicole.

"General Norman. Nicole." Frederick Kinawadi raised his good hand in a salute. "I had a feeling I'd be seeing you again."

"Good to see you too," Kal replied. If he was put off by the former soldier's appearance, he didn't show it.

"The Jadid are running scared," Kinawadi said. "My

soldiers—what's left of 'em—are tracking their movements so you can round them up when ready."

"Glad to hear you have some soldiers left," Nicole said. "When I was last here, it seemed like the Nasi had wiped you all out."

Kinawadi nodded. "They practically had. Killed or captured almost all of us. When the Jadid took over, we had a chance to escape in the chaos. Some of us got away, some didn't." He lifted his prosthetic arm. "Some *barely* got away."

"I hear you." Kal raised his own metal arm in a gesture of recognition. "When we get more settled, we can get that fixed up."

"I notice you haven't gotten fixed up," Kinawadi observed, echoing Nicole's own thoughts.

Kal frowned. "Maybe when I've had a chance to rest."

Nicole hadn't talked to Kal, but she could tell by his tone he had no such intention.

"Is there anyone in control?" Sergeant Kimathi looked over the makeshift command center. "You heard from Garcia?"

"No, I haven't heard anything. But it's only been a couple hours since the Jadid fled their bases. It'll take more time to settle. The most important thing is making sure we keep the peace. We can't afford for another civil war to break out."

"You need help from the fleet?" Nicole asked. She had to offer even though the three damaged ships in orbit couldn't provide much in the way of assistance.

Kinawadi shook his head. "No. At least not now. And

maybe never." He looked at them. "Patagonia has been invaded twice. We've had plasma cannons fired on us, been invaded, and have gone through a civil war. I think we're done with help from outsiders. If worse comes to worst, then all bets are off. But for now, we'll handle it."

There was a small murmur of agreement from the people manning the consoles around them. Nicole hadn't realized they'd been listening; they'd seemed to be studying their consoles so intently.

"Fair enough," Kal replied. "You let us know how we can help. In the meantime, you willing to help the fleet? We need materials and technicians to get the ships as ready as possible. Both the Nasi and Jadid are still out there. We won this battle, but we're not stopping until we've won the war."

The private turned revolutionary leader smiled. "It would be our honor. Anything you need, you'll get. I'm preparing to make an announcement, but my people can help." He gestured to the woman who had led them to the room.

"I'll have the fleet send you what we need," Kal said. "Let the rebuilding begin."

Nicole and Kal sat next to each other on the deck of the governor's palace, several floors above the green lawns of the complex. As the news had gone out on the planetary net of the Jadid's defeat, more and more people had begun congregating on the palace grounds. Now the green space between the buildings was practically bursting with people.

They carried small noisemakers, devices that could emit almost any imaginable sounds, though most people had set them to replicate the sound of a high-pitched horn. They were a kaleidoscope, decked out in celebratory clothes, bright colored dresses, tunics, and trousers with rainbow belts and headbands.

"He's taking his time to speak." Kal gestured to the stage that had been hastily set up across the large courtyard. Kinawadi was going to address the planet from there. His speech would be streamed to the entire planet through the net.

"Takes time," Nicole said. She squeezed Kal's hand gently. "It's not like they were exactly prepared for this."

"True," Kal said. "But we need to get moving."

"We need to *recover*," Nicole corrected. "We've got wounded and the ones that aren't injured are working on the ships. There's nothing you can do except wait." Initial estimates were another two days until the fleet would be ready to move again. After that...well that was General Samaha's job to figure out.

"Feels so real," Kal said idly.

"It *is* real."

"I know. I know. I just can't believe it. Patagonia free." Kal stood up and then started walking back toward the entrance to the building. "I can't stay here. I just—"

"What do you mean?" Nicole asked. "We have a win, a victory. The first one in a long time, and you're acting like it's torture."

"We're not done yet. Not by a long shot. We can't sit around here and—"

Kal stopped talking as a spotlight illuminated the dais opposite them in a blinding halo of light. The crowd instantly quieted and turned. As a sea of Humanity watched, a small figure, Private Kinawadi, slowly made his way up the stairs to the platform. As he reached the lectern, the dam of silence broke, and applause, cheers, whistles, and almost every other sound Nicole could think of came from the mass of people.

An alert chimed on Nicole's implant, and she activated the message. Private Kinawadi's face floated in her field of vision. He appeared more nervous than she'd ever seen; his eyes darted back and forth as small rivulets of sweat trickled down his face.

"Attention, people of Patagonia. I am Frederick Kinawadi, leader of the Patagonian Front." He shifted nervously as he waited for the crowd to calm down. "Today we have won a great victory. The remains of the Jadid fleet over our planet have been destroyed."

The crowd cheered, the noise flowing over Nicole like a wave. After several minutes of cheering, Kinawadi held up his hands to calm the crowd. After almost a minute, the noise dropped to a steady hum of excited chatter. "Today is our Reclamation Day, the day when Patagonia threw off the shackles of oppression from the stars and declared that we will no longer be ruled by others. Today a new planet arises. One that has the values of equality, freedom, and honor at its core. We've been aided by the soldiers of Samsara Fleet and

183

will remain allied with them as they prepare to continue the fight on our sister planets of New America and Mariga."

Kinawadi paused and took a breath as if gathering his courage. A few errant shouts and yells—unintelligible to Nicole—erupted from the crowd.

"I declare myself the interim President of the New Patagonian Front. Once we have rounded up the remaining Jadid and Nasi, we *will* hold free and fair elections and I hope for your vote. Until then, I will lead our people as we start the long process of rebuilding. Although the enemy is on the run, they are not defeated. My government will be posting further instructions on the net, and failure to follow them in this time of crisis can result in imprisonment or worse." Nicole glanced at Kal—who had returned to his seat—to see if he had a reaction, but he only frowned slightly.

Kinawadi gestured to a large screen behind him. "Already, we have captured the leader of the Jadid fleet." The screen burst to life and the bruised face of General Frederick Zhou appeared behind him.

"This is General Frederick Zhou. Among his many crimes are genocide, torture, and treason." The crowd hissed. "There's no doubt that he is guilty of these crimes; we've all been a victim of his actions. I will not wait to dispense the justice he so richly deserves."

Nicole felt a wash of despair as a woman, her face covered by a mask, stepped into the frame next to Zhou. Nicole had to give the general credit, he stared at the camera, his face calm, his eyes unblinking. She wasn't sure she'd be able to handle her inevitable demise with such stoicism. She wasn't sure why she felt a pang of sympathy towards the turncoat. Perhaps it was because she knew that he had been doing what he truly believed was best. Esma and Bao sought power and vengeance, but Zhou had just wanted what he thought was best for Humanity.

"What the hell is he doing?" Kal asked with alarm.

"They seem to be on board." Nicole gestured to the crowd below them. After a few seconds of stunned silence, a low murmur of appreciation—and a few jeers—had started to bubble up.

"This is the justice that awaits everyone who betrayed our people." Kinawadi turned to face the screen. "General Frederick Zhou, as interim president of Patagonia, I sentence you to death."

The executioner pressed a syringe against the side of Zhou's neck, causing him to flinch slightly. The camera zoomed out, revealing a plain white room. Zhou was seated on a bare metal chair in the center, his arms tied behind him and legs tied to the chair. His head started to loll to the side and his arms and legs twitched as the injection coursed through his bloodstream.

The woman waited patiently, her eyes focused on a tablet she held in her hand. After a few minutes of silence—during which Zhou's limbs continued to twitch—she turned to the camera and gave a thumbs-up.

To Nicole's horror, the crowd burst into a cheer.

Kinawadi turned to the crowd, his hands held high.

"Tonight, enjoy yourselves and celebrate because for the first time in our history, Patagonia is truly free."

As the crowd screamed and cheered with happiness, Nicole met Kal's eyes. She could see the same question she had in his eyes: *What is Kinawadi thinking?* The speech had been meant to be a declaration of victory. Kinawadi had also made it into a declaration of independence and a promise of retribution. She wondered how much imprisonment had changed the man.

"Our work's not done yet," Kal said grimly as fireworks exploded in the night air around them.

Chapter Thirteen
Kal | Patagonia

Kal kept thinking about Kinawadi's speech. In addition to the grisly showmanship of the execution the former private had been unambiguous the Unified Earth Government was not welcome in Patagonia. With that pronouncement, so warmly received by the audience, the idea of an interstellar Human government was most likely dead.

Kal was a Marigan. He completely understood the feeling that many colonists had. The conflicting depression yet—he couldn't think of a better word—opportunity over the destruction of Earth. The UEG had enriched Earth at the expense of the colonies, and now they could have complete freedom. There was a joy because of the removal of the Nasi and Jadid from power, yet an omnipresent dread in worrying that they may return.

As he had watched the crowd with Nicole, his emotions had been too much for him. He realized with a sense of bitter irony that the thing *he* dreaded most was an end to the war. It would be over soon, one way or another. Then what would he do? How could he live without something to fight, without another *thing* to do? His worst fear was going back to the way things had been.

After the speech was done, he and Nicole retreated to one of the guest suites of the palace. Despite the enormous crowds celebrating outside, the building was still relatively sparsely occupied. However, Kinawadi had assembled a security team and they had tight control on people entering and leaving the complex. Unfortunately, it was taking them a while to process everyone.

Almost as soon as Kal and Nicole arrived in their suite, Sergeant Kimathi called for them to come to one of the main reception rooms, saying there were visitors that they'd definitely want to see.

As soon as Kal entered the opulent receiving room with Nicole trailing behind, there was a squeal and a blonde streak darted from between a small cluster of people and barreled into him.

"Kal. I knew you'd come back. I knew it." Asha jumped into his arms and buried her face into Kal's shoulder. He felt his eyes sting. How had this happened? How had he come to care for this little girl so much? He had thought that part of him had died when his family had over a decade earlier.

"I promised, didn't I?" Kal asked. He could see more than a few people blinking their eyes in emotion.

"I met Nicole," Asha said excitedly as she looked past Kal, arms still around him, at Nicole. "You're right. She's super nice."

"If I say something, you know it's true." Kal gently set the small girl on the ground, and she immediately grabbed his cybernetic claw.

"What happened to your arm?"

"Uh…" Kal tried to think of something to say that wouldn't cause her to worry. "I forgot it somewhere." He smiled at her.

Asha looked at him dubiously.

"Asha, it's so good to see you again." Nicole knelt and the small girl ran to her and almost barreled her over.

"So you guys won, huh?" The girl's small arms barely reached around Nicole's neck.

"Well…we won today, that's for sure." Kal looked at the adults watching them. "It's not over though." Asha grabbed his good hand, her tiny pale fingers not quite encircling his own.

"Nicole, I think there's some people you might want to see," Deepta said. She gestured to a man and woman who couldn't have been further apart in looks. The man was tall, with a gaunt face and a flat-top of close-cut blond hair. He reminded Kal of the old EDF recruiting posters. The woman was heavyset and short with a mane of thick braids framing her round face which was marred by a deep scar that ran from her chin to forehead.

"Grupp. Mother Ju." Nicole grinned from ear to ear as she walked toward them and enveloped them both.

"Seems like this is a regular family reunion." Kimathi smiled at the others. "Am I gonna see my third-term mathematics professor next?"

"I haven't seen the lady who sold me candy as a kid lately," Sato added.

"Shut up." Kal scowled at the two soldiers but couldn't hold the stern expression for long.

"It's an amazing day," Ju said warmly then arched an eyebrow at Nicole. "You remember our deal, right?"

Nicole nodded. "The people of the communes will be

part of this government if I have anything to say about it."

Kal wondered if that would be the case. He knew Nicole had lived in the communes back on Earth and guessed that was coloring her judgement. But they weren't any part of the Patagonian government, and he doubted that their input would be too welcome. With victory came the inevitable process of making good on promises that might have been made in combat.

They were a price worth paying though.

General Samaha had made it clear that there was nothing Kal could do to help the fleet prepare for their next mission, and Kinawadi had been clear he didn't want outsiders participating in the rearming of the planet. Mother Ju, Grupp, and all the other natives of Patagonia had immediately started to discuss the process of rebuilding, leaving Nicole and Kal to their own devices.

Without a mission to complete, enemy to fight, or task to accomplish, Kal finally gave in and tried to relax. Asha made it crystal clear that she would not let him out of her sight, and he didn't have the heart to leave her side anyway. Instead, the three of them—Kal, Nicole, and Asha—walked through Kasongo, taking in the sites of the capital. The streets were still filled with people dressed in their brightly colored celebratory clothes.

Discovery Day had been the only planet-wide holiday on Patagonia. Despite its name, the holiday recognized the day the first Human settlers came onto the planet years earlier. Kal could already tell Reclamation Day would become the second. Banners and strings of lights had been hoisted over the streets. People danced underneath them to a rhythmic percussive music that blared from the windows of the surrounding buildings. Men and women twirled around each other, clad in traditional Patagonian outfits. Braids of cloth, covered in glitter, fanned from their bodies as they wove tightly between each other as they danced.

For the first time, Kal thought about what a life could be *after* the war. He'd always assumed he wouldn't live to see it and had to admit that *still* was the most likely scenario. But he couldn't help wondering what would happen if they survived, and they didn't have to fight anymore. The idea filled him with more apprehension than the Nasi dreadnaught.

Asha stopped to study a small cart filled with sweets while Nicole bent down next to her, placing a hand on the girl's back. The vendor, a young man with dark features and a beaming smile, glanced at them tenderly and then looked around the area as if to take it all in.

What's next? Kal wondered. *What would this look like without any Jadid or Nasi?* He felt a wave of nausea as he realized he was comparing Asha and Nicole to his now long-gone family. Would he be replacing them? He felt a wall of emotion crash into him and braced himself against the onslaught.

"What's wrong?" Nicole asked, her head tilted.

Kal shook his head, not trusting himself to say a word.

"Everyone's so happy," Asha chirped.

"First time they've had a reason to be happy in a long time," Kal said. "They're finally free."

Despite several entreaties from the people around them to join in, they only watched the festivities. They were attendees at a reception for the planet. Honored guests, but the ceremony and cheering weren't for them or about them, and it felt somehow wrong to try and be a part of it.

A small tone beeped in Kal's ear; someone was trying to reach him through the net. Whomever was calling had somehow gotten their hands on his unregistered ID.

Yes? Kal asked through implant.

General Norman, can you hear me?

Ancient Musa, Kal asked. *How are you contacting me?* The Ancients—and Jadid—did not have implants.

I need you to come to the Foothold immediately.

The Nasi had created enormous walled compounds on each of the Human colonies. These Footholds were the center of their occupation, housing not only their soldiers but their support and resources and even civilians. When the Jadid had taken the planet, they'd generally stayed out of the Foothold, preferring small bases scattered around the planet rather than a single large base.

What's this about?

It'd be better to talk in person.

Just tell me what you want, Kal said, exasperated. *Why do I need to be there?*

We're opening the gateways, explained Musa. *There may*

still be survivors on Altterra. We must bring them here before they're slaughtered by Esma and Bao.

You want to reopen a portal between Patagonia and Altterra, now? After Kinawadi closed them? Kal asked. What was she thinking? Opening the gateway would not only allow them to travel back to Altterra but would also allow any enemy forces to march right into Kasongo.

There's no time to talk, Musa spat back. We're doing it one way or another. Either come now and help or don't.

Kal thought about calling for someone to head to the Foothold and stop them. But it was unlikely they'd make it before he did, and he dreaded the thought of a firefight breaking out between the Ancients and an overeager Patagonian.

He motioned to Asha and Nicole then turned and strode towards the Foothold. *Don't do anything 'til we get there.*

Kal cut the connection.

Kal knew he needed to speak with Musa before she did anything rash. The woman's threat of "one way or another" was too ominous for him to ignore. As they made their way through the throng of revelers, he realized that her mind had always been back on Altterra.

The "children" the Jadid had left on Altterra had probably been captured or killed. However, now that Patagonia was under Human control, there was a way for them to be saved—bringing them to this universe. Of course Musa and Kingsley

193

would be determined to do whatever they could to open the portal as soon as possible.

The question Kal couldn't answer was whether it was even possible to open the gateway. Although the Ancients has told them that the Jadid were using them earlier, Kinawadi had ordered the one on Patagonia closed and Kal understood the process to reopen it could take weeks. He had no idea how easy it would be to do but remembered Bo saying one would need to have control of both endpoints—in both the Human and the Jadid universes.

After several requests from Kal, Asha reluctantly agreed to return to Sergeant Kimathi in the palace while they headed to the Foothold. Other than Kal and Nicole, he was her favorite person. A sentiment that was clearly reciprocated by the sergeant, who had mentioned that she reminded of his own little sister back on New America.

"If they open that portal then Wang and Baykara can send their armies right back onto Patagonia," Nicole said as they pushed their way through the crowd.

"I know, and I'm not sure they much care."

"Why the hell not?" Nicole asked.

"Because it's their children."

As they reached the edge of the crowd, the battered walls of the Foothold seemed to magically appear in the distance. Despite being in the center of the city, there was no one near them, not even a security detail. It was as if there was a force field around the enormous compound.

They passed through one of the gates—or at least Kal

thought it had been one. It was hard to tell since it had been shredded beyond recognition by what he guessed was orbital cannons. The interior of the base was just as ruined as the walls. Most of the structures had sustained heavy damage, their discolored weave-covered walls slashed by shrapnel.

"I remember assaulting this place," Kal whispered.

"Nasi thought they'd be here forever," Nicole said. "The Foothold was just supposed to be the beginning."

They reached the gateway, and Kal was forced to reassess his estimate of how large the building was. He'd seen it several times on reconnaissance images and from the air. But now, standing in front of it, he realized that his understanding had been way off. The light from the celebrations going on around the Foothold bounced off its slightly luminescent exterior which blotted out the clouds above. Unlike the other buildings, the large sphere looked undamaged. Kal guessed it wasn't an accident that the gateway was the only building the Jadid had left untouched; they'd had plans for it.

They entered the building's circular entrance and found Ancients Musa and Kingsley waiting for them in a surprisingly small and austere room.

"General Norman." Musa raised her hand in greeting.

"Why would you reactivate the gateway?" Kal demanded. His jovial mood from the celebrations outside had ceased as soon as they'd stepped through the walls of the Foothold.

"General," Kingsley walked forward to put his arm on Kal's shoulder. He was close enough Kal could see small gray hairs poking out from his beard. "You of all people should understand why."

"We just recaptured this planet, and you want to open a door to the Nasi and Wang?" Nicole asked.

"Not to them," Musa corrected, "to our children. You saw what we faced on Altterra. If we can bring them to safety—well, we don't have a choice."

"Why did you ask us here?" Kal asked.

Nicole stepped forward at the same time, her hand in the air. "We can't let you do this."

Kingsley turned to look at Kal. "We want your help when the gateway opens. We have no idea what we'll find. We need soldiers to help us get our people out." He turned to regard Nicole. "As for stopping us...well, you're too late for that. The gateway is already reactivated and will be opening soon."

She muttered a curse.

"Surely there's a way to turn it off," Kal said.

"I'm afraid not, sir," Bo said as he entered the room from the door directly behind the two Ancients. He glided forward to stand next to them in what Kal interpreted as a show of solidarity. "There's no shutting it down once the system is engaged."

Kal shot his friend a wounded look. "What about *after* the portal is formed?" He flung an arm toward the door where Bo had come from. "I mean, they were shut down before."

The Jadid scientist nodded solemnly. "True. But I won't close it. I'm sorry, but I just can't." His face twisted in emotion. "Not if there's a chance that at least some of my people can be saved. I know what you think of them—and perhaps you're right—but I can't do nothing."

Kal was taken aback. He'd never seen such emotion from his friend. But he didn't doubt that every word the Jadid said was absolutely true. Bo was willing to give up everything to try and save what was left of the Jadid. Could Kal blame him?

"Have you told Kinawadi?" Kal asked.

Musa scoffed and twisted her mouth in contempt. "No. Why would we? He's the one who closed it in the first place, and his only loyalty is to his new government."

Kal looked at Bo. His friend returned the look, unflinching, from between Musa and Kingsley.

Kal sighed. "Well, we're not going to be able to do this alone." He called to Kimathi through the net and told him to bring who he could to the gateway immediately. "I've got help coming. The Skulls don't leave our comrades out to dry."

Bo smiled in relief.

Chapter Fourteen
Nicole | Altterra

They walked through the door to the center of the gateway. The enormous room stretched at least sixty meters into the air. Nicole looked around the empty chamber, expecting to find a glowing portal or an enormous bank of machines. Instead it was completely empty. She was about to say something to Bo when she noticed an almost imperceptible faint line that ran across the floor and walls and bisected the room. The colors on the other side of the room seemed slightly different, more vibrant somehow. She realized the gateway was already opened, and she was seeing the other side in the Jadid universe. She was literally looking at another universe through the impossibly stable wormhole that the gateway created.

Stepping across the threshold was strange insomuch as there was no sensation at all. The only signs Nicole had that she'd entered another universe were her implant abruptly shutting off and the strange feeling of the Jadid's chaotic gravity.

"No offense, Bo, but I hate your damn planet," Sergeant Kimathi said after passing through the portal.

Bo mutely nodded back at his friend.

"How do we know that someone won't come through the portal while we're gone?" asked Kal. He flexed his cybernetic limbs, testing that they still worked. Nicole could have told him they would. He'd been to Altterra before, and they'd worked previously.

"We don't," Bo replied. "But I can't shut this down. We have to risk it."

"Shouldn't we leave a guard behind?" Corporal Sato asked.

"No reason to." Kimathi hefted his rifle. "They won't be able to stop either the Jadid or Nasi and can't even radio to us anyways. We're gonna have to find their people as fast as possible and get back. I've got guards on the other side who will at least be able to radio for help."

"Follow me," Ancient Kingsley said as he walked toward the exit, the door swishing open as he got close.

Nicole had been overjoyed when Kal had told Bo they would help. When she'd seen the pain and desperation across her friend's face, it had taken everything in her power not to run over and give him a hug. He'd done so much for them; Nicole had no doubt she'd be dead if it wasn't for Bo. If they could help him, especially with something this important, rules and common sense be damned.

No more than fifteen minutes after they'd been called, Sergeant Kimathi had arrived with the entirety of the Skulls along with a healthy component of some of the local Patagonian forces. Including Bo, there were eleven of them that had gone through the gateway, all carrying daton plasma rifles.

After passing through a small antechamber, identical to the one on Patagonia, they found themselves shielding their eyes from the orange glare of the Altterran sun. Small trees— or perhaps bushes, Nicole couldn't decide—grew in chaotic intervals, reaching to the top of her head.

"You know where we are yet?" Kal asked.

"Thankfully, yes," Musa replied. "We're not too far out. Whatever survivors there are will be around here."

"We knew that it was only a matter of time until Eden was destroyed," explained Kingsley. "We had a plan B in case everything went wrong."

"The Savage Plains?" Nicole asked, remembering their last words to Governor Huang when the two Ancients had left the planet earlier.

Musa nodded. "I just hope whoever's left was *able* to escape." She sniffed loudly and then turned to face forward, increasing her pace and seeming to steel herself for what they would find.

As they continued forward, the tree-bushes grew taller and denser. They transitioned from single ones scattered across the ground to small clumps that grew to about twice Nicole's height, to a forest that stretched tens of meters in the air.

Kingsley and Musa alternated between glancing at their comecas and scanning the ground around them as they walked forward. Following their leads, Nicole watched the ground, looking for anything that seemed out of the ordinary. She felt a jolt as she noticed a small patch where the ankle-high foliage was battered down and slightly wilted.

"Is that what you're looking for?" Nicole pointed to the spot.

"Yes." Kingsley let out a deep breath of relief.

He walked to the spot, bent down, and dragged the brush across the ground, revealing a small stairwell that had been cut into the dirt. "Follow me," the Ancient said as he climbed down a ladder. They walked through a narrow tunnel until it ended in a large cavern with a few small transports.

"At least some got out," Musa said sadly.

"Not enough," Kingsley replied.

It was impossible for Nicole to tell how many of the transports were gone, but based on the size of the room and the number of vehicles remaining, she guessed it was about fifteen to twenty. No more than a couple hundred Jadid had escaped. She wondered how many there had originally been and felt a pang of sorrow for the Jadid. Humanity had been hit and hit hard, but the Jadid had practically been wiped out in the war.

They climbed into the nearest ship. In a matter of minutes, they'd exited the cavern through a well-hidden bay door in one of the rock walls and were soaring over the Altterran countryside.

Less than an hour later, they touched down outside a tall grove. The trees were like nothing Nicole had seen. Their enormous trunks bent so far over that the tips of the trees rested on the ground and created a domed shape. Their broad blue leaves jutted out toward the sky, completely obscuring the tops of the trunks and giving Nicole the impression that the enormous structure was covered in fur like the stuffed animal she'd had as a child.

"This is the hard part." Kingsley glanced at Bo. "At least for us Humans."

The Ancients took lead and began to scale the nearest trunk. At first, Nicole was forced to use her hands and legs to climb, but as they neared the apex, the branches of the trees wove together to form a floor and the slope petered out. She was able to stand upright and weaved through the person-sized leaves as she followed the two Ancients.

Nicole heard a plasma rifle and dove to the ground as a yellow bolt sizzled next to her head.

"Hold!" Musa shouted. "It's us. Ancients Kingsley and Musa."

A green face peered from between the leaves in front of them, and its eyes widened as they set upon Musa. A Jadid guard slid through the branches and bowed deeply.

"Apologies, but we…" The man's voice faltered. It was a behavior that was completely out of tune with how Nicole had seen the Jadid before. The icy confidence that they had possessed when Nicole had first come to Altterra was gone—at least in this case.

"We understand," Kingsley said smoothly. "Much has happened. No one could be prepared for what has befallen us."

The guard nodded dumbly. With a jolt, he pushed the enormous leaves aside and gestured for them to enter.

They made their way through the leaves to find a large clearing. Small huts, fashioned from the leaves and branches, dotted the perimeter of the area. A small murmur broke out from a hundred or so Jadid as they spied the two Ancients strolling into the clearing. The murmur was cut off as a tall Jadid woman, dressed in a formfitting crimson outfit, stepped forward. She stopped in front of the Ancients and bowed deeply.

Musa ran forward and wrapped her arms around her daughter. Governor Huang, who was over a head taller than her mother, looked down in surprise. For a moment, Nicole thought the Jadid would push Musa away. Instead, she remained still for a moment then gently returned the embrace and closed her eyes before stepping back.

"Ancients Musa and Kingsley, you have returned," Huang said. Nicole thought she almost heard a hint of disappointment. With the Jadid, it was hard to tell what they were thinking; in some ways, their emotions and logic were so alien.

"Yes, we've come to bring you to the Human universe," Kingsley said. Huang's already angular cheekbones could have cut glass as she clenched her jaw. The other Jadid, who had moved to form a semicircle around them, began to whisper to each other in low tones.

"I know you don't want to leave," Musa said gently, "but—"

"I *will not* leave." Huang's words were steel. "These Humans and their cursed universe have brought about our destruction. I will not walk willingly into the predator's mouth." She waved at the others. "Others can do as they please, but I will stay right here."

"Madeline." Musa's voice rose. "You cannot stay here. I can't let you stay here." She reached for her daughter again. This time Huang stepped back. "There's only one option."

"That's not true," Huang said. Nicole could have sworn there was a note of petulance in the woman's voice. "I *can* stay here."

"Governor Huang, *please* come with us," Kal said. "There's a chance for the Jadid, the *true* Jadid to make a new life in our universe. You can always come back here when the war's over. This isn't forever, just for now."

Huang sighed derisively. "That's what you say. But you can't guarantee that, and I don't want to take the risk. I would rather die here, at home, than on some strange planet in another universe. My answer is final." Huang crossed her arms. "There are one-hundred-and-fifty-three of your children here. Think of them and take them with you."

Musa looked at her daughter in despair. Her mouth opened and shut several times like a fish gasping for air.

"Fine." The word seemed to have been forced from Kingsley. He looked around at the other Jadid. "Will you join us? There is a place for you in the Human's universe. As General Norman has said"—he gestured toward Kal—"this is not permanent. You will have a chance to return when the war is over. But for now, this is your best chance—your only chance—for survival. I won't order you, but I *am* asking you: please come with us."

"I will follow," said one of the Jadid after a few seconds of silence. The others murmured their agreement. Soon all of them except Huang had agreed to follow the Ancients into the Human's universe.

It only took a couple of minutes for the refugees to gather their belongings. As the group started to make their way to the ground, Musa asked to say a final goodbye to her daughter. Nicole gave Madeline a slight nod then turned around and climbed down to the ground.

It turned out the refugees' transports were hidden underneath the bowing trunks of the grove. They'd staged them between the trunks with their bows fanning outward from the center so they could take off as quickly as possible.

"Where the hell is Musa?" asked Kimathi, scanning the top of the grove. "We gotta get out of here."

Nicole was about to say they should leave, that the woman had decided to stay with her daughter, when she spied someone climbing down one of the trunks. It took her a moment to realize that Musa had somehow strapped Huang's unconscious body to her own and was cautiously making her way down.

When she reached the ground, Musa motioned for the others to help her. Nicole and Sato ran to the woman and helped her haul Huang's unconscious body into the back of one of the transports.

"Let's get the hell outta here," Musa instructed. She looked Nicole dead in the eye. "Damn you Humans."

Chapter Fifteen
Kal | Patagonia

"I'm not sure we thought this through, sir," Kimathi said. "How the hell are we gonna get the Patagonians to house *Jadid* refugees? You saw Kinawadi's little speech earlier."

They were standing outside the presidential office, waiting for Kinawadi to receive them. He already had a security detail manning the door and a rather priggish—in Kal's opinion—assistant manning the reception desk.

After returning to Patagonia, it had been a near universal consensus that the Jadid should remain inside the Foothold. It was at least somewhat familiar to them, and adjusting to the strange new universe they found themselves in would take time. Not to mention the fact that Kal had no idea what the locals would do if they saw a large group of Jadid walking through the streets. He doubted it would be anything good.

The doors to the presidential office swung open softly, and the sound of two men arguing swept over Kal and Nicole. The guards gave curt nods, gesturing for them to enter. As they neared the office at the end of the hallway, Kal began to make out words.

"—had no right."

The voice sounded familiar.

"I had *every* right. You were gone and the people needed a leader."

"Bullshit. You wanted to be president. You want power. You didn't care about the people."

Kal smiled. He knew who was calling bullshit.

"Karl Garcia," Kal shouted.

"General Norman!" Karl Garcia's lanky frame was silhouetted by the sunlight streaming through the windows behind him. Kal was surprised to see the man open his arms for an embrace. As he drew near, Kal involuntarily sucked in his breath as he saw what the Nasi had done to him in captivity.

He'd always been thin, but now Garcia looked and felt practically skeletal. His face looked haunted with protruding cheekbones and scars—plasma Kal guessed—raked across his face, twisting his features and completely bisecting his right eye socket. Where the eye had been was a patch. Although he'd probably get a cybernetic one, Kal could attest to the fact that no replacement felt as good as the real thing when it came to cybernetic augmentations.

"Nicole." As Garcia bent down to give her an embrace, Kal could hear a small whimper of pain escape his lips.

"It's great to see you." Nicole glanced at Kal, her face a picture of concern. "You look like you've seen better days."

Garcia straightened back up and nodded. "Yeah, I've seen better days all right." He strode back into the room with Kal and Nicole trailing. "But what really pisses me off is that when I get back, there's been a goddamn coup."

"Coup is a strong word, Karl." Kinawadi reclined in his enormous chair, his hands behind his head, obviously trying to seem indifferent to the conversation. "You weren't around, and someone had to take control."

"You declared yourself *president*," Karl shot back.

"*Interim* president." Kinawadi waggled his finger in the air.

"Well, your interim is over. I'm back. Now get the hell out of my chair." Garcia moved around the desk and tried to pull Kinawadi from the chair. The former private was easily able to fend off his attacks. After several more attempts, Garcia howled in frustration and sat down in one of the visitor's seats.

"Why don't—"

Both Garcia and Kinawadi stared daggers at Kal, their scarred faces a perfect metaphor for what Patagonia had gone through. "This is a Patagonian matter," Kinawadi said. "Samsara Fleet, allies though they are, do not have any say in it."

Garcia, still winded, simply nodded in agreement.

"You agree on one thing at least," Nicole said. "That's a start, right?"

"We've got an issue," Kal said. He explained their excursion to recover the last remains of the Jadid, emphasizing how they were almost just as much victims of the Nasi and Liberation Fleet as the Humans. It was impossible for him to gauge the two Patagonian's expressions as he talked. Both had become extremely skilled at hiding their reactions. They were becoming politicians through and through.

"You've brought the enemy here, inside Kasongo?" Garcia looked at them with incredulity.

"They're not the enemy," said Nicole "They're no more to blame than we are for what happened."

"They *let* it happen." Kinawadi had given up all pretense

208

of being relaxed. He leaned forward in his chair, his hands on the desk. "Their friends, their fellow children"—he gestured to his scarred face—"did this to us."

"Less than two hundred Jadid remain," Kal said evenly. If he was going to convince the two men with him, he needed to keep his cool. "The rest are either dead or have been twisted up in Baykara and Wang's schemes. They deserve to survive."

"Deserve." Kinawadi spat the word out. "Who gets what they deserve? I didn't." He pointed to Garcia. "He sure as hell didn't. I don't know that I really give a shit about what they *deserve*."

"Is it really that much of a problem?" Garcia asked cautiously, cutting off Kal before he had a chance to speak. "I mean, they're in the Foothold already, right? Why not just let them stay there?"

Kinawadi looked at Garcia in surprise. "What do we say if the Jadid or Nasi come back and start killing our people again?"

"The Jadid in that Foothold would be the first to be killed," Nicole said. "And they'll be the first to fight."

Kinawadi paused. "Some people might take it into their own hands to get revenge. Or the Jadid may decide to try and finish what their friends started."

Nicole scoffed. "You think a hundred and fifty Jadid are going to take over Patagonia? Your security forces must be crap."

"We could close the gaps in the walls. That'll keep them

away from our people," Garcia said. "Most people are sensible enough to know that they can't take a Jadid anyways."

Kal was shocked that Garcia, a man who had clearly been through hell and back, would be so willing to lend aid to the Jadid. He couldn't imagine how he would act in a similar situation but could only hope that he'd be as empathetic.

"And we can have patrols go in there, just to make sure they're not up to anything." Kinawadi was still rubbing his hand across the scarred side of his face and turned toward Garcia. "These are the same bastards that attacked us."

"No, not the same," Garcia replied. "They're victims, like us."

"You have the chance to be better than Esma and Bao," Kal added. "You know that there *are* good Jadid. People like Bo and Ai. You want to be leaders, then lead. Do the right thing."

Garcia limped to the window and studied the people walking past. "Damn it, I hate them so much for what they've done. You know I escaped when the Jadid took over the planet. Had more near misses than I care to count—and a few near hits. I was holed up in the woods when I found out what had happened and realized I could finally return."

Garcia turned back to look at the others in the room.

"But these Jadid aren't the Nasi who tortured me. I don't think I'll ever be able to trust them or even look at them, but I'm not gonna be the monster."

"I'm not promising anything," Kinawadi said. "I'll think

about it. He's a lot more forgiving than me."

"That's all we're asking," Nicole said quietly. "Think about it. And in the meantime, just let them be in peace in the Foothold."

"Let who be in peace?" General Samaha asked as she strode into the office,

"The Ancients brought what was left of the Jadid—the ones that hadn't been corrupted by Wang and Baykara—here to Patagonia," Kal said.

"Damn, this entire thing's a mess." Samaha strode to Garcia and gently clasped his shoulder. "Major Garcia, it's good to see you back."

"Thank you, ma'am. Glad to be back."

"We've received some intel that the rest of the Liberation Fleet has left the space around New America and is heading toward Mariga," Samaha announced. She gestured toward the sitting area. "All of you, sit down. We've got to talk."

Samaha grabbed one of the large ornate chairs from the sitting area and dragged it to sit next to Kal. It made him realize just how frail the general was. She'd been ready for retirement before the war had begun. Now she was clearly spent, physically and—he guessed—mentally.

"The interplanetary probe network is still touch and go," Samaha began. "But we have confirmation that Wang's fleet has left New America, and my sources tell me they're going to attack Mariga. My guess is the bastard is willing to risk the planet if it means Baykara loses."

"Which means *we* lose too," Kal said.

"The Nasi will keep that damn dreadnaught away from the planet until the Jadid commit to the battle," Samaha said. "Bao might be willing to sacrifice Mariga, but I'm not."

"There's *no* way to find it," said Nicole.

"Wrong," Samaha said dryly. "The Nasi on Mariga know where it is. Their flagship orbiting the planet *must* know where it is so that they can send word when the Jadid attack."

"So we just need to take the *McCullough*, speed ahead of the Jadid fleet, infiltrate the Nasi flagship, get the location of the dreadnaught, and then what? Destroy it from the inside?" Kal couldn't keep the incredulity from his voice.

"You've had harder missions," Samaha smiled weakly.

"No we haven't, ma'am," Nicole replied.

"Well, then this should be a fun challenge," Samaha rubbed her palms together. "This is our best option to save Mariga. We know Baykara won't hesitate to destroy the system if the battle turns against her."

"Which it almost certainly will," added Nicole.

"Ai feels that she might have a way for you to get the information from the Nasi flagship without having to reach their bridge," Samaha said. "She's been working on something that she said"—she held up her hands to make air quotes—"will exploit inherent and heretofore undiscovered weaknesses in the bioelectrical architecture of the Jadid ships."

"What about actually recapturing the planet?" asked Kal.

"If we destroy the dreadnaught, we're basically guaranteeing that Wang will capture it. The *McCullough* can fold ahead of the Nasi fleet, but the remains of Samsara Fleet cannot."

"We've had some of our best engineers looking at the fold calculations, and if we're willing to take some risk, we can cut down Samsara Fleet's travel time by twenty-five percent," Samaha said. "It won't get us ahead of Wang's fleet, but they shouldn't be too far behind." She sighed deeply. "Besides, I'm not like the Ancients. I'd rather have Mariga under Jadid control than no Mariga at all."

Samaha clapped her hands together, the sound ringing through the room like a gunshot. "Well, enough talk." She looked at Kal and Nicole. "Get your asses over to the *McCullough* and get out of here. I have a transport waiting on the landing pad." She turned her gaze to Kinawadi and Garcia. "As for you two, figure out what you're going to do with this planet. Make sure all the people who died to liberate it didn't die in vain."

After the meeting, the general called Kal aside. There was something about her demeanor he couldn't place. She started talking about nothing, troop levels and resources, but clearly had something else on her mind. Her eyes lost focus as she received a message on her implant, and she gave a slight nod as she turned to walk out of the office.

Samaha stopped and turned back toward Kal. "Whatever happens, you finish this. You and Nicole are the only ones I trust."

"We won't be long," Kal said uneasily.

Samaha nodded. "I'm sure. But I might be."

With that, the general strode away. Kal wanted to chase after her, but he knew Samaha well enough to know that if he asked anything she would close tighter than the gravity locks on a trading vessel.

As Kal walked with Nicole toward the presidential compound's landing pad, he called ahead to Kimathi, telling him to gather half the team for a mission and to be ready to go. Less than five minutes later the transport touched down inside the Foothold, and Kimathi led Bo, Sato, and Pham up the back cargo ramp.

As they left the planet's atmosphere and headed toward the *Ofira*, Kal explained their mission. The other's complete lack of a reaction was enough for him to know that they agreed with his and Nicole's assessment—it was a suicide mission.

"The general said Ai had a way to hack the Nasi ship. You know anything about that?" Kal asked Bo.

"I wouldn't say hack," Bo replied. "Ever since we infiltrated the *Resolute Stand*, I've been thinking about the network architecture of the ships. The Human-built ships rely on graphene-based processing, electrical in nature. However, we Jadid integrated biological components into our ships. Ai and I had discussed the potential weaknesses of this approach."

"For the love of everything, get to the damn point,"

Kimathi shouted.

Bo regarded the sergeant with an air of amused disgust. "You are quite the ass, Ekon. Is that enough of a point?"

"We all knew that already," Kal said, earning a dirty look from the sergeant. "What about this hack?"

Bo rolled his eyes. "I just hate the word hack; it reminds me of ancient Human holos. But the point is simply this, our biological systems have an inherent side-channel vulnerability that I can exploit through a series of queries made—"

"Bottom line, please," Kal pleaded.

"I'm guessing Ai has found a way to exploit the system from any console on the ship." Bo crossed his arms across his chest.

"So we *can* hack it," Kimathi said. "Was it *that* hard?"

Kal could feel the time slipping by them as they prepared for the mission. Every second they remained on Patagonia was one more second for the Jadid and Nasi to vaporize Mariga, his home planet. He tried not to let the stress show, but by the way the others reacted to him, he was doing a poor job.

The entire crew of the *Ofira* was immersed in repairing the ship as fast as possible. General Petrov knew they didn't have much time before they'd need to fold again and was making use of every second to focus on the systems that would be unavailable while they were underway. A steady stream of resupply ships glided in and out of the landing bays, bringing

215

fuel, ammunition, and parts from the planet. Kal hadn't seen a ship's crew operate with such efficiency in his entire military career; it made him proud.

It took an hour for Bo to pull together the equipment he'd need to hack—Kal didn't care if his friend didn't like the word, it fit—the Nasi system and for Chief Ramos to go through her preflight checks. As they locked the final battle suit into its cradle in the ship's cargo bay, Kal shouted to the cockpit that they were ready to leave.

"*McCullough*, you are cleared to depart." General Petrov's face was on the cockpit's main viewscreen as Kal entered. "Kal and Nicole, I figure next time I see you we'll either all be dead or have won this thing. Thank you for everything…you've done more than anyone could have expected. Just finish this last mission and you can take a rest."

Kal glanced at Nicole and noticed her eyes watering slightly.

"Thank you," Kal replied. He struggled for the words. "Uh, you too."

The net clicked off and Nicole turned to him. "You too?" she asked incredulously.

"Best I could come up with on the spot," he replied.

She patted him on the back. "Stick to shootin' and flyin' because you *do not* have a career in diplomacy."

Kal chuckled.

The McCullough glided through the bay's shimmering atmospheric shield, and Ramos spun activated up the fold drive. A moment later the screen flashed, the icons and dots

216

on the tacmap disappeared, and a new set appeared instantly as they entered the space around Mariga.

"Scanning the area now." Ramos began tapping at the console in front of her. "We've got Mariga directly behind us."

Bo hummed. "Ai and I still need to work on some of the calculations with this new drive." He looked at the comeca strapped to his wrist. "We're about a hundred thousand kilometers from our target location."

"Don't beat yourself up about it," said Nicole. "Considering how far we folded, that's not bad."

"Not good enough," Bo replied. He gave a small grunt, which Kal knew meant he didn't want to discuss the matter any further.

"What do we got?" Kal asked.

"At least seven Nasi capital ships in orbit," Ramos replied. "They're not in the standard formation." The Nasi typically kept their ships in geosynchronous orbits that allowed them to cover an attack from any direction. "Three of the ships are clustered at the north pole and four at the south."

"Any idea why?"

"None, sir."

"They're taking a risk," Nicole said. "They know they can call the dreadnaught to fold in and are clustering their ships so that they can defend en masse. If the Jadid attack from a direction that they can't cover," she clicked her tongue, "well, the dreadnaught will just blow up the entire system, and it won't be a problem anymore."

"They don't care if they win any more, do they?" Ramos asked.

"They're even more dangerous now," Kal replied. "Do we know which one of these is the flagship?"

"Thanks to General Samaha's spies, yes," Ramos said. "The amount of intel we've received about the Jadid *and* the Nasi has greatly increased." She pointed to one of the three dots near Mariga's northern pole. "It's this ship, the *Defiant Scream.*"

"That's a helluva name," Kal said. He had to admit it was appropriate for the Nasi's current situation.

"It certainly is an...interesting name," Nicole added.

"Nasi. Jadid. They're all nuts." Ramos shrugged, then turned and looked back at Bo. "Sorry, Bo, no offense meant."

He returned her shrug with one of his own. "I'd be offended, but I can't really argue with you. We've strayed so far from the people we used to be."

"Well, here's hoping the cloak Ai installed works," Kal muttered. "Get us alongside the *Defiant Scream,* and let's hope we can breach the hull."

Kimathi, Sato, and Pham already had their battle suits on. As Kal turned around and walked into the cargo bay, they started sealing their helmets. He stepped into his own suit, feeling the comforting sensation of the suit zipping closed behind him, and then put on the helmet and the suit's HUD blinked to life.

"One minute until we make contact with the *Scream,*" Ramos called out. The rear cargo bay door swung open, revealing a spattering of stars. Standing inside a ship with the cargo bay doors open was an odd sensation to him. He knew there was an energy field there that would keep the atmosphere inside the bay but still couldn't help feeling like he was going to be swept out into the void at any time.

Kal peered into the abyss, looking for their target. Finally, he saw the small gray smudge that was the Nasi ship. As they approached, the smudge grew, slowly at first, but soon it was approaching so fast he began to worry they were going to smash into the enormous ship's hull.

No sign they've spotted us, Ramos called out. The tweaks we've made to the cloak seem to be working.

Cross your fingers, said Nicole.

Not possible in these suits, Kimathi said. Guess we're screwed.

I've got you. Bo was wearing a Jadid battle suit. The jet-black suit made the ones that Kal and the others were wearing seem hopelessly clunky. Although the Human suits were equal or even superior in some ways, the Jadid battle suit gave the wearer an agility that they couldn't match.

You sure you got the right velocity, Ramos? Kal was growing increasingly alarmed as the Jadid ship had grown to fill the entire bay door opening.

Sir, with all due respect, can it.

As Ramos spoke, the rear thrusters sprang to life, and white streams of propellent shot out from either side of the bay door. Even with the inertial dampeners fully engaged, Kal had to steady himself so that he wasn't pitched forward by the

219

sudden change in momentum.

They came to a rest against the hull of the *Defiant Scream* with a small bump. Up close, the ship's hull was a brownish-gray with a rainbow sheen and irregular glow. Kimathi and Pham stepped forward, unleashed the meter-long blades from their suit's gauntlets, and stabbed into the side of the vessel. The blades sunk in a centimeter before becoming stuck. The two soldiers strained to push them in farther, clearly stymied by the ship's thick hull.

Uh, we got a problem, sir, Kimathi admitted after several seconds of trying to cut through the hull. *These blades just aren't gonna do it.*

Kal looked around the interior of the *McCullough*, trying to find something they could use. He'd assumed the battle suits would be able to cut through the hull, considering how easily they'd been able to breach the bridge of the *Resolute Stand.* Now he was cursing himself for that assumption. If he'd had more time, he would have had a plan B and C, but now he was going to have to improvise.

Although they'd been using it for missions, the *McCullough* was still an experimental ship; it wasn't meant to conduct assaults or infiltrations. The number of weapons and materials they had on hand was slim to none. After a couple of minutes of fruitlessly searching for something to penetrate the hull, an idea struck Kal.

Kimathi. Pham. I want you to start stabbing a perimeter around the hull. He circled his arm in the air while stabbing forward to indicate what he wanted. We need to perforate a hole big enough for the McCullough to fly through.

I know where you're goin' with this, sir, and I like it, Pham said as she began stabbing the Defiant Scream's hull at regular intervals.

I'm not as hot on this one, said Kimathi, *but I figure what the hell.* He was on the opposite side of the cargo bay opening stabbing as well. Although their blades weren't able to fully pierce the side of the ship, they did sink at least enough to leave slashes that looked uncomfortably like flesh wounds.

After a couple of minutes—during which Kal couldn't keep his eyes off the ship's tacmap he'd streamed to his suit's display—they had completed a large irregular circle of perforations in the Nasi ship's hull.

Ramos, you know what to do, Kal called over the net once the two soldiers stepped back from the opening.

I know, Ramos said, but I don't like.

Do it anyways.

The rear thrusters shot back to life, and they jetted away from the Defiant Scream's hull. As they shot away, the thrusters turned off and the ship spun on its axis until they were facing the opposite way; their momentum continuing to carry them away from the ship.

Okay folks, hold on, said Pham.

The rear thrusters reengaged, and Kal was pushed backward by the change in momentum. The ship slid to a halt and then began accelerating toward the Scream. This time Kal couldn't see anything except the sea of stars behind them. He watched their progress in his suit's display and began a countdown in his head as they neared impact.

Three.

Two.

One.

Chapter Sixteen
Nicole | Mariga

The *McCullough's* reinforced frame tore through the *Defiant Scream's* side with almost no sound or resistance. Nicole had expected an ear-shattering wrench of metal and had braced herself so she wouldn't be pitched forward in the collision.

This wasn't at all what—

Nicole's thought was cut short as the ship's reverse thrusters sprang to life, sending her—and everyone else—sprawling backward. The ship ground along the undulating deck of the *Defiant Scream's* cargo area before coming to a halt. *Never mind.*

Think they noticed? asked Pham sardonically.

Nah, we're like ninjas, Kimathi replied.

Shut it, Kal ordered, and get the hell out and start pulling security. Bo, do what you need to and then let's get the hell out of here.

Bo gracefully leapt from the open bay onto the deck. The battleship's cargo area was a series of large roughly ovoid cargo holds connected by intersecting tunnels. They had managed to crash into one of the holds rather than a corridor, which Nicole believed was the only reason the *McCullough* was still in one piece.

We need to get to a level-two console, Bo said as he gracefully ran toward the large door at the end of the cargo hold.

Bo, hold up, Kal ordered. Pham and Kimathi will take lead.

223

The last thing we need is for you to run into a security patrol—which is definitely on its way.

Yes, sir. Bo came to a stop while Pham and Kimathi ran past him toward the door. I've sent you the path to where I think a level-two console would be, at the entrance to the cargo area.

Nicole looked at her map. The exact layout of the ship was unknown to them, but Nasi ships generally followed the standard Jadid layout. If the tacmap was right, they had a few hundred meters of the wide hallway before they'd reach the console Bo needed.

She gave up trying to run down the undulating corridor and activated her suit's thrusters, allowing her to fly a meter from the ground. The twists and turns of the hallway were a nightmare, providing ample opportunity for ambush. As they reached the halfway point to the console, several pink dots appeared on her tacmap, indicating likely enemy targets.

You see them? she asked over the net.

We see 'em on the tacmap, not with our own eyes, Kimathi said. He wasn't that far in front of her but was out of eyeshot.

Bo, how long will it take you to hack this ship? asked Kal.

Hard to say, sir, perhaps a minute, Bo replied. I know I can do it but not how long it will take. Also, once again, I am not hacking the ship.

We don't have time to stop and fight, said Kimathi. The Nasi normally send a quick reaction team to pin any boarders down and then follow up with the cavalry.

Cavalry? asked Kal with a note of confusion. *Like horses?*

Nicole chuckled to herself. Kimathi truly was a product of another age.

It's an old expression, Kimathi said. Not like literal—never mind. We can take care of the enemy, sir. Everyone else just keep going to the console.

Will do, said Nicole.

Pham and Kimathi continued to speed ahead to pin down the enemy, while Nicole and Kal held back with Bo. A few seconds later, the sound of plasma fire came from the hallway in front of them.

Thrusters on, Kal ordered. Get past them as quickly as possible. Whatever you do, do not stop, do not engage. I don't care what you see.

Nicole tried to shake the feeling that the comment was directed specifically at her. She'd talk to him about that later. She'd run enough missions to know that you left your feelings on the ship during missions.

They flew through the battle zone, their feet centimeters from the ground. Kimathi and Pham had engaged the Nasi in a mid-sized cargo area filled with enormous mounds of sacks piled throughout the room. Nicole couldn't see the combatants, but she could see errant plasma bolts flying around and saw the blinding flash of a plasma grenade go off near one of the far walls. At least the battle was even with Kimathi and Pham fighting against two Nasi. Both of the Skulls were still green on her display, which meant they were at least holding their own.

Another blast erupted on the far side of the room and Kimathi's icon flickered from green to yellow. His body crashed against the ceiling and dropped to the floor, his landing obscured by one of the pile of supplies.

She suppressed the urge to stop and kept moving forward, trying not to think of what was happening to her friend.

Bo, Nicole, keep going, Kal shouted over the net.

She didn't need to look at the map to know that he'd had decided to jump into the fight. There would be time to tease him about it later, but for now, she had a mission.

Nicole continued through the cargo area corridors, trying to keep up with Bo. She tried not to pay attention to the status indicators on her display. The others would have to take care of themselves, there was nothing she could do to help them now.

Bo touched down at a small room at the end of the hallways and started looking around.

What are you looking for? Nicole asked.

The console.

I know that. She wanted to slap him. What does it look like? Anything I should be on the lookout for?

Normally it's against the wall, Bo said. Should look like a normal console.

Nicole wasn't sure exactly what a normal Nasi console would look like; she'd seen several of them and none would

226

have been what she considered normal. She activated her suit's full sensor suite and began to scan behind the walls, floor, and ceiling. She had no idea what she was looking for except it would be something out of the ordinary.

She found a bundle of wires—though in reality they were closer to a bundle of nerves than wires according to their composition—that ended in the ceiling near the entryway they had just come through.

Check there.

Nicole pointed to the spot, and Bo hovered to it. After examining it for a moment, he pulled a small device from one of the storage pouches on his suit's exterior and deftly sliced a small hole in the ceiling.

Not good, Bo said after a moment of examination. *This is the input panel for the console. Unfortunately, they never installed it.*

Or they removed it because they were worried about just this type of situation.

If that's the case, we're in a lot more trouble than we realized.

Nicole felt her heart sink.

I'm still going to try, Bo said. *Endpoint security on Nasi ships is rather lacking. Something I learned from your universe.*

Do it fast. Nicole glanced at the status indicators of the others. Thankfully Kal and Pham were still green. She couldn't help them, but she could make sure Bo had as much time as he needed to get the location of the dreadnaught. She studied the far entrance to the cargo area. If anyone were to come in, it would be from there. The oval portal was closed but opened automatically as she got close to it. She suspected it would only be a matter of time before a security team rushed through.

Any chance you can secure this? Nicole pointed to the door that led to the rest of the ship.

I can. But it means it'll take me longer to get to what we're here for.

Fine. Just get what we need, Nicole said after a moment's consideration.

She pulled out several proximity mines and attached them to the door then stepped back a meter and placed a few more on the floor. Hopefully, the Nasi wouldn't expect the second round after having breached the initial opening. Thinking back to how they'd been able to gain entrance to the *Resolute Stand's* bridge through the wall, she placed her last two on either side of the door. If someone tried to cut through the weaves, they'd get a nasty surprise.

How's it going? Nicole asked.

We're in luck, ma'am, Bo replied as he continued to work. The security on this endpoint is nonexistent. I've been sending neural pulses through the system to get a sympathetic signal back and have achieved—

Great news. Nicole cut him off. Keep at it.

She knelt near Bo and trained her kinetic rifle on the far door. The sounds of gunfire and explosions behind her had started to die down, but there were still occasional shots and blasts. Their indicators on her display hadn't changed, so she imagined they were in a protracted battle trying to stall the enemy while Bo did his job.

An explosion ripped through the door in front of Nicole. The blast sent them crashing into the opposite bulkhead. Nicole reflexively began firing at the door while Bo immediately returned to his work on the ceiling, seemingly oblivious to the danger.

Almost there, Bo said. Just need a few more seconds.

A few seconds is all I can give you. Nicole rattled off several rounds of automatic fire at the opening, cursing the fact that there wasn't a single piece of cover in the entranceway for her to dive behind. She activated her suit's antipersonnel missiles and waited for her suit's targeting system to kick in.

No one came through the door.

Get ready, they've got something up their sleeve.

Finished, Bo called out. I have the data but will need to further decrypt on the ship.

The far wall was ripped away in a cacophony of snapping and tearing, and plasma fire poured into the room. A second later, the two proximity mines Nicole had set against the wall went off. The explosions stunned their attackers, and the enemy's rate of fire dropped for a second.

Get out of here, Nicole screamed through the net. Whatever happens, get to the ship.

Roger.

Bo was already flying back toward the *McCullough* before

he'd finished speaking. Nicole was right behind him, blindly throwing grenades behind her as she negotiated the winding tunnel.

Get ready, we've got the cavalry on our tail, Nicole shouted over the net.

We're pinned down, Kal replied. Just make it to the ship.

I'm planning on changing that, sir, Pham called out.

As Nicole entered the small storage room where the others were, Pham launched herself from behind a pile of cargo and soared across the top of the room. Rockets flared from her shoulder launcher; their target obscured from Nicole by another small mountain of supplies. A split second later, Kal rushed from the same position and ran to where Pham's missiles had detonated.

He wasn't fast enough though.

Plasma fire streaked at Pham and hit her in the chest. Her energy shield absorbed the first hit but sputtered and died as the next ones hit her in the chest, causing her to plummet to the ground, crashing into a mound of sacks.

Her icon on Nicole's HUD went red.

Nicole knew what it meant. She saw what had happened and knew there was no chance of survival. Despite that, she couldn't stop herself from crying out over the net.

Pham! Are you okay?

She's gone. Ekon's reply was in the monotone cadence that meant he was using his implant rather than a battle suit microphone. *We need to get out of here.*

He rushed from cover just as Kal appeared with his blade

out and covered in gore.

Hurry up, Ramos called out over the net. We've got at least ten Nasi fighters coming in and I have a feeling they're not going to wait for us to get clear to start firing.

I've got him. Kal activated his thrusters and scooped up Kimathi as he flew from the room. Nicole and Bo were right behind, their thrusters at max as they navigated the twisting tunnels of the cargo area. More than once, Nicole's suit was unable to handle the rapid turns, and she bounced off the wall before recovering.

The *McCullough*'s engines were already engaged, and the ship hovered a meter from the floor. They crashed into the cramped cargo bay at what Nicole would have considered an irresponsibly high velocity, but the missiles and plasma fire that traced their path didn't leave much room.

Nicole crashed into one of the *McCullough*'s vertical supports hard enough that she felt a bolt of pain through her suit. She suspected she might have bent the pylon.

Bo, can this thing fold with the cargo door open? Ramos asked.

Ai is actually more of the expert on that, the Jadid replied. Theoretically yes as the fold drive is designed to—

The *McCullough* folded and all that Nicole could see out the rear cargo bay door were stars.

Chapter Seventeen
Kal | Deep Space

Kal stepped into the suit docking station and placed his helmet on the stand in front of him as the suit unknit itself. He felt a wave of fatigue and pain overtake him and wanted to fall onto the deck and lay there for eternity.

Now that he was safely inside the *McCullough*, his mind started replaying Pham's death. He could see her body falling to the ground after having been seared with the Nasi plasma fire. He couldn't help imagining what her burned corpse must have looked like as it hit the ground. The rest of the battle was a haze for him.

Lately, most battles were.

Kal pushed the darkness away and focused on the present. He knelt by Ekon, joining Nicole who had already brought over a portable medkit and was running diagnostics.

"Looks like you got a one-in-a-million hit." Nicole ran the device over his shoulder. "The round passed clean through both you and the suit. There's minimal spalling and the wound is so clean a bandage should take care of it."

She pulled one of the nanobot-and-medicine infused bandages from a compartment in the bulkhead and placed it over both the entrance and exit wounds. Seconds later, Ekon's face relaxed as the anesthetics started their magic.

He looked up at Kal, meeting his eyes. "Guess I should say thank you, sir."

Kal looked away. "No problem."

"I mean, you did go against your own order though."

232

Kimathi smirked. "You really should have some sort of punishment for that. I'm not entirely sure what the penalty is for disobeying a general officer's order, but I bet it's bad."

"Up to and including death," Kal replied.

"Well, that's pretty serious then, sir." Kimathi pushed himself up, winced, then lay back down. "I'll try and put in a good word for you."

"You do that, Ekon." Nicole gently placed a hand on his shoulder. "Just take a break for now though. You did just get shot after all."

"Fair enough, ma'am." Ekon lay back down. "I'll be right here if you need me."

Kal smiled weakly at the sergeant then stood and walked to the cockpit. He knew his relationship with Ekon would never be truly friendly, but there was a lot of respect between them, for sure. Bo was already seated next to Ramos and furiously typing away at the console.

"I was able to locate the coordinates," Bo said. "At least I think I did. I downloaded their entire file pertaining to the dreadnaught. There are multiple layers of security, and the ship's location is protected by the highest level."

"Can't you crack it?" Kal asked. He'd seen a few holos and the hero was always able to run some sort of program to get the data they needed.

"Crack it, sir?" Bo looked back at him in indignation. "Do you think this is some sort of holo?"

"Honestly, Kal." Nicole fixed him with a look of stern admonishment.

"You thought the same thing," Kal hissed back before slinking to the cargo hold. He sat down next to Ekon and looked at the empty space where Pham's suit should be.

"Can't believe you didn't know how hacking works." Nicole winked at sat down next to him.

"As we've fully established, the term hack is not appropriate," Kal replied. He glanced over at Ekon. The sergeant had fallen asleep. The adrenaline loss plus the drugs in the bandage had taken him out.

"They're so peaceful when they're sleeping, huh?" Nicole asked with a wink.

Her question made him think of Asha. And *she* made him think about the future. What would he do with her? She'd never had a family before—not at least until recently—but what could he offer? How did Nicole fit into that equation?

"What's up?" Nicole touched his arm.

"I'm just thinking about Asha."

"Poor girl," Nicole said. "Wonder who's watching her while we're out here."

"The rest of the squad. I guess."

"Oh, the things they must be teaching her."

"I'm trying to figure out what I'll do if, you know, we actually somehow manage to win this."

"*You'll* do?" Nicole withdrew her hand. "What do you mean *you*? I thought we were in this together."

"We are," Kal tried to sound soothing. "But she's not your responsibility. I'm the one who brought her into all this."

Nicole was clearly—confusingly—angry. "You think I don't

234

care about her? You think we don't share the same responsibilities?"

"Of course we do. It's just, well, I don't want to presume."

"There's no presumption necessary. I love Asha too. I'm not letting that girl spend another night of her life alone. She's had it hard enough as is."

"Ain't that the truth," Kimathi said weakly.

"Sorry, didn't mean to wake you," said Kal.

"It's fine," Kimathi replied. "Man, those drugs can hit like a cargo liner."

"How's the shoulder?"

"Eh." Kimathi gently rotated his arm. "Doesn't tickle but I've had worse."

"What're you gonna do if this ever ends?" Nicole asked.

Kimathi scoffed. "Not an if, it's a when and how." Kimathi closed his eyes as if trying to picture something in his mind. "The way I figure, the best we can hope for is survival. Even then, there's gonna be a lot of species out there looking to take our last few colonies since we'll have nothing left. What am I gonna do in all that? No idea."

"Everyone else got beat pretty bad too," Kal said. The Nasi had destroyed the homeworlds of every species that bordered Human space. It was supposed to have been their first step in galactic domination if Samsara Fleet hadn't gotten in their way.

"But they've had time to recover," Nicole said. "At least more time than we'll have."

"Fat help they've been for us," Kimathi said. "All of 'em

are supposed to be part of the fleet, but as soon as the Nasi retreated to our planets, their help disappeared."

Kal had to admit the sergeant was right. Samsara Fleet was supposed to be a multispecies fleet. The one that stung the most was the Kurz. Normally they were loyal to a fault, but their fleet had been destroyed, down to the last ship by the Nasi.

"Not a problem we can worry about right now," Kal said. "If anything, it's up to General Samaha to figure that out. I'm more focused on what I can control; like can Bo figure out how the hell to hack into the Nasi information about their dreadnaught so we can destroy it *now*."

Kal immediately regretted his choice of words. "It's not hack," Nicole and Kimathi scolded in unison.

"Honestly." Nicole placed a hand on her chest, "I can't believe he still thinks it's like the holos."

Kimathi nodded. "Well, duh, anyone should know that."

After a half hour, Bo announced that he'd been able to decrypt most of the information in the Nasi dreadnaught's files.

"I've got bad news and good news," Bo said. "Bad news is I can't actually decrypt the file store with the precise coordinates of the dreadnaught."

"Good news?" Nicole asked hopefully.

"Two things. First, there's a detailed schematic of the dreadnaught's design. As we had thought, it's a heavily modified battleship. Second, I've identified *where* the key to the encryption is. The Nasi added a failsafe; the key to decrypt the location must be sent from Lidice."

"Where the hell is Lidice?" asked Ramos.

"It's Mariga's orbital station," Kal reached over Bo's shoulder and trained the ship's external cameras on the station. It was an almost perfect square with docking tubes protruding from each of the six sides. The station had clearly taken significant damage but was operational as they could count at least ten transports docked.

"No one command can know the information," Nicole said. "Esma's getting worried about informants."

"Not without reason," Kal said. "Fair enough to say they've got their own spies in the Jadid fleet and maybe ours."

"Is this gonna be another assault mission?" Ekon groaned theatrically.

"I wouldn't recommend trying to assault the station," Bo said. "From what I've seen, the Nasi would have left the existing Human computer system in place and just wired their system into the station backbone. Surprisingly, your Human security is more difficult to hack than the Jadid or Nasi systems."

"Didn't need to add the surprisingly in there, Bo," Ekon called out.

"It's a byproduct of living in a galaxy with a bunch of other species," said Nicole.

"We had other species in our galaxy," Bo said. "But

they're not like what you have here. They"—he paused, clearly trying to figure out how to explain himself—"they're just nothing like the creatures in this universe. Network security was not something that we worried about." He shivered.

Kal had been to Altterra and learned some of their history. The Jadid's survival was nothing short of miraculous from everything he'd heard. He knew the battles they'd fought for survival had been brutal, but still, whatever could cause Bo to react like that had to be something more terrifying than Kal could imagine.

"So just storming in and hacking their systems is out," Kal said, earning a dirty look from Bo.

"Not to mention they'll be looking for us," added Nicole. "We just hacked their flagship."

"We didn't hack," Bo said exasperatedly. He seemed to be losing enthusiasm for correcting them.

"Maybe they don't know what we're looking for," Ekon said hopefully.

"Oh, they know, sergeant." Ramos swiveled in her chair to the face the others. "There could only be one thing that we'd be looking for and the Jadid ain't dumb."

"We'll need to dock with the station and then make our way to the Nasi controlled area," Bo said. "The information will still be stored on their systems. If I can get to a Nasi command terminal, we should be okay."

"I'm guessing we need you to actually get the coordinates too, huh?" Kal asked. "Can't just download the key?"

Bo shook his head. It would be nice if things were simple. Kal was trying to understand how Bo felt this was a good news, bad news situation. To him, it was about ninety percent bad news. The one good thing is that the coordinates existed, and they knew where they were—kinda. Not much different from when they had started the mission.

"We'll need to head back to Patagonia and get a civilian ship," said Ramos.

"We don't have time." Nicole pointed to the center of the tacmap to the large white circle of Mariga. "There's only one place we can go."

Getting onto the surface—so to speak—of Mariga was no easy task. The planet was covered in layers of ice, and there were only a few public ports available, which meant they were likely all monitored by the Nasi.

The *McCullough* was a Jadid experimental ship, which meant it would almost certainly be flagged. If they came within sensor range of the planet without their cloak, every single light in Marigan Portal Control would light up. They'd been to Mariga before though, and Kal was from the planet. He knew several utility tunnels that were off the official maps where they could land and access the network of caves that lay beneath the surface.

They were able to land without anyone being the wiser. Kal directed the chief to a flat patch of ice that was conveniently shielded from observation by an enormous dagger of ice that stabbed upwards from the ground. Unfortunately, they were already short two battle suits, so Sergeant Kimathi and Chief Ramos had to stay behind with the ship. Although he might stick out like a sore thumb, bringing Bo was worth the risk to Kal. They very likely would need the backup.

"I swear, sir," Ramos called out as Kal, Nicole, and Bo put on their battle suits, "you'd better come back soon or else I'll turn myself in just to get away from this guy." She pointed at Ekon, who was now sitting on one of the benches in the cargo area, his back against the hull.

"We're going to have a great time together, Chief, just you wait." Ekon stood and put his good arm around Ramos, who made a face.

I worry about those two, Nicole said.

I don't think you should, Bo said. I believe the chief is just being humous. Oh, you knew that, didn't you?

Bo had become so well-versed in Human culture and speech that Kal was surprised when he missed subtext or humor. Out of all the Jadid or Nasi Kal had met, Bo was the most Human, but there would always be a part of him that remained Jadid. Not to mention the fact that he was a head taller than Kal with superhuman strength and purple skin.

Mariga's surface was a barren landscape of ice and snow. Having lived on the planet, Kal knew looks could be deceiving. There were hundreds of creatures that inhabited the desolate icescape, but Humans weren't one of them. Without their suits, Kal and Nicole would die within minutes from exposure. Kal wasn't sure how long Bo could last but guessed it wasn't too much longer.

They reached a utility tunnel that led down to the warren of caves and tunnels. Once inside, they activated their thrusters and let their suit's computers handle the flying. The blue-tinged glacial surface ice gave way to a small seam of gray and then the brownish black of the planet's bedrock. As they turned a corner, a halo of light glowed against the rock in front of them as they neared an area with overhead lighting.

We need to find a place to stash the suits, Kal said. If their battle suits were found, the mission was over, and there was a good chance they wouldn't make it off the planet alive.

They found a maintenance shed, a small space that was segregated from the main tunnel and used to store equipment. Maintenance sheds were all over the planet, and the chances of anyone stumbling upon their suits inside was slim. As a bonus, they found several pieces of discarded maintenance apparel, including a large mining helmet that just fit Bo and a pair of maintenance overalls that clearly did not. After a final check for any additional supplies, they left the suits behind several large pieces of excavation equipment and returned to the main tunnel.

They were far out from any sort of major thoroughfare, and Kal's implant couldn't connect to the planetary net, which meant he had no way to reach the Odpor. They steeled themselves for a long walk toward the closest major thoroughfare. Once they got close enough, they'd be able to contact the Odpor and get someone to come to their location.

"Didn't think we'd be back so soon, eh?" Nicole asked.

Kal could tell she was trying to lighten the mood. They'd been walking for almost an hour and nerves were on edge. Bo was forced to skirt the edge of the tunnel, ready to duck aside if a transport or crawler came by. Kal felt he was being watched, and his neck was starting to ache from turning around every few seconds, expecting to find a patrol aircar barreling down on them.

"Once we contact the Odpor, we should be set and out of here," he replied. In the past few months he'd spent on Mariga, he'd done a pretty good job of getting the resistance group whipped into shape. He was confident they'd be able to get them a cargo ship and help them get off planet quickly.

They passed the time talking about their shared memories of the past few years. Not about the battles or the times where they were apart but the funny times. Like when Jae-Ho—junior, not the father—had spit up in Chief Kanumba's face when they were in the galley. Or the time Sergeant Kimathi had deactivated the biorecycler in Sergeant First Class Jones' cabin on the *Ofira* only to find all his personal belongs stuffed into a sack and stuck to the ship's hull the next day.

"Took him three hours to actually get them back in," Nicole laughed.

There were countless more times like that; bright stars of humor and friendship in the blackness of the war they were fighting. They were situations that wouldn't make sense to a civilian, too rooted in the time, place, and culture of Samsara Fleet. To explain them would invite a litany of questions that would take hours to answer. They were stories where "you had to be there" or else they just didn't make sense.

As they laughed—even Bo—and walked along, Kal heard the chime that indicated his implant had established a connection to the net. He contacted one of the Odpor's autonomous relays and had an aircar sent to them. A few minutes later, the faded black vehicle came to a jerky stop next to them, and the passenger door swung open.

"Guess rebels don't like to travel in style, huh?" Nicole arched her eyebrow at Kal.

"Budget cuts," Bo said before Kal could reply.

They climbed into the transport and were off, heading to the capital, Torgut.

When Humans had settled Mariga, they'd created Torgut in a large naturally occurring cave. Over time the cave had been widened and extended. On a map, the city looked like a person with two arms and two legs coming down from the central cavern and the main port as the head.

They arrived in the outer circles of West Leg. The tunnel was relatively low to the ground and the road was lined with high occupancy residences and shops selling necessities. As they continued toward the center of the city, the tunnel widened and the ceiling rose. Viewscreens on the ceiling created the illusion that they were in the outside with sunlight, broken up by the enormous towers of the city, saturating the area. They were still well underground of course, and the

243

enormous skyscrapers that towered above them were just images on the screens. Kal could see the telltale black line where reality ended, and the faux sunny sky began.

Their vehicle sped through the city center then toward West Arm and a few minutes later were standing outside a dilapidated building in what Kal would generously describe as an up-and-coming area.

"What is this place?" Nicole asked as she scanned the multistory structure.

"An itinerant's lodge," said Kal. "Meant to house workers who come in from the countryside. The ones who are gonna be here for more than a few days."

Nicole screwed up her mouth. Kal could tell she was bothered by the building and had a good idea of why; it looked an awful lot like a commune.

The lobby was a small room, no bigger than a scout ship's cargo bay. Everything about it screamed bare minimum, from the unfinished concrete floor and prefab paneling on the walls to the rusty metal light fixtures hanging from the ceiling at an angle.

Kal activated the viewscreen on the far wall and dialed the number for the Odpor cell in the building. They'd rewired the system so the call couldn't be traced to their unit in case anyone was listening.

"Prompt?"

"Zurich." It was the code word which meant he had not been followed and was not under duress. If he'd said anything else, the line would have cut off and every single Odpor agent in the building would be scrambling to clean the cell and get out.

The door next to the screen clicked and swung open a few centimeters. Kal pushed it open and led Nicole and Bo through the dingy hallways. After several turns and a few climbs up rickety sets of stairs, they ended at a metal door, which swung open as they approached.

"General Norman, you're back."

Kal squinted. The hallway was poorly lit, and the person cloaked in darkness, but the voice sounded familiar. He felt the hairs rise on the back of his neck.

The figure stepped forward, revealing several long black braids, which had been artfully twirled around a woman's head to create a crown of sorts.

"Gudit?" Kal was shocked. He'd thought the former Alliance boss was dead. He hadn't seen her in the previous months when he was setting up the Odpor. He'd assumed either the Alliance had gotten to her as retribution for betraying her oaths to them, or her criminal activity had caught up to her. Gudit was a woman who looked after one thing—herself.

"You thought I was dead?" She laughed. "Glad to hear it. You know I've been watching you, Kal. Watching what you and your band of merry misfits have been doing here on Mariga." She gestured to the door. "Come on in."

"What's going on?" Nicole asked uncertainly.

"Don't worry. We just need to have a talk." Gudit smiled in a way that was anything but reassuring.

Chapter Eighteen
Nicole | Mariga

Nicole trusted Gudit about as far as she could throw the woman. Scratch that; Gudit looked pretty light. She could throw Gudit *farther* than she trusted her. Although the former Alliance boss had never betrayed them, Nicole knew of plenty of people she *had* betrayed.

Before the Nasi arrived, the Alliance had been a thing of legend. They'd had a de facto monopoly on the galaxy's interstellar criminal activities. The Alliance had been smart, remaining prominent enough that people knew who they were while keeping far enough in the shadows that no one knew where to find them. They'd been criminals, but never did anything so bad that governments felt it was worth the effort to root them out. It had been a stable arrangement until the Nasi arrived and had wiped them out.

"You're probably wondering what I'm doing here in one of your Odpor cells, huh?" Gudit asked as they entered the room.

Two bodyguards stood silently in opposite corners, their faces impassive and their hands crossed at their waists. Nicole could tell from Kal's reaction that this was not going according to his plan.

"Gudit, seems like we're in business again." Kal carefully sat across from the woman. Nicole could tell he was ready to pull his pistol out at a moment's notice.

Nicole tried to feign indifference as she sat next to Kal, but she could hear her heart in her ears, and the pressure of the plasma pistol in her waistband was in the front of her mind. Meanwhile Bo gracefully sat on the other side of Kal, his movements so precise and elegant they made any Human seem like a walrus.

"I see you have a friend." Gudit eyed Bo coolly.

"Probably a good thing to keep in mind," Kal replied. Immediately after he spoke, Bo grabbed a glass that was on the table and took a deep gulp. The movement was so fast, so deadly in its precision, that Nicole knew it was a warning.

"Whoa. Whoa." Gudit held up her hands. "We're on the same side here. I've been asked to help you and your little ragtag group."

Bo made a face and started spitting onto the floor.

"What did you do?" Nicole asked. She stood up and pulled her pistol out, aiming at Gudit. "What's in the glass?"

Gudit held her hands up calmly. "It's bourbon. Distilled right here on Mariga. One of the last batches before the Nasi took the place over."

"It's disgusting!" Bo shouted in between retches.

"Most of your friends like bourbon," Gudit remarked innocently. "More than a few like it more than is good for 'em."

"This…is the…worst thing I've…ever tasted." Bo wiped his mouth with his sleeve and sat back on the couch, his air of deadly precision irrevocably punctured.

"What do you mean, you were asked?" Nicole asked.

Gudit's face betrayed a flicker of uncertainty. "Well, seems like the Alliance ain't as dead as I thought it was. They found out about some of my extracurriculars and took offense."

"You mean like killing innocent people?" Nicole felt herself getting flush with anger. "Those kind of extracurriculars?"

"They don't care about all of that," Gudit replied. "It was more about messing with their agents," She shrugged. "So they made me an offer. I can keep my life if I get back with the program." She motioned to the two guards behind her. "They sent the fun siblings over here and told me to make sure I keep my end of the deal."

They weren't guarding Gudit. They were watching over her.

"Anyway, as you know, the Alliance is heavily interested in making sure you're successful. They've told me to do anything in my power to make sure of it. So I reached out to the Odpor and joined up. All the resources of the Alliance—as they are—are at your disposal."

"Where's the rest?" Nicole asked. Although she couldn't see the entire unit, she had the distinct impression they were the only ones in the place. It didn't feel right to have a morally ambiguous Alliance boss as the only person there.

"We're alone," Gudit said. "You can check around if you'd like. The Odpor's been short-staffed since Kal left. The Nasi are getting worse, and the Odpor is losing people left and right. I told them I'd take the shift here. It's probably their least secure facility, and I think they consider me expendable enough to man it."

Nicole had the distinct impression that Gudit's story was

missing a few chapters. The coincidence that they just happened to end up in the safehouse she was manning seemed unlikely.

"We need a cargo ship," Kal said. "Like right away."

Gudit nodded her head. "I can get you that. What for?"

"That, you don't need to know," Nicole said. "All *you* need to know is that we need a standard, completely nondescript, cargo ship."

As Nicole met Gudit's eyes she was taken aback as she realized the woman's black irises were touched with small flecks of silver. She also noticed a slight tightening around the mouth. Her demand had gotten under the woman's skin. Nicole was glad.

"Context is important in my business," Gudit said evenly. "There are a lot of cargo ships. What you need it for may change what I get."

"It isn't that we don't trust you," Kal said.

It most certainly is, Nicole thought to herself.

Kal continued. "It's for your protection. We've got a high chance of getting caught and if we are, the less you know, the safer you are."

Gudit smiled and looked at Kal. "You know, I used to say that little speech to people myself. But the truth is, it's bullshit. You get caught—whatever you're going to do—and it's all over anyways. You need to tell me exactly what you're planning on doing or else this will go sideways on you."

She looked back to Nicole, and Nicole couldn't help but look away. The woman was right: she needed to know what they were going to do. Of course, that meant it would give her every opportunity to betray them. On the other hand, she might have *already* betrayed them; there could be a Nasi squad on their way at that moment.

"We're going to get into Lidice Station," Kal said. "Anything more than that is irrelevant."

Gudit's smile returned but not before Nicole noticed a flicker of something—surprise, perhaps—in her eyes.

"Interesting. I'm *very* glad you told me. You can't just take any cargo ship to dock on Lidice. The Nasi have instituted regulations, a lot of them, around what ships can access the station."

"What kind of regulations?" Kal asked.

"Well, first, the ship's got to be at least a class three, no more of the simple cargo ships like the Shreen you used to pilot. Next, the transponder must be approved, meaning that the ship has already been inspected and allowed to go the station. Finally—and this isn't strictly about the ship but is still pretty damn important—all personnel aboard the ship are cleared upon landing."

"The Nasi don't have any information on me," Kal said.

Gudit laughed. This time it was real. "The Nasi don't have information on *you*." She lifted her glass and toasted Kal. "Oh I'm sure they got a helluva lot of information on you by now. You've been a thorn in their side from day one. You're a hero of Samsara Fleet. Of Humanity. Maybe even of the galaxy. And you think they won't know it when they start scanning you and whatever identification you're planning on using?"

She placed the glass down with a clink. "Rich."

"So just get us fake IDs," said Nicole. "We can upload them to our implants."

"Aren't you listening? There's no fake ID that's gonna get you onto that station without it being in restraints. Not with the kind of screening they have on Lidice." She motioned for the guards to come over. "But I can still help you."

They two guards were an odd pair. The woman was tall, almost as tall as Bo, but where the Jadid was thin and wiry, she was solid. Solid enough that Nicole only realized how tall the woman was when she was standing directly in front of her. The man was short, only a couple of centimeters taller than Nicole. He moved with the grace of a Jadid, his muscles bulging beneath the formal tunic and vest he was wearing.

"This is Tiny and Shrimp," Gudit said, pointing at the woman and then the man.

"Interesting names," Nicole said.

"We didn't pick 'em," Shrimp said with a shrug of his shoulders.

Gudit laughed. "I did. Couldn't help myself. They'll be the pilot and copilot of our ship."

"They're not watching you?" Nicole asked in surprise.

"The Alliance doesn't do things that way," Kal said. "They're always watching, and if they decide it's time for you to… retire, then you'll never see it coming."

"Spoken like someone who's worked with them before," Gudit said with a nod. "They work for the Alliance, and now they work for you. As do I. Which means I'll be joining you as the commander of this not so little trading vessel."

"I'm going to need to talk to someone in the Odpor before I agree to any plan like this," Kal said. "You asked us to trust you, and we have. But you know that trust can only go so far."

"Again, spoken like someone who's worked with the Alliance before," Gudit said after a pause. "Fair enough. Feel free to hop on a link with the central cell and talk to them. You'll see that I'm aboveboard. Besides, it's gonna take a bit for me to get the ship you need."

As Gudit had predicted, it took the Alliance a couple of hours to secure a cargo vessel and the necessary permits for them to access the station. While they'd been waiting, Kal had confirmed that Gudit was working with the Odpor, which, though not surprising to Nicole, did make her feel a bit better.

They took a private aircar through the center of Torgut to the central port. The main entrance to the enormous facility was guarded by several Nasi soldiers in battle suits who thankfully paid them no attention as they strode through. Gudit and her guards posed as mid-level independent merchant captain and her two mates, while Kal and Nicole were their maintenance crew. They were dressed in baggy grease-stained coveralls and had a cargo bot trailing them, hauling a half-opened cargo box that was almost overflowing with parts.

Because the port was beneath the surface, the landing pads were arranged in clusters beneath large bay doors which periodically dilated opened to let ships in and out. Hallways filled with traders, crew, shops, and bars connected the clusters together.

As they walked through the crowded passageways, Nicole looked back at the cargo bin. Somewhere underneath all of the metal and grime was a very uncomfortable Jadid scientist.

Gudit led them to a bay near the back of the port and motioned toward a trading vessel that looked like its best days were *way* behind it. "Voila!"

Nicole wasn't an expert in ships, but even she could tell that it wasn't top-of-the-line; scorch marks and dents from countless atmospheric entries dotted the large miscolored hull. The ship was large, easily twice the size of the scout corvette's they used for most of their missions, and she estimated the *McCullough* could have easily fit inside the cargo hold a few times over.

"Stop staring and climb aboard," Gudit called out with mock cheerfulness. Nicole shook her head ruefully and walked up the cargo ramp. The cargo bot hovered up the rear ramp behind her and unceremoniously dropped the crate on the side of the bay with a loud metal thunk.

"Bet he felt that," Kal whispered to Nicole.

"Get ready, we're out in five," Gudit shouted as she made her way through the bay. She climbed the ladder that led to the second deck and the cockpit at the far end. "Tiny, you come with me. Shrimp, I don't give a crap what you do." She paused at the top rung. "Just be ready."

Nicole and Kal followed Gudit and Tiny to the cockpit and sat down in the jump seats behind the pilot's and copilot's chairs. The cockpit was large but just as dingy as the rest of the ship. Nicole had to shift her weight in the chair a few times until she didn't feel a metal spring poking her backside. True to Gudit's word, they launched five minutes later. As they floated out of the bay, Nicole took a moment to appreciate the landscape below. In the safety of the warm cockpit, the icy valleys and mountains below looked like an ethereal wonderland as sunlight sparkled off the jutting glacial features.

"Okay, we don't have long." Gudit's chair squeaked loudly as she swiveled to face Kal and Nicole. "We're under the watch of the Nasi air control, which means we can't change course or speed. Follow me."

She led them back down the ladder to the cargo hold where Bo had somehow managed to pull himself out of the storage container. Gudit pulled open one of the built-in storage pods inside the bulkhead and pulled out a cylindrical device about the length of her arm.

"What's that?" Nicole asked.

"Watch and see."

Gudit strode to the bulkhead next to the stairs and pushed the device against one of the rivets. In a matter of seconds, the rivet was off, and she was on to the next one. Before long, she'd detached an entire panel and set it on the deck, revealing a small space which she motioned for them to climb into.

"This isn't gonna be the most comfortable accommodations, but it should hold you. It's near the engine, so the heat, noise, and radiation should mask any signatures.

"Um." Nicole's mind was still stuck on the word "radiation."

Bo smoothly climbed in while Kal and Nicole stared at the square-shaped hole uncertainly.

"How much radiation we talkin' about here?" Kal asked, poking his head into the hole.

"Enough to mask your presence. Not enough to instantly kill you."

"Not the biggest fan of the use of instantly here," Nicole said. "How long can we be in there?"

"I guess we'll find out." Gudit banged the small tool in her hand against the metal wall. "Let's go. I still gotta close this thing up. It ain't gonna be fun, but it's the best we got."

Nicole and Kal climbed into the opening. The sounds of their clumsy efforts echoed through the piping-hot chamber. Nicole felt sweat breaking out on her forehead before she even sat down.

Gudit's hand reached through the opening with a large metal jug. "Take this. It's water," she called out.

Nicole obligingly grabbed the water and sat it on the floor next to her.

"I'm closing this thing up," Gudit called out. Nicole heard the scrape of the metal panel as the woman picked it up from the floor. "I don't know how long it'll take to get through their security and onboarding, but I'll get you out as soon as I can."

With that, Gudit slammed the metal panel back on, casting them in darkness.

The first five minutes in the hole, as they decided to call it, were torture. The stifling heat, the sweat pouring down her face, and the complete darkness made Nicole feel like she was in some version of hell. As she got used to the heat, the physical torture gave way to the mental. The helplessness of their situation and knowing that at any moment they could be caught or killed made every second feel like an eternity.

As they suffered, they tried to keep the mood light but were too preoccupied with what might be happening outside to keep up a conversation. Nicole felt a small tingle of affection as she felt Kal's hand reach out and grab hers. He didn't say anything, but his touch was enough to let her know what he was thinking.

A faint whirring emanated from the steel panel where they'd entered. Someone was coming. Light flooded Nicole's vision and she held her hand up, trying to shield her eyes while still making out who was there.

"Hey, it's Gudit. We're in."

Chapter Nineteen

Kal | Lidice Station, Mariga

Kal fought the urge to reach up and scratch his neck for the fifth time. The stevedore coveralls he was wearing were at least a size too small. The dirt-encrusted fabric was uncomfortably tight around his neck while also bunching up at his ankles and wrists.

Nicole gave a small yelp as she almost fell on the floor next to him. She was having the opposite problem. She looked like a child wearing her father's work outfit with the sleeves and legs pulled up so they didn't cover her hands and feet. Unfortunately, the pants legs kept rolling down, causing her to periodically trip.

"Come on," Gudit said sternly, barely turning her head. "I don't pay you two idiots to sit around. We've got to get this shipment and get out of here."

"Did you purposely do this?" Kal hissed at her. He wouldn't put it past the woman. She had a twisted sense of humor.

"I'm not saying." Her tone was sickly sweet.

Kal had only been on Lidice twice before: as a small child with his father and the day he left Mariga to join the Earth Defense Force. Although the station still bore signs of fighting from the initial Nasi invasion years earlier, it was clearly functioning. The hallways weren't as busy as he remembered, but there still were ship captains, stevedores, maintenance folks, security, and others striding purposefully through the station. The merchants and performers he'd seen the other times were gone and with them so was the air of fun and adventure that he remembered.

They walked through in the general direction of the cargo pickup area. According to Gudit, the Odpor had been able to provide her a general idea of where the Nasi would have established their command center but didn't know for sure. Lidice was still very much a mystery since the Odpor hadn't been able to get an agent inside yet.

The plan—if it could be called that—was to make their way toward the cargo storage areas and look for an opportunity to enter the Nasi area when they saw it. Once inside the Nasi-controlled area, they should be able to use the information from the files they downloaded from the flagship to get the dreadnaught's location.

As he walked, Kal kept his head down but his eyes up. He knew they were probably being tracked by surveillance cameras. Getting into the secure area would be tough. It wasn't their first time doing something like it though—not by a long shot. The Skulls had infiltrated Nasi areas multiple times, and they'd become relatively proficient at it as well if Kal was being honest with himself.

There were two important devices they used. The first was the skeleton key which had been developed by Chief Kanumba and Bo. It had gone through multiple upgrades and improvements since its initial design and could reliably override most Nasi locks. The other device was their portable optical cloak which rendered them invisible to the cameras and casual glances.

It had been months since they'd last tried an operation like this, and Kal had two concerns. The biggest one was that a guard or AI noticed a door magically opening on their security consoles. The second was that the Nasi might have updated their systems so their tools no longer worked. That was the way of war; each side developed new weapons and tools, and the other side figured out ways to nullify them. A constant arms race.

"Where's that cargo bay?" Gudit asked loudly. "I think we're turned around."

She turned and led them around the other part of the hallway, still looking for some sign of where the Nasi controlled part of the base was. It was maddening. They'd seen a few Nasi soldiers walking through the hallways or standing at intersections with their datons at the ready. But they hadn't seen any evidence of them going in or out of any specific area of the station.

Unfortunately, Kal couldn't speak. There was a good chance the hallways had audio monitors as well. Instead, he and Nicole were forced to follow Gudit's lead, hoping they would have some luck.

Kal jumped as the utility door next to him slid open with a whisper of brushing metal. Two Nasi guards strode into the hallway, shoving Kal and Nicole to the side.

Per their plan, Gudit mumbled an apology and kept moving forward, now making a beeline to the cargo pickup area. They quickly loaded up several cargo bots and made their way back to the ship with a small train of bots trailing behind them. As soon as they entered the ship, they made their way to the galley where Bo was already waiting for them.

"Sent you the coordinates for the target," Kal said.

Bo looked down at his comeca and nodded. "Ready, sir."

Kal caught Gudit's eye, and she nodded back at him.

"Let's do this." Kal flicked on his optical cloak. His vision dimmed, letting him know that the device was working.

Nicole and Bo had switched theirs on as well and had disappeared.

Kal carefully made his way through the cargo bay, avoiding the bots as they meticulously stacked and strapped down the cargo. The optical cloaks were great inventions, but they had their drawbacks. Most notably, the wearer had to be careful not to get close to anyone or anything. Otherwise, things would start to magically disappear as they came inside the range of the cloak. Additionally, it could be hard to see where one was going since the cloak blocked out a good portion of light. Thankfully, Lidice Station was well-lit, and Kal had been recording the interior layout with his neural implant when they'd been searching for the Nasi command area.

Kal took lead, with Bo and Nicole following behind at regular intervals. As he walked down the cargo ramp, he dragged a foot on the decking, letting the others know he was stepping off the ship. They'd developed a sort of shorthand for communication when using the cloaks, little sounds to let the others know where they were.

The station's cargo bay, which had seemed empty only minutes earlier, now felt like an obstacle course. Kal had to jump and dodge as he made his way through people so he wouldn't give himself away. The hallways were less occupied, but even more treacherous since there wasn't much space for him to move out of the way as people walked past. More than once he was forced to dodge through a doorway or even double back to get out of the way of a group of people.

Kal arrived at their target door and dragged his foot on the ground, making a slight squeak. He waited for any responding signals but didn't hear a thing. After a tense wait, he heard a small metallic knock against the far wall. He responded with his signal of dragging his foot on the ground. Another metallic knock sounded from right next to him. They were all there.

The security access pad next to the door disappeared as Bo got to work with the skeleton key. Suddenly the door sprang open, and Kal started to move forward before he saw two Nasi stepping out. He jumped to the side and saw one of their arms disappear as it entered the field of an optical cloak. The Nasi stopped and looked around, clearly sensing something was wrong. He hefted his daton with both hands as if to swing then stopped and reassessed the hallway.

Kal froze with his back against the wall. He could hear his heart beating as the two Nasi looked around.

"I thought I felt something," said the Nasi who'd been scanning the area.

"I did not hear anything," the other replied. "We can still log it though."

"No, there's no need. I do not have anything to report,

and I do not want to deal with the report. Always second-guessing us. Did you investigate? Why not? What makes you think anything was wrong?" He groaned. "I can't wait to get back to the surface."

The other laughed and slapped his friend on the back consolingly, and they headed toward the cargo bay. As soon as they'd turned the corner, the pad security disappeared again. This time, it was only a matter of seconds before the door slid open. Kal double-checked that no one was coming in before rushing through—and collided with Nicole on the way in. As the fields from their two cloaks merged, he was able to see her clearly while the area around them dimmed to an almost complete darkness. They hastily moved apart, hopefully before anyone noticed the large cloud of black from their two cloaks interfering with each other.

The Nasi had completely retrofitted the section of the station. The Human terminals had been ripped from the walls and floors. In their places were the Nasi equivalents, rounded and misshapen devices with screens formed from loose particles, connected by loose bundles of brown and green cables which dangled from the ceiling.

"Follow me," Bo whispered from somewhere in front of Kal.

Bo moved forward, occasionally tapping on a nearby wall to let them know where he was. As Kal followed behind, he realized the Nasi hadn't just removed the Human consoles, they'd removed almost every vestige of Humanity from the area. Viewscreens, doors, furniture. All removed and replaced with their Nasi equivalent.

Kal heard a metallic clink to his left then saw the open doorway to his right, revealing a small room with a large console in the center. It must be the console Bo was looking for. Kal stepped into the small room and knelt in a corner, pistol raised to cover the door. The top of the console disappeared and reappeared as Bo got to work.

Small groups of Nasi occasionally walked past the room. Thankfully, none of them looked inside. If they had, they would have seen half the console miraculously gone.

"Got it," Bo hissed. "Lets—"

A Nasi guard walked by and stopped, whirling his daton out and firing in a smooth motion. The bolt hit the console and vaporized it to slag. Before the soldier could get off another shot, he disappeared and then reappeared in a heap on the floor, unconscious or dead. Kal couldn't tell.

"Let's go," Bo whispered.

Kal ran back the way they came, trusting the others were running along with him. When he got to the entrance to the Nasi command area, he saw it was open and two Nasi guards were laid out on the floor. He rushed through and ran toward the cargo bay. A klaxon burst to life, loud enough to be almost painful. Kal rounded the corner to find that the entrance to the cargo bay had been closed by a large security barrier.

"Damn." Kal couldn't help himself.

"You can say that again." It was Nicole.

"Indeed." Bo whispered.

A small door on the side of the large security barrier opened, and several Nasi guards stepped out with their datons at the ready. They knelt in a semicircle with their weapons up blocking the way.

Think. Think.

Kal brought up a map of the station in his implant. He started looking through the utility corridors for some way they might enter the bay. *There!* He saw a small maintenance tunnel that led through the ceiling from two levels above them. If they could manage to get to it, they might be able to somehow drop down into the bay. He opened their channel to let the others know about his idea.

I think—

The small door in the security barrier opened again and Kal was jolted out of his thoughts by a bloodcurdling scream that erupted next to him. A moment later, the Nasi who'd been walking through the door was on the ground, his back bent at an unnatural angle. The four Nasi guarding the entrance were just as startled as Kal. They fired at where the scream had come from, but by the time they reoriented themselves toward the door, plasma was pouring on their positions from thin air. They didn't have a chance.

Shots continued firing inside the bay, and Kal rushed through the door, again running into Nicole on the way through. When he got to the other side, he found chaos waiting. Nasi guards lay on the ground, their bodies charred from plasma fire. Although Bo was a scientist, he'd learned a lot about fighting in his time with Kal and Samsara Fleet. He put those skills to good use now. He was a phantom, screaming around the bay, killing, and then moving on.

No matter what Bo's skills were, he couldn't match an entire station of trained Nasi soldiers. They had to leave immediately. Bo's path was taking him toward the dilapidated cargo vessel they'd used to enter the station. However, the ship was old and slow; there was no way they'd make it off the station in it—not when they'd been discovered.

Kal looked around and spied a Nasi fast-attack assault ship, one of the newest models, sitting nearby.

Head toward the assault ship, Kal called out over the net as he sent the location to the others. *Let's go.*

Gudit and the others poured from the back of the cargo vessel as plasma fire continued to crisscross through the parked ships. Tiny was hit, the bolt dissolving her leg almost instantly and sending her to the floor with a shriek of pain. The other two made it to the ship, which was thankfully open, and jumped in.

Kal wasn't far behind. He dove in headfirst to find Bo already inside. As he sat up, he was knocked to the deck as Nicole barreled in after him, the door slamming shut behind her.

Precious seconds ticked by as the ship's engines spun up. Kal and everyone else in the crew area were slammed against the rear bulkhead as the ship catapulted forward.

They'd cleared the station.

Chapter Twenty
Nicole | Mariga

Nicole's head throbbed. When she'd dove into the assault craft, it had collided—quite squarely—with some part of Kal. She wasn't sure which, but from the pain it had clearly been hard. Elbow, knee, skull. She had no idea.

The combination of the blow to her head and the second blow to her entire body from cartwheeling into the far bulkhead had taken their toll. It took her a little bit of time to get up and make her way to the cockpit.

Assault ships were designed to transport soldiers quickly and discreetly into a battle. They were simple, a back crew area for the soldiers with benches and nothing else. The cockpit normally sat two but now had four people crammed inside—Nicole, Kal, Bo, and Gudit—all talking at once.

"We're going to need to head to the *McCullough*," Kal shouted over the others. "There is no way we can outrun a Nasi *fleet*."

"Fine," Gudit said. "How are we"—she pointed to Shrimp and herself—"going to escape then?"

"You're coming back with us," Kal said.

"Not an option. I need to stay on Mariga."

"You can either come with us or die on Mariga," Nicole said. "Your choice."

Gudit grunted angrily. She didn't like it, but she knew Nicole was right. "Fine."

Thankfully, assault ships were designed for quick atmospheric entry. As they plummeted towards Mariga's surface, the friction caused the front of the ship to glow an angry red and the fighters following them began to drop back. Nicole held on for dear life as the ship bucked back and forth. She wasn't sure she'd entered a planet's atmosphere at such a steep angle before.

Kal managed to climb into the copilot's seat and reached the *McCullough*, telling them to get ready to take off and fold.

"I'd suggest you all strap in," Bo said calmly as the ground approached. "There's no clear landing place in walking distance of the ship. Due to the severe weather conditions on the surface, I'm forced—"

Nicole dove back into the crew area and quickly strapped the padded restraints around her body and waist.

Only a few seconds after she'd heard the final click indicating all restraints were attached and activated, the jolt of them hitting the surface nearly knocked her out. The ship slammed into the ground, and the sound of snapping and tearing came from all around her. They scraped along the snowy ground for several hundred meters before coming to a halt.

Bo ran from the cockpit to the side door and opened it. The temperature inside the ship plummeted almost instantly, sending small electrical thrills up Nicole's arm. Smoke and a smell that reminded her of burning flesh came in right after.

"I forgot how damn cold the surface is," Gudit said as she released her restraints.

Nicole nodded toward the woman dumbly, not trusting

herself to form a coherent sentence. She tripped on her way out of the vessel, landing in the snow with a crunch. As she pushed herself up, she wanted to scream in triumph as she saw the *McCullough* soar over a nearby rise, heading directly toward them.

The repurposed science vessel landed meters away, its rear bay door already open. Nicole and the others ran inside. The ship's energy shield kept the freezing cold air out, and the warm air of the cargo bay hit her felt like she was being blasted with thrusters.

As soon as she was inside, she collapsed on the floor, exhausted.

"What happened?" Kimathi asked, kneeling next to her.

"We had to infiltrate Lidice Station," Nicole said. "We almost got caught and had to fight our way out, then steal a ship, and then we crash landed on the planet's surface." She wrung her hands together, trying to get the sensation back. "I can barely feel my hands."

Ekon frowned. "I can't believe I missed it. Being injured sucks."

The *McCullough* was forced to fold as soon as it left Mariga's atmosphere. Once they were safe, they checked out the coordinates Bo had downloaded from the station. As expected, the dreadnaught was located extremely close—in galactic terms—and was clearly waiting for Wang's Liberation fleet to arrive.

The question that immediately came to Nicole's mind was whether the coordinates were accurate. There was a good chance the Nasi may have anticipated their actions and changed the coordinates to send them to a trap. Bo was firm in his opinion that they had the genuine coordinates, and after a short conversation, Kal voiced his agreement.

The *McCullough* folded within a few light minutes of the dreadnaught's location and conducted a deep sensor scan of the area.

"Yup, that's the ship alright," Ramos confirmed after reviewing the sensor readouts.

"Now what do we do about it?" Nicole asked. She knew that as Tac-Is their entire job was boarding ships and stations, still it felt like their luck was going to run out sooner or later.

"We reload and get ready," Kal said. "The fleet's left Patagonia so we need to head there and get what supplies and reinforcements we can and board that ship."

"It's what we do best," Ekon called out, poking his head in from the cargo bay.

'You were just shot boarding a Nasi ship," Bo said.

"I didn't say well, I just said best."

A few minutes later, they were rapidly descending towards Pangea, Patagonia's main continent. Nicole marveled at what Ai and Bo had done when they'd created the *McCullough*. The very concepts of distance that had constrained all species were gone. Whatever happened after the war, nothing would be the same again.

An idea struck her.

"Bo. Do you think that the Jadid could build a ship like this?" she asked. "I mean, you and Ai were working on it with them. Surely your files are still there."

Bo smiled. "Esma and the Nasi taught me a few things." The smile faded a bit. "One of them is that you have to be *very* careful who you trust. Outside of this ship, there are only a handful of people that I would trust with this information. We've made sure to keep our calculations and findings under our own security. We left a few things in there to find, but anyone who knows anything about interdimensional physics will soon realize they're worthless, rehashing existing research that we simply tweaked to look new."

"That's good to know," Nicole said, relieved. The thought of their enemies having this technology in their hands was terrifying.

"It's only a matter of time before someone else discovers it," Kal said. "Now that people know it's possible."

"Lots of people would be willing to pay anything for a ship like this." Gudit ran her hand along the bulkhead.

One thing at a time, Nicole thought to herself.

"Interesting," Ramos said. "We're being asked to land directly at the presidential palace.

"Guessed they missed us," Kimathi said.

"Or else there's something up."

The crowds were finally gone from around the palace, and normalcy had started to return to Patagonia. Paper and rubbish littered the pathways that wound between the buildings and more than a little of it had found its way into the unmanicured gardens.

When they reached the entrance to the palace, the guards immediately ushered them towards the presidential office. Nicole wondered who they would find when they entered. Already there were two desks in the office. However, neither one was occupied. Instead, Kinawadi and Garcia were seated at the plush sitting area talking with a small group of people.

She did a double take.

"Sandra! Taisha!" Nicole ran towards Chief Taisha Kanumba and Sergeant Sandra Chedjou. The two women had been lost on New America when the Jadid had betrayed them. Kal, who had been captured there as well, hadn't said anything directly, but Nicole knew he believed both women had died in the fighting.

"Nicole," the women said in unison as they stood.

Nicole relished how wonderful it felt to see the two of them. It had been months, months of wondering if they were alive and then the sinking feeling that she would never see them again. The fact that they were there in front of her was amazing.

Kal was right behind Nicole, beaming from ear to ear. She saw a small tear make its way down his cheek as he grabbed the two women in a bear hug and brought them close. Ekon was next in line and then Ramos, all of them taking a moment to appreciate the pure joy of finding out their friends were still alive.

271

"You able to see Jae-Ho yet?" Nicole asked.

Taisha shook her head. "No, not yet. The fleet had left already."

Nicole squeezed her shoulder. "You'll see him soon enough."

"You both look like you've been through hell," Kal said.

"Long story," Sandra explained. "When the Jadid attacked the Fridge, we were sitting together at the edge of the landing area. Their orbital fire was like nothing I've ever experienced. One minute we were talkin' and people were celebrating around us, the next I was bleeding from the head and almost trapped in rock and ice."

"We found a way out of there," Taisha continued, "and followed it for what seemed like forever until we ended up in a valley on the surface. We had no idea where we were, and our implants were no help either, so we just started walkin'. Eventually, right when we were givin' up, some locals picked us up. They knew enough not to ask questions, but we ended up in Xin Chengdu—eventually." Nicole's ears perked up. She could tell there was more to that story, but she wasn't about to ask. "We ended up getting caught up in the wrong place at the wrong time and were sent to a Jadid work camp."

"How'd you survive that?" Kal asked. "They didn't know who you were?"

"Apparently not." Chedjou shrugged. "Finally, we got our chance and escaped and linked up with the resistance. When everything went down and we knew you were alive, we got here as fast as we could."

272

"I'm just glad you're here," Nicole said.

"Sounds like we arrived just in time for the fun," Chedjou said.

Nicole nodded.

She looked at the faces in the room. All of them were members of the Skulls. They'd been together for years, but in reality, it was so much longer than that. The things they'd seen and done transcended explanation. "You've come just in time for the battle to end all battles."

"I'm assuming you've been brought up to speed," Kal said. The two women nodded. "With the fleet on its way to Mariga, we got to find a way to disable that dreadnaught before they arrive. We know where it is. We also know that we don't have too much time until Wang's fleet reaches the planet as well."

"If they get there and the dreadnaught isn't disabled, we can be sure that Baykara will stop at nothing to make sure he doesn't capture the planet," Nicole said.

"How are you gonna take the ship out?" Chedjou asked.

"Still working on that," Kal said.

"I'm still of the shoot first ask questions later opinion," Sergeant Kimathi quipped.

"Too bad that ship has a lot longer weapons range that you, sergeant," Kanumba said.

Nicole knew from personal experience that infiltrating a ship or station was one thing. Destroying it in the process, especially one as large as the dreadnaught, was almost impossible. Their best hope was to somehow disable it for a

273

period, but the window would be short.

"Is there any way to reach the fleet?" Kal wondered out loud.

"For what reason?" Garcia asked. "You want to send them to the dreadnaught."

"We're not going to be able to take it on our own," Kal replied.

"We captured the *Resolute Stand*," Nicole said hopefully.

"Yes, with several more teams and a fleet helping us out," Ekon replied. "This would be a single squad with no backup."

Bo glanced down at his comeca and muttered something to himself. "There may be another option," he said. "But we need to go to the Foothold and talk with Ai."

Bo wouldn't tell them what they were going to see, only that he wasn't sure it was even possible. Kinawadi and Garcia offered their personal aircars as transportation, saying that they would be happy to help the fleet with whatever was required. Nicole had a sneaking suspicion that curiosity had gotten the best of them as well.

When they arrived in the Foothold, Ai, Red, and Governor Huang stood in front of one of the few buildings that hadn't been destroyed in the fighting. Bo practically leapt from the aircar and rushed over to Ai.

"What you're saying shouldn't be possible," he said. "The field would be too large."

Ai's mouth twitched. "Yes, that's what we'd thought, but

274

then I realized our assumptions about how we extend the field were erroneous."

The conversation became a flurry of technical terms as the two scientists talked back and forth with Bo challenging a statement and Ai coming right back to explain how he hadn't considered something or other.

Finally, Bo raised his arms in supplication. "It makes sense. I admit it. If true, this is amazing. More than that, it's revolutionary."

"We've had a lot of those lately," Nicole said.

"Can someone fill us in on what the hell you're talking about?" Kimathi asked.

Bo turned and looked back at the rest of them. "Absolutely. Among the Jadid, I am considered the foremost authority on inter-universal travel. I have to admit that I took pride in this, wore it like a badge of honor. However, if what Ai has said is true—and I believe it is—then my reputation was a gross injustice to her."

"Can you stop making this about you, Bo and just tell us what she discovered?" Nicole asked. Honestly, the Jadid was getting as melodramatic as Ekon.

"She's found a way to take our drive and extend the range so it can be used on a capital ship."

"So what? We could actually take a battleship across the galaxy?" Nicole asked.

"Well, not that big," Ai said quickly. "At least not yet. But it can be much larger than a ship like the *McCullough*."

"But it *could* be a ship big enough to carry say a hundred-

and-fifty Jadid," Huang said.

"What are you suggesting?" Nicole was confused. Huang had wanted to die on Altterra, and now she seemed to be proposing that they attack their own people.

"You know exactly what I meant, Colonel Bergeron," Huang replied, seeming angry more than anything. "We have been told about your plan by Ai. You cannot hope to capture that ship on your own, but with our help, you might have a chance."

"But you hate it here," Kal protested.

"From what I can tell you hate us," Nicole added.

Huang nodded in acknowledgement. "True, I do not want to be here on your world." Nicole wanted to retort that it wasn't *her* world. That *her* world had been destroyed by the Nasi. "But I also do not want to be a pawn of Ancients Wang and Baykara anymore. They have slaughtered their own children until all that remains is us few. I—and everyone in this Foothold—are tired of hiding and of trying to defend ourselves. We will fight. Not for you or for your fleets, but for us. We will destroy that ship so that there is at least a chance that this entire war can be over."

"What do Ancients Musa and Kingsley think?" Nicole asked. She couldn't help noticing they were not outside.

"They accept our decision," Red said. "Their time as leaders of our people is over. They have lost that right."

Kal rubbed his hand through his hair. "You say this is possible, but has it been built?"

Ai shook her head. "No, it hasn't. But we have the ship

identified, and we have a drive."

"How do we even board the dreadnaught?" Ekon said. "An optical cloak won't work on a capital ship."

An idea struck Kal. It had worked once. There was a good chance it could again.

"We don't need to sneak in," he said. "They'll let us on board."

Chapter Twenty-One

Kal | Mariga

Kal walked around the ship, trying to understand exactly what it was.

"Is this an assault corvette?" he asked. An assault corvette was essentially a beefed-up version of an assault ship. It was built to get several assault teams to a single location without relying on a carrier or battleship to get them there. Perfect for their mission.

Huang nodded. "Yes. Exactly."

The Jadid ship had the same organic sheen and materials as their much larger capital ships; however, where those were round and misshapen, this one was sleek and aggressive-looking. It was clearly designed to operate in atmosphere as well as space and had more than a touch of Human styling.

Huang told them that the ship had been found completely intact outside of Kasongo. From what they'd been able to tell, the ship hadn't been shot down. Instead, one of the thrusters had simply stopped working and the Jadid had decided to abandon it. Kal was glad to hear that they had had the same problem he'd faced countless times in the EDF, broken equipment. The bigger puzzle was why the ship hadn't been repaired *after* the battle.

Knowing the way that Jadid minds worked, Huang's forces were combing through the ship as they spoke to ensure there were no surprises waiting inside.

Bo and Ai stepped out of one of the troop ramps and walked to where Kal and the others were standing.

"It'll take about a day to retrofit and install the fold drive from the *McCullough*," Bo said. "The drive itself can be lifted out of the ship and placed in this one. However, there are some changes that will need to be made to adapt it to the other ship's systems."

"Excellent job, let's get started," Kal said and turned to Huang.

Bo turned back to the ship, but Ai held her ground. "Governor?" she asked.

Huang nodded. "Yes, scientist. Begin work." Ai turned around and quickly closed the distance toward Bo as she walked back to the ship.

Kal studied the two scientists as they walked away, talking softly to one another. Were they a couple? They'd spent an awful lot of time together, but he had no idea how romance among the Jadid worked—or if they even had romance. He knew that it wasn't anything like Humans.

"What about Ancients Musa and Kingsley?" Kal asked, turning towards Huang. "Are they coming with us?"

"No. They do not agree with what we are doing." Huang's lip curled in displeasure. "They will not stop us, cannot stop us, but they have made their displeasure known. They feel we are throwing our lives away."

"What're our chances? Assuming we don't get vaporized before making it to the ship."

"I am assuming that you want me to give an estimate. Or do you want me just to reassure you?" Huang had made several statements like that as they'd been talking the past couple of hours. It seemed like she was trying to understand Humans, studying them almost.

"I'm just looking for a rough estimate."

Huang nodded in understanding. "About a twenty-five percent chance. Fifty percent that we will be allowed to board the vessel and fifty we are able to prevent it from destroying Mariga."

"That's not too bad—"

"Now if you're asking about surviving the mission," Huang continued. "Then according to our analysis"—she glanced down to the comeca on her wrist—"the percentage drops down to five for any one person and zero that all of us will make it."

"I get the picture," Kal said.

As he spoke, a gout of plasma erupted from the side of the assault corvette, arced to the ground and landed near a group of seemingly unperturbed Jadid. The Humans in the area ran for cover.

"So the ship has to look damaged?"

"Not just look," Huang said. "It *must* be damaged. They will easily be able to tell if it's a facade."

Kal had remembered their success in getting the *Defiant Scream* between the two Jadid battle cruisers above Patagonia. The same concept could work again. All they needed to do was fool the Jadid long enough that they could get on board.

They would fold to the dreadnaught and send out an immediate hail on the open net. Their story would be that

Mariga had been attacked, and Ancient Baykara had ordered them to fold to the dreadnaught and be on standby. They had access codes that should at least make them seem legitimate. However, their ship's computer would automatically interface with the dreadnaught's and relay key information. If that exchange happened and they weren't damaged, the jig would be up as Kimathi liked to say.

"I don't think we'll get another chance at this," Kal confessed. "If we fail, Mariga will be destroyed, and Ancient Wang and his *Liberation Fleet*"—the words came out in a bitter rush—"will have won. Samsara Fleet won't be able to stand against them."

"Even if we are successful, I doubt your fleet will be victorious," Huang said unhelpfully.

"Thanks for that," Kal said.

"I do not think that false optimism is healthy. Especially when one is about to go into battle." Huang sniffed. "You must be realistic about your chances; it allows you to make rational decisions."

"Perhaps that's where Humans and Jadid differ." Kal knew there was no perhaps about it. "We need that optimism. It lets us to do things that our rational minds tell us are futile. And sometimes we're able to overcome those odds."

The Jadid governor hummed in thought. "Interesting. I think I understand what you're saying. Empirically, your forces have already accomplished more than I ever thought they could. Based on what I have read of the past couple years, it seems to be a pattern."

"Will your soldiers be ready for the assault?"

"Of course. We have been at war for almost the entirety of our existence."

"So one could say that you were *born* ready?" Kal raised his eyebrows in anticipation.

"I suppose. Yes. Though the phrasing is odd."

Kal groaned and rolled his eyes. He hated when jokes were wasted.

"So I told her that you could say they were *born* ready." Nicole chuckled.

"Thank you." Kal wasn't sure if she was humoring him, but she at least had the appropriate response.

Nicole grabbed her glass and took a slow sip. They'd given the Skulls a few hours of leave while the fold drive installation was completed. The team would assemble at the Foothold and go through final preparations for the mission. Nicole had spotted the small restaurant they were sitting in as they'd been wondering through the streets. When the portly owner had realized who they were, he'd brought a bottle of wine to the table and beseeched them to order whatever they wanted.

After the Torgham War, there'd been a similar outpouring of gratitude towards the EDF. Kal had felt extremely uncomfortable about it at the time. This night, he was willing to put aside his pride and enjoy the man's hospitality. There was a very good chance that this was his last meal, at least according to Huang.

"What are you going to tell Asha?" Nicole asked.

"About what?"

"Why you're leaving. I mean you and I both know that"—
she took a sip of her drink—"there's not the best chance of us
coming back."

Kal would be lying if he said he hadn't thought about it.
Frankly he didn't understand how the girl had become his
responsibility. But somehow, amidst everything else, she had.
She had picked *him*. Despite everything he was, everything
he'd done wrong, she looked up to him and believed in him.

"I'm not sure. Maybe we can talk to Kinawadi and Garcia,"
Kal said. "I mean, it's a small ask and I know they'd make sure
she was set for the rest of her life."

"Maybe," Nicole said doubtfully. "Though I doubt there's
a single person in the galaxy that can guarantee her safety.
Not with this war going on."

"You have a better idea?"

She sighed. "No, not really. Practically everyone Asha
knows is either dead or going to be with us on this mission. I
just hate the idea of leaving her alone. Again."

Kal imagined the small girl standing by the landing pads,
watching their ship leave with tears streaming down her face.
The image was so visceral and painful, he had to put down his
water and look away.

"I know what I want," Kal said.

"What *do* you want, Kal Norman?" Nicole smiled and
grabbed his hand.

283

"I want this war to end, and then I want to find some place where we can just be alone. You me, and Asha. She can have the life she's always wanted and so can we."

"A little family?"

That was the word Kal had been dreading. He'd had a family: Li Na, Stephen, and Lan Fen. When he'd lost them, he'd thought his life had been over. Until suddenly, it had started again. Ever since he'd realized how he'd felt about Nicole, he'd felt a sense of guilt. That guilt had only grown when Asha entered his life. Who was he to have another family, to have happiness? But he'd realized something amidst the death and sorrow of the war. He had the right to be happy, and his happiness wasn't a betrayal of the family he'd lost. There was a part of him that was missing. He was damaged, but he wasn't broken. Not unless he chose to be.

"Exactly," Kal replied with a smile.

Nicole smiled back and pulled him toward her.

A few hours later, Kal and Nicole returned to the Foothold. They'd already become well-known enough that the guards didn't check their IDs and simply waved them through with a smile. The smiles vanished as soon as they spied the Jadid on the other side of the Foothold's perimeter wall.

They made their way through the battered compound to the small building that had been set aside for the small contingent of Humans that would be going on the mission.

The door had been destroyed in the fighting, so no one noticed them as they entered. Kal pulled on Nicole's sleeve, stopping her in her tracks after they'd cleared the threshold; he wanted to be a fly on the wall for just a moment.

Deepta and Mother Ju sat together in a corner laughing and slapping each other on the back. Frederick Kinawadi seemed to be having an intense conversation with Sandra Chedjou in another corner. Sergeant Kimathi knelt behind Asha, braiding her hair while Chief Kanumba talked to both earnestly. They were all there, together for that one moment. So many people who had fought for or with Kal and Nicole were in that room, ready for the last mission.

It made him think of the people they'd lost as well: Sakata, Kondari, Pudari, Jae-ho, and many more. For once, it didn't fill him with complete sorrow. The depression and the darkness were fading, replaced by something else, acceptance perhaps.

"Sir." Kal looked up and realized that every eye in the room was on him. "Sir," Sergeant Kimathi said, "you ready to get this started?"

"Let's do it."

Kimathi kissed the intricate mass of braids on Asha's head. "You look beautiful. Like a proper princess." He stood up and faced the room. "Line up, folks. We got an hour and then we launch. Time to make them bleed."

"You're going again?" Asha asked. "I thought the last

mission was it."

She'd been waiting patiently as Kal and the others had gone through their final walk-through. Thanks to the schematics Bo had downloaded, they knew the ship's layout and where they needed to go.

"It's not like I want to go," Kal said. "It's my duty."

Asha giggled. "Duty."

Kal smiled. "You know what I'm saying."

She frowned. "You don't *have* to."

"I do," said Kal. "There are bad people out there, and I have to protect the good people from being harmed."

"There's already a buncha people going," said Asha. "They won't miss you."

Kal wished she was right but had a sneaking suspicion they would.

"I'll be right back. You won't even know I'm gone." Kal forced a smile. "You get to stay at the presidential palace, you know. That's a big honor."

"I don't care. I wanna go with you."

"I wish you could."

Kal wrestled with what to say. "When we come back, me and Nicole were thinking the three of us find a home and settle down somewhere. Would you want to be part of our family?"

Asha's blue eyes opened wide, and she smiled from ear to ear. "That would be the best thing ever. It's everything I ever wanted." The girl was practically vibrating with excitement.

"It's everything I ever wanted too." Kal pulled her in for a hug, and her small arms made their way around his waist. "We'll play games and just have fun adventures together."

"Yes. Yes. Yes!"

Ekon stepped out from behind a corner and motioned toward the waiting Jadid ship with his head. Kal nodded in acknowledgement.

"Listen, it's time for us to go." Kal pulled a small paper-strip photograph from his pocket gently placed it into Asha's hand. "Can you hold on to this for me?"

She looked down at the picture, her nose wrinkling in confusion. "What's this?" Her eyes widened. "Hey, that's you, 'cept younger. Who are they?"

"That's my family. My family that I lost."

She held the photo in both hands with a small look of reverence. "You lost your family too?"

"Yeah."

"Well, I know what that's like. I'll take good care of them."

"Thank you." Kal kissed her forehead and quickly walked toward the waiting ship. He didn't want her to see him cry.

Chapter Twenty-Two
Nicole | Patagonia

The Jadid assault corvette had been called the *Eternal Vengeance*, but everyone had agreed the name just didn't seem to fit. When Ai decided to rename it the *McCullough*, no one had any reason to argue.

The bliss that Nicole had felt in the past few hours was pushed to the back of her mind as she entered the dark hold of the ship. One thing she'd learned as a soldier in Samsara Fleet was to enjoy moments when you could because things could change quickly. Another was to know when to push everything else to the side and focus on the mission. There was unfinished business she had with Kal. Wonderful unfinished business. But that had to wait. Her only focus had to be the mission because if they failed, nothing else would matter.

The Jadid pilots announced their departure over the ship's public address system. Nicole couldn't feel or see anything as the ship lifted off from the pad. She was already in her battle suit—helmet off—as was Kal, Kimathi, and several other Skull soldiers. Since they only had ten of the suits, about half their small group would be assaulting the ship with nothing but a kinetic rifle.

"You ready?" Kal asked.

Nicole nodded. "You?"

"As ready as I'll every be." He gave her gloved hand a quick tap and turned back to the group with a smile on his face.

"Looks like it's inspirational speech time," Ekon shouted across the bay.

"Damn right it is," Kal shouted back. "There's no better time than now."

"We all know the drill," Deepta shouted. "Save your breath."

"Hey," Kal's shout brought the entire room to a standstill. The only sound Nicole could hear was the hum of the engine. "I practiced this speech and I'm gonna say it, dammit."

The group laughed and more than one person shouted an assessment of Kal's intelligence.

"I say we let him give it," Mother Ju said, still laughing. "I meant the poor man clearly spent all this time on it."

"Not all of it," Nicole said, immediately blushing.

A cacophony of whistles greeted her comment.

"Thank you," Kal said. "I appreciate the support." He cleared his throat. "Look, this is it. This is the last thing we need to do. There're three ways this ends. We all die." Another chorus of catcalls came from the group. "Or we survive, and the dreadnaught still destroys Mariga and either Wang or Baykara"—a few hisses erupted from the group—"control our galaxy. Or." He paused dramatically.

"Or what?" Grupp shouted.

"Or we win the whole damn thing." Kal yelled it out, rapid fire. "We take out that dreadnaught, we let Wang and Baykara take each other out, and we win the whole damn thing."

There was a weak cheer. Like Deepta had said at the

beginning, they all knew the drill. It was tough to motivate a group like that.

"I know. I know. A simple speech is going to get you fired up," Kal said, raising his gauntleted hands in the air. "But here's the thing. Every single person here right now has been through hell. You've been through more than any one person should have to endure. We're all soldiers, even if some of us don't wear a uniform. We'll win this because we've been fighting to survive for years, and we've had to win every single battle we fought to get here."

"We lost a bunch too, sir," Corporal Sato called out.

"You survived, that's winning," Kimathi called back.

"We're going to be landing soon," Kal said. "I want each and every one of you to know that you're family to me. This *is* our last battle, one way or another. We must win it. We've made it this far because of every single one of you, and we will win one more time because of you."

To Nicole's surprise they did let out a weak cheer. They were all too experienced to be nervous—or more accurately, *show* that they were nervous—but Kal's speech had touched something in them. Purpose perhaps. But Nicole thought it was more likely that it was hope. They weren't being marched off to the butcher. They were the butcher.

"We've folded next to the dreadnaught," announced the pilot. "Prepare for boarding."

Nicole placed her helmet over her head and quickly synced her suit to her implant. What had seemed foreign a couple of years ago was now as natural as putting on her socks.

The *McCullough* had several troop bays lining the exterior of the ship. Each one could fit about fifty people. At capacity, it would allow almost a thousand soldiers to disembark from the ship in seconds. With around two-hundred, it would take even less time.

Nicole patched her suit into the *McCullough's* computer to listen in on the communication between it and the Nasi dreadnaught.

"—we've received direct orders from Ancient Baykara. We are to stay with you until the—"

"Your authorization codes are several cycles out of date."

"This ship has been damaged. We were the only one that the command felt could be spared."

"Which still doesn't explain why you do not have current codes."

"Again, our system was damaged. Scan our ship and you will see that this is accurate."

There was a pause.

"Fine. You may land. Coordinates being transmitted."

They bought it? Nicole wondered.

Apparently, they had because the assault corvette was allowed to enter the dreadnaught and touch down within one of the many bays inside the enormous Nasi ship.

Wait, I've got to do one more thing, Kal said and ran toward the cockpit, his suit thudding along the soft weave floor of the troop bay. He was back as the bottom of their ship touched the landing bay floor, and the doors opened.

Nicole joined the others in running down the ramp with her weapon at the ready.

She expected to see the bay filled with ships and mechanics running to and fro as they realized they were being boarded. Instead, it was completely empty. The only thing breaking up the unremarkable walls of the cavernous room was a door easily large enough to fit a small ship through. The bay door through which the *McCullough* had entered was shut, leaving them trapped.

Dammit, Kal shouted over the net. *Be ready for an attack.*

Guess they didn't buy it.

"General Kal Norman," boomed a voice. "It seems like I will finally get a chance to meet you. I'm going to ask, just this once, for you to order your soldiers and *my* children to stand down."

Nicole recognized the voice. It was Grand Ancient Esma Baykara.

What do you want to do? she asked Kal through the team net.

I suggest you do as I say, Esma hissed over their net. In case you haven't figured it out, you are completely outmatched.

What are you waiting for? Kal asked. Why don't you send your Nasi children to kill us?

Oh, I don't think we need to start out that way. The glee in Esma's voice was unmistakable.

Nicole looked around, expecting to see automated weapons pop out of the walls or soldiers stream through the door, their rifles raised. Instead, there was nothing, just Esma's voice inside their heads.

"My children, you've been led astray," the Ancient called out over the net. "We can stop further bloodshed now. You do not have to be a part of this treason."

"You are the one guilty of treason, Ancient," Governor Huang shouted, brandishing her daton. The pain and anger in her voice was unmistakable. "You have betrayed everything that you taught us. Now you tell us to stand down?" She paused, searching for the words. "Screw you."

"I'm sorry to hear that." As soon as the words were spoken, several slugs flew from the wall, cutting down a cluster of Jadid in battle suits. Nicole had to turn her head away as she saw what the projectiles had done to the bodies—despite them wearing some of the most advanced and well-armored battle suits in the galaxy.

I'm going to say this again, Kal. Tell them to stand down. Place your weapons down, exit your suits, and lie on the floor.

At least she sounds angry, Nicole thought with trite satisfaction.

Stand down, Kal ordered over the team's net.

Screw that, Grupp said. He unleashed a barrage of everything his suit had—missiles, plasma, kinetics—at the far wall. An energy shield flared to life, absorbing the plasma bolts while the kinetic rounds and missiles went through. None of them had any effect. The brown weave walls weren't even scratched.

Again, several bolts flew from the wall, cutting Grupp

down before his missile launcher had even retracted back into his suit's shoulder.

Damn you, Ju shouted over the net.

I assure you, the walls are impenetrable, Esma said. You can fire whatever you want at them. It doesn't matter. You could fly your ship into them, and it still wouldn't matter. Did you think I didn't know who you were the second you folded in? I know exactly who you are, Kal Norman. You think you're doing something grand, something great, but you're only a spoiled child who's causing death and destruction. You've fought well. Even I can admit that. But you're fighting for the wrong side. Her voice softened on a dime. I want to help Humanity, to bring your people, my people, out of the stupor that has held them still for the past century.

When I left Earth hundreds of years ago, we expected great things, Esma continued. But only a small fraction of that has come true. When I returned, Humanity was just a weak species that was bullied and dominated by its neighbors. I can change that. The Nasi are here to help. Think about how much Humanity has already advanced in the few years since our return.

Nicole had to admit the woman wasn't wrong about the progress. Humanity had made enormous leaps and bounds, mainly in its military capabilities. But the cost had been insane. Earth and Wudexingqiu destroyed as a start. She wasn't sure if Esma truly believed what she was saying. If she did, she was insane.

Esma, you're right, your return has made us have to adapt

294

faster than we ever did before, Nicole said. Maybe we can work with you.

Kal turned to look at her. She couldn't see through his visor but could imagine the look he was giving her.

You know I worked for you before, she continued. Unwittingly, but still.

I can't imagine you take pride in that. Esma sounded doubtful and suspicious. That was okay, the speech wasn't for Esma; it was for someone else—Ai who was sitting in the cockpit of the *McCullough.*

We truly have made amazing strides in the past few years. Did you know that one of the Jadid scientists, Ai, developed a new fold drive? It can actually fold from anywhere, even from inside a ship. And the drive has almost pinpoint accuracy. Why you could even fold fifty meters forward without an issue.

I know you are trying to communicate something, Ms. Bergeron, Esma said. And I suggest you stop. I think have fully illustrated to you how far—

It's actually Colonel Bergeron, Ancient. Ai's voice cut through the net. And there's no way in hell we're stopping now.

The *McCullough* folded, instantly shifting position so that the ship was embedded in the wall, half of it inside the bay and half on the other side. The displacement of air knocked several people off their feet and the ship emitted several loud shrieks as the illumination from the weaves flickered.

Don't just stand there, Nicole yelled. Get out of the bay through the McCullough.

Everyone rushed forward and began running through the assault corvette's open troop doors as kinetic rounds streaked from the walls. They ran together, a smooth movement of Humans and Jadid fighting for their survival as one. The wall the ship had folded through lay on the ship's deck inside like a rug. As Nicole came out the other side, she was immediately struck by a plasma bolt. Her suit's shield flared a brilliant green, and the power reading dropped by half.

Let's move, Kal said. Orders remain the same. Remember this net is not secure.

The Humans, along with a large portion of the Jadid, rushed toward the ship's command center while the rest headed towards other locations to destroy the dreadnaught's main weapon.

As they made their way toward the command deck, Nicole was surprised by how little resistance they faced. There were a few groups of ill-equipped Nasi that tried to ambush them using bends in the corridors or intersections as cover, but they were quickly overwhelmed by superior numbers and weaponry.

The net was deathly quiet since everyone knew Esma could hear every word they said. The only sound Nicole heard as she ran through the corridors were the hydraulics and servos in her suit whirring away.

The dreadnaught's interior was like an insect's nest with countless tunnels crisscrossing and looping through each other. It made progress slow going but allowed their team to split into smaller groups and assault their objective from multiple directions. Nicole could tell from her tacmap that all three of the assault teams heading toward the command deck would reach it at the same time. After avoiding disaster, it was all going according to plan.

As her team neared their objective, all hell broke loose. The Jadid in the front of their formation were greeted with a wall of plasma and kinetics. The missiles followed right after. As she topped a rise in the tunnel, Nicole used her thrusters to dodge to the side, barely avoiding a Nasi missile that flew past her and detonated in a cluster of people. She didn't have time to look back and frankly didn't want to. Hopefully, they would have time to mourn later.

"Flank them," Kal shouted through his suit's external speaker as he motioned to the left.

Nicole started to move when her tacmap flickered.

No.

McCullough, are you there? Nicole asked.

No response.

She tried again.

I'm here. There was a raspy edge to Ai's voice as she slurred her words.

Nicole worried for her friend, but there was nothing she could do.

Did we just fold?

No response.

Ai, Nicole shouted into the net. She knew her friend must be injured but she had to know. *Did we just fold, dammit?*

Yes. A pause. We're at Mariga.

Nicole felt a sense of nausea. They were too late.

Chapter Twenty-Three
Kal | Mariga

Kal pushed aside the momentary pang of panic when he heard Ai say they were in Marigan space. Although the *McCullough* was no longer able to fly, its sensors and computers were still online, so he patched his suit to the ship's computer to scan the area.

As he'd feared, the only ships surrounding Mariga were Nasi. Now Esma had an entire fleet's worth of soldiers available to stop them. Already the call must have gone out asking for reinforcements as several assault craft, including a few assault corvettes, had started to move toward the dreadnaught. The ship would be inundated with thousands of enemy soldiers in a matter of minutes.

Time for a Hail Mary, Kal thought to himself, remembering Ekon's saying.

We're out of time, he called over the net. Nothing matters except destroying the ship before the reinforcements arrive. You hear me?

Screw it. Who cared if Esma could hear everything he was saying?

He could see on the tacmap that the other three assault teams on the command deck were bogged down. The Nasi clearly had been trying to delay them the entire time, and now with reinforcements coming, they'd taken positions boxing in every single one of their teams. What had been a relatively quick march had turned into a bloody mess. With time, he knew they could break through, but time was not something they had.

How much longer until those assault ships reach the dreadnaught? Kal asked.

No one answered. He'd heard Ai's response to Nicole, the scientist must be severely injured. Who knew what the effect of folding the *McCullough* into the walls and infrastructure of the dreadnaught had been?

Kal motioned for Sergeant Kimathi to come toward him. The sergeant rushed across the narrow room and took a knee next to Kal, plasma fire following him like a tail.

"We need to break through now," Kal said. "Those reinforcements get here, and this is all over. You understand?"

Kimathi gave a thumbs-up. "Got it. I'll take care of it. Just be ready to move." He turned then looked back at Kal. "Last time, huh, sir?"

"I don't know about that, but it's been fun either way. You get us on that bridge and we make it, the first round'll be on me."

Kimathi nodded then ran to a side of the corridor and knelt by a fire team. Seconds later he rushed to the opposite side and dropped to talk to another team. Kal had to admire the man's bravery. Every time he got up to move, he was greeted by a hail of slugs, plasma bolts, and a smattering of missiles. Still, he didn't hesitate as he marshaled their forces for the assault. Sergeant Jones would have been proud.

Now, Kimathi shouted over the net.

Every soldier began unloading their ammunition.

Grenades, missiles, even mines—which could do in a pinch—were hurled over the portable barricades the Nasi defenders had used to block the approach.

Before the smoke had dissipated, Kimathi shouted for them to advance, and the soldiers in battle suits leapt up and engaged their full thrusters, heading straight toward the enemy. Those without battle suits followed, looking for targets of opportunity as they rushed forward. The Nasi, though taken aback, greeted the assault with a wave of fire of their own.

The corridors lit up with the light of plasma bolts and the glare of flaring shields. Kal jumped up and joined the attack, aiming at the center of the Nasi formation. The few seconds he was in the air felt like an eternity. He heard several slugs bounce off his armor, and his shield registered at least one direct hit, dropping it to less than ten percent of capacity.

He collided with a Nasi barricade, sending both it and the soldier holding it catapulting back. Half his suit's status indicators were now red; he'd lost thrust, most of his shields, and most of his weapons. But he was alive.

Kal unleashed the blade tucked in his suit's gauntlet and began slashing at nearby Nasi while firing his sidearms with his other hand. For a moment he felt like he'd been swallowed in a sea of black Nasi battle suits. But then he saw that others had made it through the Nasi lines as well, and together, they were able to push back the tide and overwhelm the defenders.

Kal looked at the mission status in his HUD. All six of the

assault teams—three on the command deck and three in engineering—had sustained heavy casualties. They now had a path forward though.

He looked at his display and saw the assault teams in engineering were being pushed back by the Nasi.

"Kimathi, send two teams towards engineering," Kal shouted.

"Sir?" The disbelief in the tone was palpable.

"We need to take both," Kal said. "If we just have the bridge, the plan won't work."

Kimathi grunted in annoyance but obeyed the command and ordered the rest to press forward.

The bridge was less than ten meters from their position. As soon as they reached it, the five people remaining in their team, out of their group of about twenty, pulled out plasma cutters and started to slice through the access panel next to the door. Kal studied the tacmap feed from the *McCullough*. They had a minute or two, max, before the other Nasi ships reached their location.

General Norman, you must realize that this is futile. Esma sounded annoyed. *This—*

Three green icons appeared in the tacmap feed from the *McCullough*. It was Samsara Fleet. Somehow, they'd arrived before Wang's Liberation Fleet.

Ai, Nicole practically shouted through the net. *Can you hear me, Ai?*

Kal continued to focus on trying to enter the bridge. He had to hope Nicole could get through to the *McCullough* so the rest of the fleet knew they were taking the dreadnaught. None of it would matter if they failed and the dreadnaught destroyed the system.

"We're in," Kimathi shouted as the bridge door dilated open. Kal rushed through. It was completely empty.

"Where the hell is Baykara?" Nicole asked.

"She must have escaped," Bo said with disappointment. "I never thought she would do something like this."

Kal realized the disappointment wasn't that they hadn't been able to capture her or that she was planning on killing several billion innocent people. It was that she'd chosen to run and sacrifice her children. That was not something the Jadid did.

Kal looked around the bridge while Nicole continued to call for Ai over the net. The enormous chamber was littered with consoles, their viewscreens made from a sort of shifting sand that moved to create three-dimensional images. It all looked foreign to him, and he couldn't make heads or tails of anything around him despite having been on a Nasi ship before.

"Bo, any chance you can activate the ship's defenses?" Kal asked.

Bo shook his head. "Given time, sir. Yes. But there wouldn't be enough time for me to stop the assault ships."

Ma'am? Ai drawled.

Can you patch us through the McCullough so we can talk to the fleet? Kal shouted.

Fleet?

Yes, the fleet has arrived. Samsara Fleet. We need to tell them we're onboard the dreadnaught.

Already the fleet had launched several waves of fighters, which were zooming toward the dreadnaught. On their way over, they started taking out the Nasi assault craft, their red icons disappearing from the tacmap as they were destroyed.

That is why you never launch assault ships without an escort, Kal thought to himself grimly.

The Samsara Fleet fighters kept coming and began to strafe the side of the ship, while the three capital ships started to power up their main weapons.

Kal heard a click over the net.

Samsara Fleet, do you copy?

He tried again.

General Norman? It was General Petrov.

Yes. Kal felt relief wash over his body. Stop attacking the dreadnaught. We've captured the bridge. We just need time to disable the weapons.

Hot damn, sir, Petrov said. Nice job.

Thanks. But we're not done. We're holding the bridge, but engineering is still occupied and—

One of the lights affixed to the wall began flashing red.

"Sir, we've got an issue," Bo shouted out. "They're overloading the engines. We have about a minute until this entire ship goes."

Everyone, get off the ship, Kal shouted over the net. He

turned to Bo. "Are there escape pods?"

Bo shook his head. "No. Not on a Nasi ship."

Get to the nearest landing bay now, Kal ordered. Take whatever you can and get out of here.

The rest of the team had already started running back through the ragged hole Kimathi had cut in the bridge and were headed back the way they had come. Kal checked the map of the ship. The closest landing bay was two decks below them. It was going to be a close call.

"What about the *McCullough*?" Nicole asked.

Their ship was another two decks below the closest landing bay. There was no chance they'd make it.

"There's no time," Kal said. "It would be guaranteed suicide, and we don't even know if they're still alive."

As they neared the landing bay, they ran into another one of the assault teams that had come with them to the command level. They reached the main bay entrance as the third team appeared in the hallway in front of them and entered the bay en masse.

Kal said a silent word of thanks when he saw that the bay was filled with Nasi ships. The other two teams split off and ran to the closest two. Kal started to follow them and then noticed something in the corner of his eye.

"What's that?" he asked, pointing to a sleek vessel with a Human-like profile but made from Nasi materials. Something about it was familiar.

"My guess is that the Nasi have been doing experimentation of their own," Bo said.

"I'm not sure I wanna be trusting my life to an experimental ship," Kimathi said.

There was something about the ship. Kal felt drawn to it. "We're gonna do it anyways."

He ran toward the ship, confident the others were behind him, climbed up the back ramp and activated his suit's emergency exit procedures. He pulled off the helmet while the seams along his arms, legs, and back sprung open. Clamps that held the suit to his arms and legs popped open, and in seconds, he was out. Bo's Jadid battle suit was even faster though, and he was already in the cockpit turning on the ship's engines by the time Kal, Nicole, Kimathi, and Kanumba reached him.

"What the hell?" Kimathi said as he reached the cockpit.

Kal dove into the copilot's seat and assisted Bo in getting the ship's engines spun to life. As his fingers floated over the console with the speed and familiarity of muscle memory, he realized something. Although they were in a Nasi ship made from Nasi materials, its design and controls were identical to a Samsara Fleet Scout Corvette, the type of ship the Skulls had flown for almost all their missions.

Kimathi's confusion made sense now.

"They copied us," Nicole said.

"I guess we should be flattered," Chief Kanumba said.

The bay doors were already opening in front of them, revealing a field of stars tinged blue by the bay's atmospheric shield. The other two teams rocketed out of the bay, not even bothering to fully clear the deck before leaving.

"Get as much distance between us and the dreadnaught as possible," Kal ordered.

No sooner were the words out of his mouth than the enormous ship burst into pieces behind them with a brilliant flash. Their ship let out a groan and the consoles flashed red as the radiation and energy from the blast struck the ship.

"If we'd been any slower, we'd have been vaporized." Kanumba let out her breath.

"Just another mission for the Numbskulls," Kimathi said airily. "Now let's get to the *Ofira*."

They changed course and headed toward the three Samsara Fleet ships. They'd exited the dreadnaught on the opposite side from the fleet so Kal had to plot a course that would keep them safely out of the range of the radiation the wreck was emitting.

"Samsara Fleet, this is General Norman. Are we glad to see you." Kal was surprised to see even the communications systems were the same as on the Human models. It meant he could upload the encryption keys on his implant and speak over their private net.

"Likewise, general." It was General Petrov. "The Nasi fleet is heading toward us now. We've got to get out of here. As soon as you and the other teams from the dreadnaught are aboard, we'll fold out."

"Roger."

The seven-ship Nasi fleet easily outmatched the three Samsara Fleet ships. They'd split their force with five ships bearing down on the fleet and the remaining two staying in positions at either pole of Mariga. "I should tell you. Ancient Baykara was somehow able to break through the encryption on our tactical net. I don't know if she can intercept this communication or not."

"Thanks for the heads-up, sir." Petrov paused. "Esma, if you're listening, you can go screw yourself. We're sending you to hell where you belong."

No one answered, which Kal took for a good sign.

As the Skulls rounded the debris field that had been the dreadnaught, Samsara Fleet continued to move away from the planet, trying to prevent contact with the Nasi while still allowing the assault team survivors to land.

All six teams had been able to make it out of the ship before it exploded. A minor miracle considering how little time they'd had to escape. Kal's happiness over their success was dulled by the fact that the teams were only at half strength, and they'd lost the *McCullough* and its crew, including Ai.

He looked over at Bo. The man stoically monitored the viewscreens in front of him. Kal wasn't sure what to say. Did Jadid even talk about things like loss? Adding to Kal's hesitation to say anything was the fact that he didn't know the nature of the relationship between Bo and Ai. He suspected it was more than just professional, but how much more, he had no idea.

He also wasn't sure what they would do once they landed aboard the *Ofira*. Where was Wang and his fleet?

"Can you put General Samaha on a personal net?" Kal

asked. The net's encryption was something only he and Samaha had access to. Even if Esma had been able to infiltrate their other nets, it was highly unlikely she could access a private link.

"That's not going to be possible," General Petrov responded. "Get to the ship, and I can explain more."

"What does she mean it's not possible?" Kimathi asked.

"Means the opposite of possible," Kanumba retorted. "Like, it is not something that is in the realm of possibility."

"Sure missed your helpful feedback, Chief," Kimathi said. "But my question is *why*."

"We could sit here and speculate, or we could just get on that ship and then they'll tell us."

Kal realized that out of all of them, Kanumba had to be the most eager to return to the *Ofira*. She hadn't seen her son in months, and he was there, tantalizingly close. He doubted he would have been able to keep it together nearly as well as she was.

"Shit," Bo swore.

Kal turned to see what had caused the uncharacteristic reaction. The tacmap was lit up with a cluster of red icons. All of them right between them and Samsara Fleet. Liberation Fleet had arrived.

"There's Ancient Wang," Kal said. "Wonder what took them so long."

"Time to adjust our plan," said Kanumba. "No way we're making it to the *Ofira* now."

She was right. Samsara Fleet was no match for Wang's

Liberation Fleet. They would get slaughtered if they stayed where they were.

Unfortunately, the small scout corvette they were in was between Liberation Fleet and the Nasi. If they stayed where they were, they'd get crushed like a grape.

"We need to get the hell out of the way," Nicole said.

"We're working on it." Kal looked for the best possible avenue of escape. All he could hope was that Wang and Baykara's fleets would be so focused on each other that they'd ignore the small scout corvette between them.

Chapter Twenty-Four
Nicole | Mariga

Nicole watched as the two groups of red dots moved toward each other with their ship in the middle. As both disgorged fighters, the tacmap grew saturated with red.

Kal had shifted their course, moving them away from the two fleets and hoping to get enough distance from the planet and the conflict that they could fold away. The fleet had a backup rally point that could be used for situations like this; they just needed to get there. Thankfully, the Liberation Fleet seemed to be focused on the Nasi. Nicole couldn't blame them. If they were to win here, then they could just come back and clean up Samsara Fleet. What Wang didn't know was that General Zhou, his top Human lieutenant, was out of the picture. Subduing a population was much harder if you didn't have a familiar face at the lead. A lesson the Nasi had learned already.

"We got an open net transmission coming from the Liberation Fleet," Kal said. "Putting it on the screen."

Ancient Bao Wang's smiling face appeared on one of the viewscreens. "Esma, oh Esma. Where are you?"

Nicole wanted to punch the smug bastard. Hopefully she'd get the chance. Where Baykara was naked rage and vengeance, Bao was something much worse. A sociopath hellbent on gaining power for power's sake. He didn't believe in any ideology that Nicole knew of, rather his only allegiance was to himself.

"Come on, this is it," Bao continued. "The final fruition of our plans. Seems a shame if we don't at least talk before we finish it. We've known each other for so long."

Esma's scowling face appeared on the net. "Bao, you piece of shit. You backstabbing traitor. What could we possibly have to talk about."

"Just wanted to see your face," Bao said. "After all this, I feel like it'd be a tragedy if we didn't have a final chance to say goodbye. We had some good times, didn't we." His smile widened.

Esma seemed to be almost apoplectic with fury. Nicole imagined that over two hundred years of being together had given the Ancients ample time to understand exactly how to push each other's buttons, and Bao was smiling with glee as he pushed Esma's.

"You know we can still end this peacefully. Just tell your fleet to stand down. Our children don't have to die in this needless fight. We can still work together."

"You don't give a shit about our children," Esma snarled. "This has never been about anything but you. I can't believe I didn't understand that when I first told you about my plans."

"You went overboard," Bao said. "You destroyed the very thing you were trying to save. I can't let you continue. We can still lead the Humans and our children to a brighter future."

"You're not going to lead anything." Esma clicked off the line, and Bao clicked off a moment later.

"Man, those two have some issues to work out," Kimathi said. "Wish they didn't have two system-killing fleets to work them out with."

"We just need to figure out how to get out of here," Nicole said. Looking at the tacmap, they had a very small window before the two fleets would close around them.

"Looks like the fleet isn't folding out just yet," Kal observed. Samsara Fleet had received the other assault teams and moved orthogonal to the path of the two fleets. They could've folded away but were waiting for something or someone.

"They're not waiting for us," Nicole said. "So what are they waiting for?"

"They're sticking to the plan." Kal pointed to the tacmap. "See, their path is moving them around the planet. They're waiting to see how things develop, and then they'll attack whichever fleet seems to be winning."

"Or they're waiting for Samaha," Nicole said. The general's disappearance was more than just notable, it was completely bizarre. They were in the middle of the most significant battle the fleet had ever faced and their commander wasn't even there.

Kal nodded. "Probably both." He ran a hand over his hair.

When the clouds of Nasi and Liberation Fleet fighters merged and the capital ships entered each other's weapons range, the battle began in earnest. Though it looked like small flashes in the vast distance of space to Nicole, she knew that weapon systems of unimaginable destruction were being unleashed on each other. It was strange for her to think that all the weaponry, posturing, and fighting came down to looking like flickering stars on her screen.

"We're clear," Bo said. "We're at eight nines."

"Hold," Kal ordered. "Let's see what happens. We're clear enough we should be able to get away if they decide to focus on us."

Rather than engage thrusters to slow them, Bo let the ship coast through space as they watched the battle unfold. As expected, the Nasi fleet was outmatched. Enjoying a three to one numerical advantage, the Jadid belted away at them. The two ships that had maintained positions around the poles abandoned their positions to flank the Jadid, but their additional firepower had little effect on the progression of the battle.

"Never thought I'd be rooting for the Nasi," Kimathi said.

"Ain't that the truth," Kanumba muttered.

One of the Jadid ships went up, a temporary sun causing their viewscreen to dim. Another one exploded in a similar burst of light not long after.

"They're holding their own," said Nicole. "Might be our chance to head back to the *Ofira*."

"I feel like we have more options where we are," Kal said. "We'd still have to weave through quite a bit of the fighting. Right now, they've forgotten about us. I'd like to keep it that way."

That might have been true, but Nicole had the sneaking suspicion that there was another reason that he wanted them to be out there on their own. She'd always been shocked that he'd had a full career in the EDF. He bristled at the concept of command and was much more at home traveling through the galaxy in a small ship than being part of the leadership of a large fleet. He felt most comfortable and in control when it was just their small crew. When things were tough, Kal would much rather be in a small ship with a few people he trusted than on a capital ship.

"I'm gonna check out the suits," Kimathi said.

"Good idea. I'll join," Nicole said. She wanted to inspect the ship anyways. It was like nothing she'd ever seen before, a faithful recreation of a Human ship—their ship—using Jadid technology. Besides, there was nothing for her to do anyway. She was just a passenger.

They dropped down to the ship's bay and heaved the suits into upright positions and activated the boots' locking mechanism. Thankfully, the suits were all seemed serviceable, but Ekon still inspected each one in detail to make sure there was nothing they were missing.

Nicole took the time to study the ship's interior. She was shocked to see exactly how faithfully the Nasi had replicated their old ship.

Kimathi looked up from the suit he was working on as she reentered the bay. "How many of these ships have we crashed, ma'am?"

Nicole thought back, counting on her hands. "Four, I think?"

"Be nice to make it five," Kimathi said, tapping a foot against the weave decking. "I just like the number better."

"I really hope it doesn't come to that," Nicole said.

"They really did think of everything," Kimathi said. "I

mean other than the strange walls and lights and stuff, you wouldn't know this wasn't one of our ships."

"So other than what it's made out of?" Nicole arched her eyebrow.

"I'm surprised there aren't battle suits docks," Kimathi said. "Seems like this thing is ready to rock. A scout ship needs battle suits."

"It's experimental, they probably haven't had time to install them." A thought occurred to her. "I wonder what other experimental features are in here."

She returned to the cockpit. "Anything new?"

"We had four more Jadid ships and two Nasi ships go down," Kanumba said. "They're keeping us on the edge of our seats. Esma ain't goin' out without a fight."

"Have you had a chance to look through the computer?" Nicole asked. "They built this thing for *something*. I'm guessing there's more to it than meets the eye."

"I've been looking at the systems," Bo said. "The ship is remarkably similar in almost every aspect to the scout corvettes we've always flown." He frowned. "There's a different operational tree within the onboard computer though."

Nicole tried to look over his shoulder, but he was going through the menu so quickly that she couldn't keep track. On Human ships, much of what he was doing was accomplished through a link between the ship and the pilot's neural implant. Since the Jadid didn't have those, he had to page through the directories and manually fly the ship.

"There's options for cloaking on this thing," Kal said. He tapped the panel a few more times but nothing happened.

"Is it on?" Kanumba asked.

Bo tapped a light in the center of the console. "According to this it is."

There was another large blast as a Nasi ship went supernova. The battle was starting to clearly lean in the Jadid's favor. With only three ships left, the Nasi were fighting a stalling action against the much larger fleet of ten Jadid battleships and carriers.

"Samsara Fleet's moving," Bo said. "They're moving going in."

Sure enough, Samsara Fleet was barreling towards the rear of the Liberation Fleet. The Jadid remained focused on the Nasi, training every weapon they could on their mortal enemy. Nicole's guess was they were hoping to finish them off before Samsara Fleet was within weapons range. The Nasi had clearly noticed what was happening and were moving behind the planet, using it to stall the Jadid.

"General Samaha." Bao's face appeared on the screen again. "I see you've decided to join our little party. I also see you also have one of my ships." His face flickered in annoyance for a moment. Bo looked at Kal to see if he wanted to respond, and Kal shook his head. "I'll find out what happened there. But I'm afraid that this is the end of the road for our little alliance."

"It ended when you tried to kill us," Kal muttered at the screen.

General Petrov's face appeared on the screen. "Ancients Bao Wang and Esma Baykara, this is General Irena Petrov of Samsara Fleet. I'm ordering you to stand down."

"General Petrov," Bao chuckled. "Why am I talking to you? Where's your commander?"

"I repeat again, stand down." Petrov scowled at the camera.

"You lost your mascot, General Norman, and his entire crew. Now you've lost your commander?" Bao smirked.

"I'm taking your lack of acknowledgement as a refusal to comply. Under section three, article four of the United Earth Government code I am authorized in using legal force."

"Did she just make that up?" Nicole asked. She'd never heard of a UEG code.

Kal chuckled and nodded.

"Come and get me." Bao laughed.

Petrov smiled back, a look of anticipation on her face. "Oh, I plan to."

The net went dead.

❖

"Let's go," Kal ordered. He stood up and looked at Kanumba. "Chief, you want in here? You're a better pilot in your sleep than I am."

"It would be my pleasure." Kanumba sat down. She tested the controls, feeling for how the ship performed. After a moment she gave a contented sigh. "This'll do just fine."

Fighters streamed from Samsara Fleet's three capital ships

318

and jetted ahead to meet the enemy.

"This ship—" Kanumba paused and tilted her head as if realizing something. "We gotta name it."

"It already has a name in the system," Bo said. "*Righteous Victory.*"

"I think *Victory* will work just fine," Kal said. "I'm not too sure about the righteous part of it. Now let's see if we can make sure it lives up to the name. Get us as close as you can without putting a target on our backs."

The *Victory* sped toward the Jadid, its speed easily outpacing the rest of Samsara Fleet. Meanwhile the Jadid continued to press toward the Nasi, pushing them to the other side of the planet.

"We're nearing their estimated weapons range," Kanumba reported.

"The cloak seems to be working, they don't seem to be tracking us." So far, so good. But Nicole didn't want them to base their safety on a single light in the cockpit.

"Let's hold back for now," Kal said. "Stay out of the direct path between the fleets. We're going to have thousands of fighters saturating the area very soon."

Kanumba nodded, moved them to the side, and cut the thrust. As the three ships of Samsara Fleet approached the Jadid, they began disgorging another wave of fighters. Unfortunately, the *Victory's* computer system wasn't linked to the fleet's, so they couldn't see a real-time update of the fighters' status. But they could see that there were at least a thousand ships flying at the enemy.

"How the hell did they get that many fighters all the sudden?" Kimathi asked.

"They didn't." There was something in Kal's tone, but Nicole wasn't sure what it was. "Those aren't just fighters. They're scouts and merchant ships. They must have crammed every single ship they could get their hands on in there."

"Damn."

It was a desperate move. Then again, they *were* desperate. The average civilian freighter wouldn't stand a chance against a Jadid—or Human for that matter—fighter. The pilots in those ships were effectively going out there to be targets or distractions, a fact that Nicole was sure they knew.

As the crush of Human ships sped toward the rear of the Liberation Fleet, half of the Jadid fighters turned around and headed to intercept. The Nasi capital ships used the opportunity to turn as well and began firing at the Jadid with what Nicole figured was the last of their ammunition.

Icons started disappearing from the tacmap as the swarms of fighters collided. Flashes of red, green, and blue flashed across their viewscreen as plasma bolts collided with energy shields and missiles detonated.

"Sir, permission to engage." Kanumba spoke quickly, her hands balled up in anticipation on the console.

"Go ahead," Kal ordered.

Kanumba's hands danced across the screen as she activated their weapons systems and accelerated into the thick of the fighting. The one thing she didn't turn on was their shields.

"You're trusting the cloaking device?" Nicole asked.

"Yes, ma'am," Kanumba said. "I figure we can get a few good kills before they realize where we are. We put up those shields, and we might as well forget about the cloak."

Nicole wasn't sure she agreed, but then again, she wasn't the pilot. There was no point in having Chief Kanumba if they weren't going to trust her judgement. Another lesson she'd learned as a leader: you had to trust your soldiers to know their jobs better than you did.

As they approached, their targeting computer began identifying Jadid ships. Kanumba didn't fire though, clearly waiting until they were in plasma range. They would run out of missiles way before they ran out of targets. Provided they weren't killed first.

Finally, she let loose a small snarl as she fired a salvo of plasma rounds at a Jadid fighter. The rounds hit midship, and moments later, the icon disappeared from the tacmap.

"Get ready, everyone." Kanumba chuckled. "This is gonna be fun."

They swept along the front of the Jadid fighters, unleashing plasma as they went. Kanumba was a machine, her hands flying over the console and her head swiveling to from side to side. More than once, a fighter noticed and turned to face them. But Kanumba was faster and lit them up before they'd had a chance to fully react.

After several more kills, they'd attracted the attention of several Jadid fighters, which were on their trail. With a sigh,

Kanumba flicked on the *Victory*'s shields just as a bolt hit their tail.

"Hey, Chief, you sure you know what you're doing?" Kimathi asked.

"I never said I did," Kanumba said. "Besides, shouldn't you be somewhere else on the ship? Like the galley?"

"I figure this may be my last chance to see...well anything," Ekon said. "I don't want a food fabricator to be my last vision in this life."

Kanumba continued to weave through the Jadid, generously dispensing whatever plasma fire she had. Nicole was in awe of the woman's skill. The chief was an engineer; being a pilot was supposed to be her secondary function. But in this battle, she was a master of her craft.

Occasionally, one of the Samsara Fleet fighters would try and engage them, forcing them to send a quick message over the net. There was the chance that the enemy would intercept, but Nicole doubted Esma was able to get any useful information from their transmissions. Besides, they weren't exactly keeping under the radar.

The *Ofira, Merrimack,* and *Resolute Stand* reached weapons range and let loose with salvos of plasma and skip and conventional missiles. The Jadid fleet responded with fire of their own while also using their energy shields, gravitational shields, and point defense systems to absorb Samsara Fleet's attack.

The fleet's offensive started to have its desired effect. Three Jadid ships went up in brilliant rapid succession.

Although the three Human ships were banged up, they were staffed with veterans at every position. Almost every single person in the fleet had been fighting for years. Those that couldn't keep up had already been winnowed out.

"Chief, I should warn you that we're below twenty-five percent power on our shields," Bo said. "If we continue to fly in the middle of this, we're not going to survive."

"I don't really care if *we* survive, Bo," Kanumba said. "How many people we've fought with have died? Too many. It only matters that *he* survives."

No one needed to ask who she meant by "he."

Kanumba threaded the *Victory* between two Jadid fighters then spun the ship on its axis and took both out. As the two ships exploded, their engines going critical, another much larger explosion blossomed behind them.

Nicole looked at the tacmap. "The *Merrimack*," she said, the color draining from her face. "We just lost the *Merrimack*."

Chapter Twenty-Five
Kal | Mariga

Kal tried not to think about the thousands of lives that had been lost aboard the *Merrimack*. How many people did he know who had just died in that explosion? Too many to count. Perhaps more than he would ever really know. He pushed the images in head to the side and focused. The past year had taught him that. Originally, he'd been compartmentalizing the losses, burying them deep inside. He'd learned—finally—that he had to accept and move on.

The loss of the *Merrimack* changed the nature of the battle. The Jadid doubled the pressure and started to encircle the two remaining ships. From what Kal could tell from the sensor readings, the *Ofira* and the *Resolute Stand* were both in a bad place. Errant radiation was leaking from both.

The Nasi were also being beaten back. Their last three ships were also leaking radiation and emitting unstable energy signals. In contrast, the Jadid had eight ships remaining, and all seemed fully mission capable. If things continued the way they were, it was clear the Jadid would win.

Kal tried to hail General Petrov on a private net. They had to do something different if they were going to stand a chance.

"Sir?" Petrov's face was matted with sweat which had started to soak into her uniform.

"We're gonna need to shake some things up," Kal said.

"Like what, sir?"

He explained his plan. The first part was the most dangerous. As Kal thought about it, he realized the last part was as well. It finally dawned on him that the entire plan was entirely suicidal. Still, they weren't going to win by playing it safe.

"Just press through the fighters," Kal said. "Head straight at Esma and around Wang's fleet."

"We'll be exposing the *Ofira's* broadside to the Jadid," Petrov said. She didn't mention the *Resolute Stand* since Jadid and Nasi ships were almost spherical and didn't have broadsides.

"True," Kal admitted. "But if you've got a better idea, I'm all ears."

"I'm not sure I could come up with a worse one."

"Irina, I'm gonna ask you to believe in me. Just one more time."

General Petrov peered back at him, unblinking. "I'll always believe in you." She swallowed. "We'll make it happen."

Kal cut the net and walked back to the cockpit from the stateroom. Samsara Fleet's two remaining ships started moving around Wang's Liberation Fleet. As they moved, the Jadid fleet turned and began to blast them with fire while their fighters moved to block their path. Several missile salvos flew from the Jadid fleet toward the *Ofira* and *Resolute Stand*.

"Fleet's getting torn up, sir," Kanumba reported. "We gotta do something."

"There's nothing we *can* do," Kal said. He hated to admit it, but a scout corvette couldn't take on enormous capital ships. "We have to trust in their defenses."

"There is something," the chief seethed. "We can't sit here while our friends and families are being shot at."

Kal couldn't imagine what she was going through with her son was on the *Ofira*. A son she hadn't seen in months was so tantalizingly close, yet she risked losing it all. What would he do to try and give his own children a chance.

Anything.

Kanumba flipped off the shield, turned on the ship's cloak, and activated their thrusters. They headed toward the area between the two ships of Samsara Fleet and the Liberation Fleet.

"We did this before, sir," Kanumba said. "And damned if not I'm not gonna try my own hand at it." Jae-Ho, her husband, in one of the most masterful displays of piloting Kal had ever seen, had taken out several missiles in a span of minutes. Still, it was a move of desperation. But what were they if not desperate?

"Attention, fighters," Kal called out over the net. "Target all the Jadid missiles heading toward the fleet. Protect them at all costs."

A chorus of acknowledgments swept over the net. The men and women who answered knew what that order meant. They were being asked to sacrifice their lives in the hope that they would make enough of a difference that the fleet got through. Yet hundreds of ships acknowledged his orders and began to target the barrage of missiles flying from the Jadid.

Small pinpoints of light erupted on the screen, and icons

faded from the tacmap as Kal's orders had their effect. The Jadid missiles exploded as fighters and civilian ships blasted them. The maneuver also made those ships easy prey for the Jadid fighters. They began disappearing in small bursts of light as they were taken out from behind.

Kanumba was a woman possessed. She flew from missile to missile, taking them out, oblivious to the Jadid fighters on their tail. Although the Jadid clearly knew the *Victory* was there, they didn't seem to be able to get a good lock, their shots missing by a hair's breadth.

"Watch out," Bo shouted. He pushed the controls to the left.

Kanumba turned and shouted, but the words died in her mouth as a plasma bolt flew through the space they'd just left.

"We're not the only ones cloaked out here," Bo said.

They adjusted the rear cameras just in time to see the cloaked fighter turn away and move through the line of Human ships, picking them off.

"That sneaky bastard," Kanumba muttered to herself as she reoriented them toward the last sensor reading they had of the ship.

It became a game of cat and mouse. The *Victory* and the other ship danced through the missiles and fighters. Occasionally they'd see a faint icon on the map and steer toward it. But mostly they relied on Kanumba's anticipation of the enemy ship's actions.

"Dammit, I've lost them." The chief slapped her hand against the console in frustration.

"I'm not seeing anything on the tacmap," Bo said.

Kal looked at the map at his command console. He didn't see anything either. They were an island in the sea of ships and munitions. The battle raged around them, but there was not a single ship close to them. Putting it another way, they were sitting ducks.

"We need to get out of here," Kal said. "There's nothing hiding us from anything else out here. If that ship's tracking us—"

Kanumba abruptly slammed the yoke up, flipping them completely backwards, then maxed out their acceleration and let loose with a barrage of plasma fire. That's when Kal saw it; the enemy ship. It had just let loose with a volley of fire of its own. The shots streaked past the *Victory,* but Kanumba's fire hit the cloaked ship directly in its prow. Kal could see the plasma searing through the hull as the ship sailed past them. A moment later, it exploded in a burst of light.

"How'd you know?" Bo asked.

"I didn't," Kanumba said. "It was just a feeling." She shrugged.

"I'm glad you're the one flying," Kal said.

"Me too, sir." Kanumba flashed him one of her trademark smiles, accentuating the scars across her face. "Looks like the fleet's made it around the Jadid."

"Let's catch up."

Kanumba altered course to follow Samsara Fleet as their two ships headed directly toward the center of mass of the Liberation Fleet ships currently engaged with the Nasi. They had circled around had turned and were chasing after them and closing fast.

Kal shook his head as he studied their situation on the tacmap. The Samsara Fleet fighters had done their job, preventing the Jadid missiles from destroying the *Ofira* and *Resolute Stand*, but the cost had been tremendous. He estimated less than a quarter remained.

He realized that they were all going to collide at the same time. The paths of the Liberation Fleet, Samsara Fleet, Nasi, and the *Victory* would intersect almost exactly at Mariga.

The portion of the Liberation Fleet which had been facing the remaining three Nasi ships continued to fire on them, ignoring the two Samsara Fleet capital ships that were approaching fast. As the *Ofira* and *Resolute Stand* came close, they unloaded a volley of skip and conventional missiles. On the tacmap, the missiles appeared as small dots, but Kal knew any one of them had the potential to destroy a Jadid ship. The Nasi, understanding what the *Ofira* and *Resolute Stand* were doing, picked up their rate of fire, replying to the Human's barrage with one of their own.

Everyone in the cockpit shouted in glee as a Jadid ship disappeared from the tacmap and then another a few seconds later. The Jadid changed direction, but it was too late. The two remaining Human ships were among them and began to fire with every weapon they had, strafing their sides, while the Nasi assaulted them from the front. Two more Jadid ships went dead, leaving one remaining from the portion of the fleet that had been engaging them.

329

The Nasi reoriented their fire and directed it at the portion of the Jadid Fleet that was trailing the two Samsara ships. The Jadid were ready for it and were also in a much better position than the ships that had just been destroyed. They'd already slowed down and immediately responded to the Nasi fire with their own.

One burst of light, then two more in quick succession, and the final Nasi ships were gone. As their icons faded from the tacmap, a Jadid battleship went up as well; the Nasi had gotten in one last good shot before their demise.

"They're gone." Kal jumped at Kimathi's voice in his ear. He wasn't sure when the sergeant had returned. But there he was staring at the screen.

"Good riddance," Kanumba said.

"So that's it? Esma's gone?" Nicole asked.

"I guess," Kal said. It seemed so sudden, so anticlimactic. He'd always imagined Esma Baykara dying in a blaze of glory. In a way, he guessed she had.

The Nasi had been destroyed, but the Jadid were still very much a threat. There were five Jadid battleships and only two Human ships remaining. Besides that, both the *Ofira* and the *Resolute Stand* were clearly barely operational. They were emitting spikes of radiation, and their engine output readings were unstable. Zooming in on them on his console, Kal could see small clouds of debris around portions of the ships, places where missiles or plasma had made it through their defenses.

"This is not looking good," Nicole said.

"We've just got to keep fighting." Kal knew the reality of the situation. But he refused to give up hope. He scrambled to think of some way they could even the odds, but nothing came to mind. They were outnumbered, outgunned, and on the edge of losing everything. If the Jadid won this battle, there would be no coming back.

Think. Think.

Kal continued to draw a blank even as he watched the remaining Jadid ships accelerate to chase the *Ofira* and *Resolute Stand*. Even as he saw the Jadid fighters, now unchallenged, swarm the two ships. Even as he saw the last two ships in Samsara Fleet turn and slow to face their Jadid pursuers for a final time.

Three icons appeared on the tacmap directly behind the five Jadid ships, and General Aamina Samaha's smiling face appeared on the viewscreen.

"Oh, Bao," Samaha called in sickly sweet voice.

Bao appeared, looking as serene as ever. "Aamina, so nice to see you."

"Last chance to surrender, my *old friend.*"

"Surrender?" Bao laughed. "I don't think so."

"I'm so happy you said that." The transmission cut off.

"What are those ships?" Kal asked.

"I think they're...Kurz?" Kanumba could not have sounded more confused if she'd tried.

Kal was also confused. The Kurz fleet had been destroyed. How were they now there with three new battleships?

However, the Kurz *were* there, and they had folded in close—very close. They released their fighters and accelerated towards the rear of the Jadid formation. Caught between the two forces, the Jadid chose to take on the weaker two fleets first, blasting the *Ofira* and *Resolute Stand* with every weapon they had. The two ships adjusted course and accelerated away from the planet while also firing what few weapons they had left. Their rate of fire dropped as they were forced to divert energy from their weapons to their aft shields in a bid to stave off destruction.

The three Kurz ships reached missile range and immediately sent what seemed like every missile they had at the Jadid. Kal held his breath as he watched them pass through the cloud of Jadid fighters and start getting picked off, one by one.

Finally, one made it through the fighter swarm and burst apart a Jadid carrier like a piece of rotten fruit.

"Sir, the *Resolute Stand*'s emissions are starting to spike," Kanumba shouted.

It meant the ship's engine was becoming unstable. The first signs of death.

"She's changed her acceleration," Bo said wonderingly.

"She's gonna ram—"

Nicole wasn't able to finish her sentence before the Jadid-turned-Human ship exploded in a blast of light, unable to reach its target.

"Damn." Ekon shook his head.

Kal zoomed his console on the *Resolute Stand*'s remains.

A large chunk of the now destroyed ship continued forward and crashed into a Jadid ship. The front of the Jadid ship bowed in, bending for a moment before exploding outwards in gout of atmosphere, bodies, and debris. It swung to the side and its engine went dark as its power failed.

"Made 'em pay at least," Ekon said softly.

"Not a lot of help to them now." Kanumba switched the viewscreen to face behind them.

The Jadid moved away from the planet, their final four ships trying to get some distance to escape the battering from the three Kurz ships. As he watched, Kal realized the Kurz battleships were still not fully armed. After the initial onslaught, they'd been using plasma and kinetic fire exclusively. Their shields, though strong, were already faltering under the weight of the regular missile fire from the four remaining Jadid ships.

Another of the Liberation Fleet ships split, bursting apart at the seams. The three remaining ships turned and concentrated all their fire on the Kurz, trying to prevent their inevitable destruction.

Suddenly, one of the Kurz ships starting listing, its thrusters stopped, and it began drifting away from the field of battle. The Jadid redoubled their efforts on the remaining two ships, trying to knock them out before the *Ofira* was able to get back within missile range. They were too late though, the *Ofira* launched a volley of skip missiles, which appeared and disappeared on the tacmap, and headed straight for the remaining three Jadid ships. A moment later, one of the missiles hit true, and another one of the Jadid ships disappeared in a brilliant flash.

"They're running," Nicole shouted, leaning forward to stab a finger at the screen. "The bastard is actually running."

It should have been a glorious moment, but Kal's fury overwhelmed everything else. Bao Wang. The man had been at the center of it all, scheming with Esma while at the same time planning to betray them all in a senseless bid for power. And now he was running away. Worst of all, the Kurz ships and the *Ofira* were not giving chase.

Kal stabbed at the console and went onto the fleet's net.

"What are you doing? We can't let the bastard get away."

"Kal, we split our forces and we risk everything." Samaha regarded him evenly over the net. "We can pick them off one by one. We chase now and we're playing right into their hands."

"Ma'am," Petrov said. "I know what you're saying is true. But I just don't care. We let them get away, and they'll come back. We *can* end this here and now."

"Or they could end us," Samaha said. "A lucky shot or a dumb mistake and it's all over. Our forces are even, but we lose a ship, they'll outnumber us. This is our window of opportunity, and I don't want it to shut."

Kal tried to remain calm, but Bao's smirking face crawled into his field of vision. He couldn't let the smug asshole get away. He turned to Bo. "Do you know which ship Wang is on?"

Bo shook his head. "I tried to triangulate the signal when

he was transmitting. As expected, he was communicating through his fleet's net. There was no way to isolate which ship he was on."

"Could you now though?"

"Could I track him now? Not unless he transmits." Bo tapped a finger on his console thoughtfully. "I doubt he would do that though. The Ancient is too careful to hide his tracks."

"Never underestimate the power of ego," Kal said. "And Ancient Wang is all ego."

He slapped a grin on his face and started broadcasting on the open net.

"Hey Bao, where you goin'? After all the scheming and plotting, betraying everyone you cared for. Scratch that, who cared for you, you still lost. You couldn't even kill me when you had me right in your grasp."

Kal forced himself to laugh. "Oh, and now you're stuck here. So even your precious immortality is gone. Your people, what are left of them, will continue without you. You'll either die in the loneliness of space or find yourself shot in the back by one of your children.

"When you do die, I just want you to remember who sent you to hell. I hope you die knowing that your name will forever be associated with evil and failure. Your dream of—"

"Kal Norman, you do keep turning up, don't you?" Bao looked less than pleased at the fact. "It's like stepping in dog crap."

"You think you're going to escape?" Kal asked. "You

sacrifice your fleet and get away?"

"I'm willing to play the long game, Kal." Bao smiled. After everything that happened, the man was still smiling. "You have this victory, but I'll be back. My flagship is faster than anything you've got, and I'm not stranded here, not by a long shot. Just remember that I have all the time in the universe."

"His ship is this one." Bo pointed at the tacmap. "He's not lying; that ship *is* fast. Their last fighters are trickling in and then they can fold away."

Kal felt his heart sink. Could Bao have a way to travel back to his universe? Kal wouldn't be surprised if the man had a plan for the next hundred years. He was right: if he escaped, Kal would always be looking over his shoulder waiting. The worst part was, there was nothing they could do about it.

"Just remember as you declare victory and have your little celebrations, I'll be out there. And I will return."

"The hell you will." Esma's face appeared on the net. Her lips locked into a snarl, her brown hair matted around her round face, and her eyes wide with what Kal could only describe as mania. "You thought you were gonna get away, Bao?"

"Uh, what is this?" Bao waved a hand in the air.

"This is vengeance, Bao. I told you before, I'd rather you lose than me win. Guess we both lose." She laughed. "After everything—surviving the landing, having our children, building a society—this is how it all ends. Not the way I would have chosen, but at least we'll be together in the end."

Bao dropped the smile and his eyes widened as he

realized what was going on. "Esma, whatever you're thinking of doing, just stop. It doesn't—"

"Yes, it does."

Both their faces disappeared from the net.

Nothing happened. Kal watched all three Jadid ships continue on their courses away from the planet with the sharp pain of defeat gripping his heart. Bao would get away. There was no way to stop him.

A bright ray of light glittered on the hull of one of the ships. Kal zoomed in. It looked like the ship had sprung a leak and light was escaping into space. The leak turned into a rupture and the ship's skin peeled apart as an explosion tore through the hull. It became too bright to watch, and the viewscreen dimmed to black. When it was all over, the devastation was complete. All that remained of the vessel and the two Ancients was an expanding mist of debris.

Chapter Twenty-Six

Aamina Samaha | New America

Retired General Aamina Samaha stared out of the ritzy penthouse hotel room she was in. It had been six months since Samsara Fleet had finished off the Liberation and Nasi Fleets. The relief of victory had been short. They'd won, but they'd lost even more. Their homeworld and one of their colonies were gone. Billions of Humans were dead, not to mention billions more of other species.

She'd wanted to immediately go into her retirement; she'd spent three straight years traveling through space in various battleships and carriers and would be delighted if she never stepped into another one. However, there were some things she had to do before she could hang up her uniform for good. Now she had fulfilled her duty and could finally relax.

The news feeds on the interplanetary net—which had been fully restored—had hailed her a hero. Defender of Humanity. Supreme Commander. The Great Negotiator. But she felt like nothing more than an old woman. What the news couldn't capture, and what people didn't want to hear, was that she wasn't a hero. She was a woman who'd done what she could as best she could. She'd made decisions that she'd have to live with the rest of her life. Decisions no hero would have ever made.

As soon as she'd announced her retirement, the presidents of all three Human colonies had approached her to ask what her plans were. Aside from Garcia and Kinawadi, the only thing they cared about was whether she was going to run for office or if they could use her in their campaigns. Her popularity was such that no politician could ignore her.

She'd told them to leave or else she'd do everything in her power to make sure they lost their next election. Except for Garcia and Kinawadi. She'd reminisced with them for a while and *then* told them to leave.

At least she'd been able to secure assurances that she could have a small parcel of land in the countryside of New America. She'd been taking day trips and found the perfect little vineyard to take care of. The land with its cool breezes, sloping hills, and high altitude was perfect for a vineyard. It was the fulfillment of a dream that she and her husband had had years ago.

Except he wouldn't be a part of it.

A small bell chimed, and Aamina padded to her door. General Irina Petrov, resplendent in her formal Samsara Fleet uniform, stood on the other side.

"You mind if I come in, ma'am?"

"Just call me Aamina."

Petrov shook her head. "Apologies but I just don't think I can bring myself to do that."

Aamina rolled her eyes but appreciated her former subordinate's gesture. She waved her into the room and poured a glass of wine.

"So how goes the fleet?"

Petrov shrugged as she took the glass of wine offered her. "Chaos as aways. Only a different, better kind of chaos."

"Ah, the life of a soldier."

"We've had a few Jadid submit applications to join the fleet."

Aamina whistled. "I bet that was received well on *all* sides."

"Yup." Petrov sipped the wine, made a face, and set the glass down. "The two Ancients were furious, and my staff says it would be a security risk."

"What do you think?"

"There's no fighting the future, and the Jadid are part of our future whether we like it or not. There's already significant evidence of an oncoming Jadid population boom."

"Like bunnies, eh?" Aamina arched an eyebrow and smiled.

After Esma and Bao had wiped each other out, or more precisely Esma had wiped them both out, the remaining Jadid and Nasi had surrendered quite peacefully. Something about the loss of their two leaders had extinguished their will to fight. The process of rounding them up and determining how they would be integrated into society had been a long one and had been almost as draining as the war itself. Many of them were still in camps, but they were in the process of being released and seemed to want nothing more than what Aamina did: to find a quiet spot and settle down.

The gateways between the Human and Jadid universes had been reopened but surprisingly few of them wanted to return to their home.

"Of course, we also have the question as to what the fleet will even be," Petrov continued. "Seems like the planets want our protection but don't want our authority."

Aamina took a small drink of the wine produced by her new estate. A bit tart, but one got used to it after a while. "Sounds like you've got a lot to work on."

"I'm sure you do too."

"Oh, I think tending to the vines will be challenging, just in a different way."

"Tell me, how did you get the Kurz to come to Mariga?"

The former general sighed; so many people kept asking her this question. She kept giving the same answer. "Simple. I just explained what was happening and asked. For all their issues, among them a distinct lack of humor, the Kurz always adhere to their treaties. I reminded them of that fact and that if we failed, the Nasi or Jadid would certainly be coming after them eventually."

"It was their only three ships, and they weren't even fully finished."

"The Kurz had made a commitment, simple as that."

Petrov looked at her skeptically, then took another sip of the wine and shuddered. "Where did you get this, ma'am? Gift from an enemy?"

Aamina couldn't help smiling. "It's from my new vineyard. Unique, isn't it?" Petrov nodded. "Don't worry, whenever you're here on New America, I'll make sure to send you a case."

"Lucky me."

Petrov was a bad liar.

❖

Consul Madeline Huang | Patagonia

Madeline Huang studied the Foothold. They'd done a lot of work in the past half-year. Rebuilding the compound to working order had been a full-time job. Thankfully, a steady trickle of Jadid survivors and reformed Nasi had helped to make the work go faster.

"They're doing well," Huang said to Red.

The former senior officer nodded her head. "Yes, I agree. Everything is going faster than expected." She looked pleased.

Opening the gateways had sent the reconstruction into overdrive. The resources and workers from Altterra had been invaluable. Despite her misgivings about coming to the Human's universe, Madeline was ashamed to realize that she was starting to prefer it to her home. The strange way things worked in the universe now felt normal to her, and for the first time in her life, she felt at peace.

Of course, she'd had to grapple with a new concept: aging. It had become apparent that whatever had allowed her to live for hundreds of years wasn't present in her new home. She, like most of the Jadid, was okay with that. She'd lived what she'd considered a full life and the chance to have a future—even if it was finite—that was full of hope was worth the cost.

Madeline dismissed Red and walked along the Foothold's reconstituted wall, studying it as an artist would look at their work. She'd decided not to rearm the camp, not that Kinawadi or Garcia would've let her anyway. Instead, she saw the wall as a temporary structure. As Jadid and Human continued to integrate, she hoped it would be torn down, the last vestige of the separation between two races which were long-lost cousins.

"Madeline!"

She turned around to see Presidents Garcia and Kinawadi approaching, their security detail in tow. It was amazing that they'd found a peaceful way to reconcile their desire for power. They harped at each other, but the banter was clearly friendly. Somehow, they'd found a way to make it work. And their people loved them for it.

"Hey."

"How are things going, Madeline?"

"Not bad. We should be done soon."

Another thing that astonished her was how quickly she was developing Human mannerisms. Strange to think how much they had annoyed her at first. She wasn't going to pick one of those inane friend names like many other Jadid did, but still, she was becoming more Human whether she liked it or not. And she was ashamed to admit she did kind of like it.

"We were thinking. We should have a ceremony to celebrate the completion of the Foothold and broadcast the holo over the net," Kinawadi said. "Let the people know that we are one planet, one Patagonia."

Huang considered it. Already there were Jadid that were intermingling with the Humans. Her people's futures were tied to them, one way or another. And vice versa, the defunct United Earth Government wouldn't be returning, and each planet seemed to be charting their own course. Patagonia would be no different.

"I think that may be a good idea," Huang said. She forced a smile; that always seemed to make the Humans pleased.

There was a lot for them to work out. Who would take the lead. What the actual message would be. Who would be in attendance. But for now, there was a ray of hope for Madeline and her people.

Her smile became genuine.

Command Sergeant Major Ekon Kimathi | Lidice Station, Mariga

"They're ready, Sergeant Major."

Staff Sergeant Cho stood at parade rest at Ekon's door. She looked like a noncommissioned officer from a recruiting holo, her uniform perfectly tailored and not a single hair out of place on her blonde head. He looked down at himself. He'd forgotten to shave this morning, there was a trace of breakfast on his lapel, and he'd somehow managed to untuck his shirt despite having just adjusted it only minutes before.

She hesitated. "There are some Jadid among the recruits."

"And why wouldn't there be?" Ekon asked. "They'll want to protect our planets as much as we do." He raised an eyebrow. "You got a problem with them being here?"

She hastily shook her head, her professional veneer wavering for a moment. General Petrov had warned Ekon there would be recruits in the class. He hadn't mentioned it to his staff because he wanted to see their response. Samsara Fleet was about to also get Kurz, Z'Ta, Qudoru, and even Torgham recruits in the upcoming weeks. It would truly be a multispecies force.

"Let's do this." Ekon stood and followed the young staff sergeant through the station's hallways towards the new recruit area.

What wasn't clear was what Samsara Fleet's relationship would be with the planets it was sworn to protect. Already each colony had asked about how they could send people and materials to help the fleet while also making crystal clear that they retained their sovereignty. The Jadid and Nasi were gone but the galaxy was still a dangerous place, and Humanity needed their protectors. The planets were definitely grateful for the fleet's help but equally unwilling to be under their control.

He'd thought that he would go back to New America after the war. Perhaps stay with his parents a few months and then resume his studies. However, after a two-hour conversation with General Petrov of which he remembered very little, he found himself as the new command sergeant major of the recruit training facility on Mariga 's Lidice Station, The Crucible.

Already they had more volunteers than they knew what to do with. Petrov had told Ekon to start training them and they'd figure out the rest, like pay and equipment, later.

He walked into the bay they'd turned into a training area.

Rows of fresh recruits, at least five hundred, were assembled at parade rest. The cadre stood around them, their faces impassive, as if they were looking at something they'd just run over.

It was exactly as Ekon had planned.

He saw Captain Sandra Chedjou smiling and winked at her. He couldn't wait to hear what she would have to say at dinner that night.

Next to her stood Bowen Nguyen. The scientist had also been roped into the training center. He'd be teaching the communications recruits defensive and offensive network warfare. It wasn't his specialty, but Bo was basically a genius at everything and could do the job in his sleep. Since the battle, he had retreated into his shell. One night, after a few drinks, Bo had admitted that he and Ai had been in love. The loss of his companion, as he called her, had been devastating.

Ekon guessed that was why the Jadid had agreed to work at the Crucible. It gave him something to do while he worked out his loss and found what he wanted to do in the new universe he found himself in. The one thing Ekon would make sure of was that Bo never felt alone.

"Recruits, attention," Cho barked.

The formation came to attention in fits and starts as young faces looked at each other hesitantly. The four Jadid at back smoothly snapped to attention, their faces as impassive as the cadre.

"Listen up," Ekon shouted. "I'll only say this once. Thank you for volunteering to defend our planets. Choosing to be here took a lot of guts, and you should know that you have my respect for doing so. However—"

He paused a nice languorous pause.

"You will be our front line of defense. So any gratitude I might have is greatly outweighed by my desire to make sure you don't screw up and get someone killed. Every single member of my team is here to make sure that doesn't happen. If you don't do what we say when we say it, I'll make your life a living hell."

Ekon quickly provided some examples of the great things Samsara Fleet had done. Telling them stories about the missions they'd been on and stressing how teamwork and training had been the key to their success. His goal was simple. Make sure they knew what they were getting into and inspire them to do their best at it. The Nasi and Liberation Fleet were gone, but Samsara Fleet could never afford to go soft.

Based on the crescendo of guttural shouts at the end— even from the Jadid—it sounded like he'd been successful.

With a flourish he turned on his heel and walked back to his office. He was starting to realize that Petrov hadn't exactly been forthcoming in his duties. It looked like it was going to be equal parts paperwork and speeches with a dash of actual training thrown in.

But he wouldn't want to be anywhere else.

Nicole | Mariga

347

Nicole checked the time again on her implant. Kal should be done shortly. They had to leave soon. Jae-Ho and Asha ran circles around the table as she and Taisha sat drinking their chai.

"So you found them," Nicole said.

"Yes, turns out some of Jae-Ho's family is on New America," Taisha said. "I've been talking with them, and they've offered to take us in."

"That's amazing." Nicole placed her hand on her Taisha's reassuringly. "You deserve it after everything that's happened."

"Not sure if I do, but he does." Taisha nodded towards her son as he ran past. "Already got a few leads on some local piloting jobs. I'm not taking anything interstellar, but they need people to help with commerce and transportation in the system."

"There's a lot more ships flying already," Nicole said. "The traders are making up for lost time."

"Rebuilding takes materials. I'm hoping maybe I can see a little of that post-war profit for Jae-Ho and me."

"I'm sure you will." Nicole wouldn't be surprised if Taisha was running her own trading company by the end of the year. Sure she seemed mild when you first met her, but the former chief was one of the most determined people Nicole knew.

"Where's General…Kal?"

"General Kal *should* be along shortly," Nicole replied. She'd noticed that the man was taking his sweet time to do the simplest things lately. He saved the galaxy one time and felt like everyone needed to align to his clock.

"Strange to think that after everything we've been through, we end up here." Kanumba gestured to the bar around them.

Nicole remembered something General Samaha had said to her a long time ago. That people like Kal Norman would be forgotten by history. She'd been partially right, Nicole had realized. Kal Norman, the man, was somewhat forgotten. But Kal Norman, the legend, lived on throughout the galaxy. She'd heard countless tales of his exploits, each more fanciful than the last. Some of them even had a slight ring of truth to them. Most were complete fabrications.

"Not that strange I don't think."

"I can't believe Petrov let the two of you go."

"She got Ekon," Nicole replied. "She knew there was no way she was gonna get Kal and me. We're a package deal."

"Son of bitch." Kal appeared as if from thin air, sweat beading off his brow. "Goddamn port controls took forever…"

"You ready, sir?" Taisha raised an eyebrow.

"Eh." Kal shrugged. "Ready as I'll ever be. Time to see a little bit of the galaxy."

After everything he'd done, the only thing Kal had asked for was a new ship. A Shreen, just like the model he'd had before, albeit with several high-end modifications. They wouldn't exactly be traveling in poverty. They'd also been given false identities so they could escape the notoriety and attention their names would carry.

"Sir, it's been a pleasure. You gonna stop by?" Taisha stood with her arm extended.

To her clear surprise, Kal walked around the table and hugged her.

"Damn straight we'll be there. You let us know anytime you need us."

"Will do. You too, sir."

"Asha, say bye to your friend," Nicole said. "It's time to go."

After she'd given a final hug goodbye to Jae-Ho, Asha grabbed Nicole's and Kal's hands, and they walked off towards the landing bay.

Kal Norman | Mariga

It had been over thirty years since Kal had first left Mariga. He had the same sense of cautious optimism as they made their way through the crowded port. He didn't know what was going to happen, but he was hopeful, and that was what was important.

He looked down, and Asha met his eyes and smiled.

The *Yonder* wasn't much to look at, but beneath the Shreen's simple exterior was enough advanced hardware to rival a top-of-the-line fighter thanks to the Alliance and Samsara Fleet. Kal stopped to admire his new home.

He looked back at Nicole and Asha and felt his eyes start to burn. What was this? What was he doing there? Hadn't he lost everything?

"Kal," Asha whispered, holding something up to him.

He took it from her hand. It was the paper photo that he'd given her. His other family, the one that he'd lost, was still there, smiling back at him. He delicately placed the photo back in his pocket, a promise kept.

The rear cargo door opened, revealing a bay filled with crates destined for the far side of space. Together, they stepped up the ramp and into the ship.

Hand in hand.

Author's Note

25 May, 2023

Writing this book has been a significantly more laborious process than the previous ones in the series. I've grown to think of the characters in these novels as real people and strived to give them all a resolution that felt both earned and real.

In writing these books, I tried to incorporate many of my own experiences and feelings from my own experiences in combat. Unfortunately, war often is not a very interesting or compelling read, and the situations you experience can be more complicated than someone like me can ever adequately express. Hopefully though, I've done some justice to this so you feel like you've been living in this world I created if just for a bit.

For me, I am not sure what I will do next with regards to writing. I've begun my Central Worlds series, which is a lighter series though still filled with action. I also have some thoughts around future tales I'd like to tell but for now I think the world of Samsara Fleet will continue without me writing it.

Thank you to all my readers. Seeing people reading my books and hearing your feedback means the world to me.

Thanks,
Riley

Glossary

Organizations / Species

Council of Ancients - The ruling council of the Jadid. Consists of the Humans who have survived since the original experiment stranded them in a new universe.

Domespat - The Domestic Patrol is a repressive police force on New America.

Earth Defense Force (EDF) - Former military force for the UEG. Ended shortly after the destruction of Earth and the capture of the four Human colonies by the Nasi.

Jadid - A race descended from Humans who were unwillingly used as test subjects in the development of the fold drive. When the Humans, now called the Ancients, arrived in a new universe, their offspring had mutated due to the unique properties of their universe. The mutations changed their appearance and greatly increased their physical strength, dexterity, and endurance. The Jadid also were found to have ceased aging within their universe once they reached adulthood.

Nasi - A sect within the Jadid. Let by Ancient Esma Baykara. They are dedicated to returning the Jadid to the Human universe and leading Humanity against the other species of the galaxy.

Not Bergeron's Boneheads (aka the Bones) - An elite scout team formed from members of the Skulls. Led by Lieutenant Colonel Nicole Bergeron.

Not Norman's Numbskulls (aka the Skulls) - An elite scout team formed immediately after the initial Nasi attack. Led

354

by Brigadier General Kal Norman.

Odpor – A resistance group on Mariga.

Patagonia Front - Rebel group on the planet of Patagonia that's led by Frederick Kinawadi, a former member of the Skulls.

Samsara Fleet - A multispecies fleet dedicated to the defeat of the Nasi forces. Originally made up of the surviving species of the Nasi attack, it was greatly supplemented by the inclusion of the Jadid Liberation Fleet under Ancient Bao Wang.

Tac-I - Tactical Insertion. Soldiers that are trained for clandestine missions, such as capturing bases and stations.

Tiradentes Liberation Front (TLF).- One of several rebel groups on New America. Located in the area around the planetary capital and split into distinct operational cells.

Unified Earth Government (UEG) - Former interstellar government of Humanity. Ended when the Nasi destroyed Earth.

Planets

Altterra - Home planet of the Jadid. First discovered by the Ancients when the experiment they were part of failed, sending them into another universe.

Earth – Home planet of Humanity. Destroyed by the Nasi in their initial invasion.

Mariga - Human colony. Extremely cold surface temperatures have forced all Human settlements below ground into large subterranean cities. Controlled by the Nasi.

New America - Human colony. Centrally planned with large zones for various activities, such as industry, mining, housing. Capital is Tiradentes. Controlled by the Nasi with the New American Empire as their puppet government.

Patagonia - Human colony. Has one large continent, Pangea. Capital is Kasongo. Controlled by the Nasi with Foyleton, led by Karl Garcia, as the Human government.

Wudexingqiu - Human colony. Planet is almost completely water with isolated islands. Most cities and development occur under the oceans. Controlled by the Nasi.

Key Characters

General Aamina Samaha - Former EDF General. Highest ranking member of the EDF who survived the Nasi invasion. Current commander of Samsara Fleet.

Ancient Bao Wang - One of the original Ancients stranded on Altterra. Commander of the Jadid Liberation Fleet forces.

Bowen Nguyen - One of the Jadid's foremost experts in fold drive technology. Originally captured by the Nasi to assist them with the development of skip ships, he was rescued by the Skulls and joined their team.

Staff Sergeant Ekon Kimathi - Tac-I squad leader for the Bones. Originally from New America, he joined the EDF shortly after the Nasi invasion.

Grand Ancient Esma Baykara - One of the original Ancients who was stranded on Altterra and founded the Jadid. Esma harbors a deep grudge against Humanity for being stranded and created the Nasi.

General Frederick Zhou – Former Executive Officer to General

Samaha. He joined with the Liberation Fleet and became their top Human general, reporting directly to Ancient Bao Wang.

General Irina Petrov – Commander of the *Ofira* and executive officer to General Samaha.

Brigadier General Kal Norman - Former EDF colonel who retired when his family died in a tragic accident. Spent a decade as a free merchant, transporting cargo across the galaxy. When the Nasi attacked, he returned to the EDF and then helped lead the initial resistance against the occupiers.

Lieutenant Colonel Nicole Bergeron - Former diplomat for the UEG. Initially held as a prisoner for unknowingly trading secrets to the Nasi. Given a direct commission into Samsara Fleet by General Samaha.

Cell Chief Rafaela Pham – Commander of the largest operational cell within the Tiradentes Liberation Front.